Simmer

STEPHANIE ROSE

To Alypsa,
enjoy!
Stephanie Rose

Cover Design:
Najla Qamber Designs

Interior Design and Formatting:
Christine Borgford at Type A Formatting

Editing:
Mitzi Pummer Carroll

Proofreading:
Marisa Nichols

Dedication

TO MY MOTHER,

I'll never know everything you did for me; all I know is "thank you" will never be enough. I love you more than words could ever say.

JODI AND JULIA,

For pushing for Sara's story in the first place and your tireless efforts to help me give it roots and wings.

Soundtrack

Because of You—Kelly Clarkson
Chasing Pavements—Adele
All The Same—Sick Puppies
When I See You Smile—Bad English
Good Enough—Sarah McLachlan
Sara—Starship
Best Friend—Jason Mraz
Feel Again—One Republic
Right Here Waiting—Richard Marx
Secret Garden—Bruce Springsteen
To Make You Feel My Love – Billy Joel
Slow Hands – Niall Horan
Starving – Hailee Steinfeld
The Cure – Lady Gaga
Jealous – Nick Jonas
Teenage Dream – Katy Perry
Bad at Love – Halsey
Naked – James Arthur
Can't Help Falling in Love – Pentatonix
Big Girls Don't Cry (Personal) – Fergie
Praying – Kesha
Never Stop (Wedding Version) — SafetySuit

Prologue

SARA

"GET OUT! AND I don't want you near Denise. Bad enough she idolizes you. The last thing I need is for her to think being single and pregnant is a cool thing to do." Her chin jutted to the front door.

"Why would you do that? I know you hate me, but don't you care about her at all? What will she think if I don't come back?" My hand shook as I rubbed at the sting along my jaw from where she slapped me. I wouldn't cry and give her that last satisfaction. No way in hell.

"I said 'get out,' Sara! You and that baby aren't welcome here. If you come near this house, I'll have you arrested." Her cheeks reddened as rage spread over her features—features that were almost identical to mine. What was wrong with me for my own mother to detest me this much?

A hysterical laugh bubbled out of my chest. "Was I ever welcome here? Even when I *lived* here? I'll figure out how to see my sister. You have a nice life being miserable, Mother."

I wrapped my hands around my torso and bolted out the door, ignoring the sharp pain piercing across my gut at the sound of my baby sister's sobs behind me. I guessed she'd heard it all. My heart broke, but I wouldn't turn around. One look at her and the emotions I was holding in would boil over.

I raced outside and down the front steps, tearing across the ten blocks to the bus stop. The adrenaline wore off right before I stepped onto the bus and fell into a seat. My eyes flooded with tears that I wouldn't let streak down my face as I rubbed my still flat stomach.

"It's just us. I don't have much, but you'll have all of me." I splayed my hand over my stomach and squeezed, hoping somehow that would make it listen to me. "I promise."

One

Nine and a half years later

"MOMMY!" VICTORIA BARRELED into my legs, wrapping her arms around my thighs in a death grip.

"Hey, baby." I bent to kiss her forehead and rub her back. Bolting out of our apartment in a white-hot rage wasn't a smart or responsible thing to do when you had a little girl watching your every move—especially lately. The poor kid clammed up whenever she tried to speak to me for fear of setting me off since I was always *this* close to losing it. I raced to her father's apartment too infuriated to think.

I promised her before she was born she'd always get the best of me. Since her father stumbled into our lives, I'd only shown her the worst.

"Hey, cookie. Everything . . . work out?" Mrs. Lillo, our neighbor who became the only thing close to a family member we had over the years, studied me with a wary stare. I'd been awful to Josh and his girlfriend, Brianna, all the while making my daughter suffer solely for enjoying their company.

All those years ago, I'd made the decision not to find my daughter's father but he ended up finding *us*. One look at Victoria six months ago was all the confirmation he needed to know she was his. Those haunting emerald eyes they shared gave their connection away in an instant. I should have been relieved. Josh turned out to be a great father, and Brianna adored Victoria as if she were her own.

I hated it—and reveled in showing exactly how much.

"Yeah, fine." I darted my eyes to Victoria and back to Mrs. L. She nodded in reply, understanding I couldn't get into it with little ears listening.

I cupped Victoria's cheek and forced a smile through my exhaustion. "You can put on the new Wonder Woman pajamas we bought the other day and slip in a DVD. I'll be in in a bit after I talk to Mrs. L. Give her a kiss goodnight and thank her for watching you."

"But you said I couldn't put those on until Saturday. Extra wash, remember?"

I nodded and pressed a kiss to her forehead. "It's a special day. Go on."

She went over to Mrs. Lillo, burying her face in the plumpness of her hip. Mrs. L was the poster woman for grandmothers. She had a nurturing voice with a chubby frame that enveloped you in the best hugs.

"You never have to thank me for watching you. You're a sweetheart and I love it." She kissed Victoria's cheek before my daughter raced down our tiny hallway to her room.

"You're pretty calm. I'm hoping that means you talked it out and there'll be no talk of lawyers and such." She raised a brow as she slid into one of my cracked dining room chairs and took a sip of her tea.

Being served custody papers was my worst nightmare realized, and to hold them in my hand this afternoon made my blood run ice-cold in my veins. But deep down, I didn't blame Josh at all. I'd made things so difficult for all of us, but my tantrum after Brianna took Victoria to the mall and bought her a toy was the straw that broke everyone's back. He only wanted to be a part of her life, and even I was disgusted with my behavior the day I yanked her out of their apartment. My poor girl cried for hours thinking I was angry with her. She deserved better than a mother too bogged down in her own insecurities to realize how much she was hurting her own kid. Josh had every right to make a legal play for his child after how I'd acted all these months.

"We did. He threw the papers in the garbage, so custody of Victoria isn't an issue. He can see his daughter whenever he wants. They both can." I grabbed a mug from the cabinet and drained what was left in the tea kettle.

"I have to say, I'm impressed by Josh." Her brow raised as she took another sip. "He really stepped it up. Not many men would find out they had a child and run toward her instead of away from her faster than hell in the other direction."

At first, I didn't trust Josh or Brianna. I figured they'd hang around until the novelty wore off and pull away, hurting her as my parents had hurt me. Then—to my horror—they became a permanent fixture in our lives. Josh embraced his newfound fatherhood and . . . just wouldn't go the hell away. He wanted to make up for all the time he missed—the time I took away from him by not searching for him all those years ago. I knew his last name and had an idea of where his army base was. Finding him wouldn't have been difficult—had I tried. But I hardly knew him and had no clue what his reaction would have been.

"Very true," I agreed. "I give him credit. He really loves her, you know." The offer he made me echoed in my ears the entire bus ride home. Despite the shit I'd given him, I trusted him. She loved him instantly right back, and the rift I fought so hard to put between them was cruel, plain and simple. I realized that now with painful clarity. Shame scratched at my throat as I forced down a gulp of tea. My eyes drifted across my table, lingering on the enrollment forms for Champlain College stacked on top of my third past-due notice for my electric bill. I almost cracked up at the irony.

"I ended up telling him about Champlain. He offered to take Victoria for a year so I could finish up my credits and get my degree."

Mrs. Lillo dropped the mug onto the table and let out a gasp. "That's wonderful!"

I grunted around the rim of my mug. I applied for the paid internship on a whim, thinking I could take Victoria with me. I'd even found a nice elementary school not too far from the college. For the days and nights I had to work, I hoped I could find some sort of child care, but that dream was flushed down the toilet as soon as I found out she couldn't live in on-campus housing with me. I still couldn't bring myself to throw the forms out, even though I knew my answer had to be no.

"I even agreed for a second, but I can't."

"Why can't you?" She glowered at me. "You just said Josh was a good father, and you know he'd take good care of Victoria. It's only temporary, not forever."

"She's my everything. How can I leave her, even for a year? It would be selfish." I waved her off with my hand as I stared into space across the table.

She scooted her chair toward mine and peeled my hand away

from the mug's handle. "It's not that you wouldn't see or speak to her for a solid year. Charlie does that face box thing with the grandkids every Sunday so I can see their faces."

"FaceTime?" I quirked an eyebrow as I held in a laugh.

"Yeah whatever, and there are holidays you'll have off. It's a long drive upstate but it's not across the country." She draped her hand over mine. "Sara, honey, I love you. Like you were my own. I've seen you struggle. You're stubborn, a little bit of a loner, and not all that friendly sometimes."

"You *are* getting to a sort of compliment, right?" We shared a laugh before she swatted my arm.

"I've watched you skip meals to be able to afford presents for Victoria. Nod off mid-sentence because you worked for almost twenty-four hours straight. You've worked yourself to the bone trying to support that little girl. The one thing I'd never call you in a million years is selfish."

I threw my head back in laughter. "The way I acted all this time. I've been an animal, for Christ's sake. That's not selfish?"

"No, sweetheart," she whispered as she squeezed my shoulder. "That's being human. Could you have handled it better? Maybe. You would cut your arm off before you'd hurt Victoria intentionally. But, you need to learn how to accept help. This is a great way to start."

"I have an interview tomorrow. For my new second job. Pays less than the first." I shook my head, warding off the stinging behind my eyelids. "I'm so delinquent in rent, it would take four jobs to catch up."

"How long do you think you can keep going around and around in the same endless cycle? You may not get this opportunity again. If you want to *really* take care of your daughter, sacrifice a year of both your lives." Her gray eyes bore into mine. "To not take Josh up on this, to barely keep your head above water until the one day comes when you drown for the sake of your own pride. That, my darling—that is selfish."

"Mommy, I was waiting for you. If you're not still mad, can you come watch the movie with me?" Victoria's voice was small as she climbed into my lap. I cinched my arms around her and buried my head into her neck.

"I was never mad at you. I love you more than anything in the world." My voice cracked as I kissed the top of her head. "I'll be right in." A smile lifted her cheeks as she hopped off my lap and headed back into her room.

I let out a long sigh as I grabbed my phone and punched out a text to Josh.

Me: Did you mean it when you said Victoria could live with you?

In three seconds, the message reply bubble popped up showing someone typing. What scared me more? That maybe he changed his mind or that he didn't?

Josh: Absolutely. It's the least I can do. Did you contact the school?

My head fell back in the chair as I prayed I was doing the right thing.

Me: No, but I will tomorrow. Thank you.

Josh: My pleasure, Sara. We'd love to have her.

"Well?" Mrs. L pressed, tapping her finger on the table.

"I'll do it. For her."

Mrs. Lillo's mouth split in a wide grin. "No. You'll do it for both of you."

Two

"DO YOU HAVE your own room?" my daughter inquired from behind me. This was a new foray for us. Me in a driver's seat and her strapped in the back seat—in a car. A car that was mine. For her entire life, I dragged Victoria on buses and subway trains. Sometimes we were offered rides, and on occasion, I'd splurge on a cab, but owning a car? Never in my wildest dreams. By some miracle, I remembered how to drive.

Mrs. Lillo gave me her son's old car as a going away present since she planned on moving to South Carolina in a couple of months. She insisted I couldn't ride the Amtrak all the way to Plattsburgh, and public transportation to and from school and work was hard to come by upstate. We shared a teary goodbye, but I promised to send her as many pictures and updates as I could. Everything was firmly in place for me to take back the dream I'd always wanted, but all I did was cry about it for the past three days.

"I have a roommate, so I have to share a room." I tried my damnedest to keep my voice even. Everything revolved around Victoria, and I wasn't sure how I'd handle being without her. I wouldn't let myself think about it until I had to. Today . . . I had to.

"Is she nice?" She winced in the rearview mirror. My heart squeezed at the worry in her eyes.

I turned to her after I put the car in park and squeezed her hand.

"We talked on the phone. She's very nice. Maybe when I call you later, I can introduce you." My reply cracked at the end. There was no way I was making it out of the city without waterworks. I hoped I'd be able to hold them off until I drove away.

How was I going to do this? She was my baby. What kind of a mother leaves her baby? The urge to grab my phone and cancel everything was so overwhelming it choked me.

I stepped out of the car and fished her suitcase and bag of toys out of the trunk. The watery smile I forced as we strode to their outside door caused pain in my cheeks. Her hand clutched around mine as I rang their doorbell.

"Hey, Sweets!" Josh extended his inked arms as he gave our daughter a smile. Instead of running toward him like she always did, she burrowed into my side and dropped her gaze to the floor.

Biting my quivering lip, I gave Josh a shrug. He answered with a sad nod before crouching in front of her.

"I know you're sad that your mom is leaving today, but she's only a call away. You'll talk to her every night and she'll be here on Thanksgiving. And . . ." he leaned in and told her in a loud whisper, "Bri and I have been setting up your room all week. Want to come see?"

He held out his hand and quirked an eyebrow until she took it. Josh was tall with a broad muscular frame and covered head to toe in ink. He was almost unrecognizable compared to when I'd first met him. Then, he was a twenty-one-year-old soldier visiting for a weekend—only "passing through" as he'd said. Neither of us thought he'd leave a permanent souvenir behind. As big of a man as he was, he crumpled into a big teddy bear around his daughter. Her eyes stayed glued to mine as she followed her father inside.

"Hey, Vic!" Brianna rushed over to her and planted a quick kiss on her forehead. "You won't believe all the Wonder Woman stuff we found. You even have your own desk!" She lifted her gaze to mine and gave me a half smile. "Hi, Sara."

Her greeting was laced with genuine sympathy and concern. Brianna was effortlessly beautiful, with golden hair flowing down her back and warm, brown eyes. She had been the target of my rage since the day Josh came back into our lives. She never returned any of the venom I spewed in her direction, and even back then, I knew deep down she didn't deserve it. My hatred evolved into tolerance, but lately the strongest emotion I'd felt toward her was gratitude. Josh somehow found the most forgiving and understanding woman on the planet to not only stay by his side after she learned he had a surprise kid, but to love his child without the slightest bit of resentment.

I had a difficult time allowing a second strong mother figure in my daughter's life. But now, I supposed, she'd be the *first* mother until the year ended. My gut twisted at the thought, but even though I wouldn't be here, Victoria would have all the love and care I'd ever want for her while I did something for us and our future.

This was only a year. I repeated the word "temporary" a thousand times in my head since awakening. One year. Two semesters. I could do this. All I had to do was kiss her goodbye and hit the road.

But how?

I followed all of them into her bedroom. They'd only just

moved in but prepared for Victoria's arrival quickly. My mouth fell open as I looked around the room. Her new bedroom was bigger than our old living room was, with Wonder Woman curtains and bedding, an adorable desk in the corner, and shelves that I was sure would be filled with toys and books the next time I came back. A lump formed in my throat so large it became difficult to breathe.

I took in a quick breath through my nostrils and knelt before my daughter. She didn't seem to notice the details of her amazing room, her eyes searching mine instead. I cupped her cheek and planted a kiss to her forehead.

"This is an awesome room. You should thank Josh and Brianna for working so hard." I lifted my head and gave them both a tight smile. A stopwatch ticked in my head. I was running out of time before I had a full breakdown and needed to make a quick exit. "Listen to your father . . . and Brianna. Be the good girl I know you are. I love you and I'll call you when I get there."

She flung her arms around me and buried her face into my neck. Her tears dampened my shirt and tore my heart in half.

"I love you, too," she whispered in my ear.

"Hey," Brianna crooned as she crouched next to us. "You'll see your mom on FaceTime in a few hours. It's okay." She rubbed her back as Victoria nodded without turning around.

"I better get going." I clutched her shoulders and eased her away. "Remember," I kept my voice stern, trying not to collapse in sobs at the sight of her tearstained face. "Be good. I love you."

My voice cracked on the last word I would be able to say before the sobs rolled through me. I gave Josh and Brianna a quick nod before standing and heading for their door. The car was close, I needed a minute to get outside and jump in. I stabbed the unlock button with my thumb and reached for the door handle before a hand cupped my shoulder.

"You need to do this."

I nodded in response, keeping my gaze forward and not turning to Josh's voice.

"For you, and for her."

I craned my head just as my first tear escaped. "That's a great room."

Josh shrugged with a laugh. "I have a lot of time to make up for. I was happy to get the chance to do it. For both of you."

I huffed as I turned around and leaned against the car door. "The two of you are always so fucking nice." We shared a laugh before my smile faded. "I don't deserve it."

"Yes, you do. You took care of our girl—and now for the next year, it's my turn." He gave me a warm smile before he jutted his chin to the car. "Go. You have a long drive."

"I do. Thank you, Josh."

He waved me off before strolling back inside. I started the car and allowed myself to cry until the highway entrance. Josh was right. We deserved this.

I owed it to both of us to find the guts to see it all the way through.

Three

SARA

"WHAT'S YOUR NAME again, dear?" I sank my teeth into my bottom lip to delay my response enough to take the nasty edge off. After being in the car for four straight hours, I was exhausted and missed my daughter so much it hurt; I didn't have it in me to be nice.

"Sara Caldwell. My room is in this building. This is the on-campus housing, right?"

Her lips pursed as she flipped through the file on her desk at a glacier's pace. I was reminded of that movie Victoria loved with the sloths at the DMV, although they were a bit faster than this lady. The thought of my daughter and the wave of sadness that followed expelled some of the frustrated air from my lungs. I didn't come all the way out here to be miserable. *Patience, I needed patience.*

"Ah, yes, here you are. Second floor." She pointed her bright pink fingernail to the flight of stairs behind her. I forced a smile and nodded a silent thank you before trudging up the stairs. I was sure I'd be one of the oldest students here because of my long absence from school. I had two years of culinary credits and managed to get into the accelerated program. I'd have my degree in a year and—God willing—a job paying well enough to support both of us. Then the real grunt work would begin, but I wasn't afraid. To spend hours in a grueling kitchen learning something beat the hell out of jumping from table to table at one of my waitress jobs. I would have a career, not just a job. My fists flexed at my sides as I made my way up the stairs, excitement and terror rushing through me.

My suitcase, duffel bag, and purse weighed on me with every step. How steep was this flight of stairs? By the time I arrived on the floor, I was a huffing and puffing sweaty mess. I dropped one of my bags and scoured every door for my room number when I plowed into something.

"Sorry." I lifted my head to a deep baritone and winced in embarrassment. The something was a some*one*.

"No, it was my fault . . ." I trailed off. My tired eyes glossed over the full lips tempered by stubbled cheeks, thick black hair, and chocolate eyes and then landed on the broad chest I'd bumped into. My victim shot me a sly grin and shook his head.

"I'm always in a rush and end up knocking someone over." His throaty chuckle vibrated through me as his eyes searched mine. "Do you want some help?" He reached for the bag I dropped on the floor, but I jerked away, unsure of why I was so damn jumpy.

"No, thanks. I just, um, need to find my room." I took a wide step back, the heel of my sneaker catching on the edge of the bag and I—in torturously slow motion—fell back as I slipped on the fabric like a damn banana peel. Chiseled arms wrapped around me right before my backside bit the dust.

"Easy there. Are you okay?" Concern flashed in his eyes followed by amusement, only adding to the humiliation. I grabbed onto his shoulders for purchase as I righted myself, too embarrassed to look him directly in the eye.

"Yeah, sure. Sorry."

"I've never seen you before. You're new here, right?" He tilted his head as he studied me.

"Yes, why?" My eyes darted to his as I squirmed under his heavy stare. Five minutes here and I already made a complete idiot of myself, and this guy wasn't letting me escape his hold. His strong hold against his hard body. Not that I noticed or anything.

"I think I'd remember you." A flirty smile curved his lips.

I spied "226" over the stranger's shoulder and let out a sigh of relief. "And there is my room. Thanks for your help." A nervous laugh bubbled out of my chest as I grabbed my bags and skirted around him, this time unscathed. I didn't understand why I was so damn flustered and blamed it on the long trip and my new role as a gasping fish out of water.

"Have a good day," I blurted before fishing the key card out of my pocket.

"Drew." I heard the smile in his voice before I turned around.

"Excuse me?" I craned my head as I fiddled with the lock.

"My name. It's Drew. And you are?" He cocked a sexy brow. *Oh, for God's sake.*

I didn't have time for him, or this. *This* being men or socialization in general. I didn't come this far to fuck around and fuck it up. Been there and done that and sure as hell wasn't going back.

"Sara. See you around." I opened the door and rushed through, slumping against it as I tried to shake off the humiliation. I studied my surroundings; the two beds with a bathroom at the far end of the room. One side was already claimed, the bed furnished with a quilt and surrounded with pictures. I plopped my stuff on the vacant side and fell onto the mattress. Hopefully I'd feel less awkward once I found a routine, but uptight and standoffish were more or less who I was. At least that was what a prior manager had told me as part of a well-meaning "why don't I loosen up" speech. I was always darting from one job to the next and had to manage where my kid was in between, so I didn't have time for small talk.

I'd held onto my bad attitude for so long, I had no clue how to be even a little social. I'd never cared about that, but I guessed now, if this was all going to work, I had to. I dropped my head into my hands and pinched the bridge of my nose. The mere prospect of it exhausted me.

"Sara?" I lifted my head to the squeaky voice and click of the lock. "So nice to finally meet you!"

Lisa, my new roommate, rushed over to me and tackled me with a hug before I could fully stand off the bed. She pulled back and grabbed me by the arms. "And you look normal! I haven't had too much luck with roommates. Welcome! How was the drive from . . . Oh, God, I forgot where you're from . . . Brooklyn?" She winced in shame and I couldn't help but laugh. The glint in her hazel eyes seemed genuine and kind. It'd been a long time since I attempted to make an actual friend, and the few seconds in Lisa's easy presence highlighted how lonely I really was all these years.

"Queens. Long but okay. Happy to be here and get settled in." I gave her a tired smile. "This is my first time living at school. I commuted in my first two years . . ." I trailed off, omitting the "before I got knocked up" part. It shamed me, but it was nice to just be Sara for a moment. Not Sara, the single mom with no family and hardly any friends.

"I'm so psyched we have our own bathroom. I mean, they aren't suites or anything, but this room already beats the hell out of where I stayed for the past three years. The building is co-ed, too, so that will take some getting used to."

"Right." I nodded. I knew that but bumping head-on with an attractive man who most likely lived here had me a little twisted. Why couldn't I have at least looked him in the eye? I'm sure he wouldn't be the only good-looking guy here I'd put off by my prickly personality.

"I'm starving," Lisa groaned and pressed her palm to her stomach. "You're in the culinary program, right? After we eat, I can show you the test kitchen. It's where we have our lab classes, but you can use it on your own."

My eyes went wide as I gaped at Lisa. "You can use the lab kitchen anytime you want? My old school never let us do that."

"None really do. It's an unusual perk, that's for sure. They should put that on the Champlain College website. I go there a lot to practice or sometimes only because I feel like cooking something for myself. It's pretty cool."

"A state-of-the-art kitchen I could cook in anytime I want . . . that is pretty damn cool." I dug my palms into my legs and pushed off the bed. "I'm starving, but after we eat, I need to make a quick phone call . . . I promised my daughter I'd let her know when I got here." My smile faded as I braced myself for the inevitable awkwardness.

"Aw, how old is she? Do you have a picture?" Lisa's smile was genuine and took me by surprise.

"Um, yeah. She's eight, almost nine." I reached into one of my bags and dug out the framed photo of her and me at her last recital. She always resembled her father more, but I'd loved this picture because our smiles looked identical. I glanced at it with a wistful grin before handing it to Lisa. She was my happiness, my purpose, and the reason I was here. That needed to become my mantra for the next two semesters.

"She's so pretty! Looks just like you. I hope she comes to visit." Lisa set the frame on the bare end table next to my bed.

As I followed Lisa out of our room and descended the stairs behind her, I attempted to shelf the guilt for a bit and force myself to believe it was okay to be here. This wouldn't be easy, but I needed to make the most out of this new turn my life had taken. I'd find a way to enjoy it all if it killed me.

I could do this.

Four

SARA

FOR THE FIRST couple of weeks, I was too busy to worry about fitting in. I was sure I'd forgotten the basics I'd first learned all those years ago, but I worked my ass off to remember. It was exhausting but fucking fabulous. The prospect of learning skills to earn a living—not holding a job—excited me. Or *jobs,* as the case used to be. The memories of my old life, although it wasn't so old yet, exhausted me.

Thursdays were my evenings off from my paid internship at McQuaid's, a local restaurant affiliated with Champlain. I met quite a few culinary students there, working their way through school or doing an internship like I was. The salary wasn't much, but I'd managed to qualify for free housing and was able to hoard every cent. I loved being a part of something, *working* toward something besides keeping my head above water. I missed Victoria like crazy and spoke with her every day, but I drifted off each night to an untroubled and satisfied sleep.

My phone vibrated in my pocket after I shut the door to my dorm room after a full, but great day of classes. I didn't recognize the email address popping up on the screen and was about to let it go to voice mail when I realized it was a FaceTime call. I pressed the button, a huge grin stretching my lips when Victoria's adorable face filled the screen.

"Hey, baby!" I crossed my legs under me and held the phone at eye level. "What number are you calling from?"

"Mine!" She gave me a big smile. "Dad and Bri got me an iPad so that I could text you and FaceTime you whenever I want!"

"That's great—" My stomach dropped from my delayed reaction. *Dad?* When I left her a few weeks ago, she still called her father Josh. Why did hearing her call him "Dad" unnerve me so damn much? That's what he was to her, right? Plus, for all intents and purposes, he was her main parent now. I should've been happy and relieved she was acclimating to her new normal so well. And I was, but the rotten, sour feeling—an emotionally bitter aftertaste—was hard to shake off.

My daughter's smile evaporated. I was ashamed whenever thoughts of how I'd behaved where Josh and Brianna were concerned fluttered through my mind. Whenever Victoria would try to talk to me about them, I'd shut her down, drilling it into her they would only be around temporarily. I thought it was the truth at first, but when I realized it was the opposite, full-on panic set in. She'd suffered enough for my insecurities, and so did they.

"It's good that you call him Dad. I'm sure he really likes that."

Her lips curved back up as she nodded. "I asked him at his birthday party, right before he asked Bri to marry him. She said I could be her flower girl!"

I had to suck in my cheeks to keep my mouth from falling open. Of course they were getting married. They practically were already. Victoria had the perfect family now, married parents and all. I inhaled a quick breath as my nose burned. I'd struggled all those years to keep her fed and clothed, managing to somehow afford dancing classes as a treat. She had the perfect life now—a huge room, an iPad of her own, and two parents. She had it all, only she had it without me.

Victoria frowned as she tilted her head at the screen. "Are you okay, Mommy?"

"Of course!" I held in a laugh when her head jerked back in surprise at my boisterous reply. "This is all great. I just really miss you, that's all. But Thanksgiving will be here before you know it, right? And now, we can talk all the time." My voice squeaked as I laid it on as thick as I could without bursting a blood vessel. Perky was never one of my personality traits, even before Victoria. I didn't blame her for studying me with a confused gaze.

"You're sure, Mommy?" Her mouth twisted in a frown. The sorrow and guilt mashing together at once were about to suffocate me.

"Absolutely. You're going to be the prettiest flower girl in history. I can't wait to see pictures. When are they getting married?"

"Dad said soon. Bri is taking me to buy a dress tomorrow."

My gut twisted as I tried to think of a time I took my daughter to pick out a dress that wasn't on sale. I skipped lunch the weeks before buying her dance recital costumes to make sure I could afford it.

"I can show you tomorrow night!" Victoria broke the long silence.

A sad smile lifted my cheeks as I shook my head. "I have to work tomorrow night. I'll be home past your bedtime. Show me Saturday morning. Deal?"

"Deal! How's school? Is your roommate still nice?"

"Lisa is very nice. School is fun." I laughed at her disgusted scowl.

"How could school be fun?"

"When you get older, you'll understand."

Her head twisted toward something behind her. Josh's deep laugh mixed with Victoria's whispers.

"Couldn't wait, huh, Sweets? Hi, Sara!" He waved a tattooed hand at me, and I couldn't help but laugh at his goofy grin.

"Hey, Josh. Congratulations."

His smile widened as he settled next to Victoria. "Thanks. Not exactly sudden, but it's time. Can you come back for a weekend next month? You're more than welcome to come."

Again, they were always too nice to me. If only once they'd told me to fuck off, my conscience would have been more at ease.

"Thanks for the offer, but I work every weekend through Thanksgiving. I'll look forward to the pictures." My eyes met Victoria's. She bounced next to her father, and as I looked between them, an unexpected warmth flooded my chest. Our struggles were just as taxing on her, even though she never made a peep about it. We were both happy in our new lives, and I hoped my time at school would eventually lead us to a place where we could enjoy all the things we'd missed together.

"Are you done with your homework?" I glanced at my watch. "It's almost bedtime." My heart squeezed at the familiar jut of my daughter's bottom lip whenever I mentioned bedtime. "We'll talk tomorrow, and every day after that. Okay?" I was soothing both of us. I didn't want her to hang up either.

"Okay, goodnight, Mommy. I love you."

"I love you, too." I kissed my index finger and touched the screen over her face. She blew me a kiss back with her father chuckling next to her. Heaving a long sigh when the screen went black, I gazed up at ceiling, trying to get my bearings from all that information. I never had a problem making sacrifices for my daughter, and this time should've been no different. I was giving up a piece of her, so she could thrive and be happy with her father while I attempted to make a future for us.

"Hey, is something wrong?" I raised my head to Lisa's concerned stare as she ambled through the door. "Is Victoria okay?" Her gaze stayed on me as she sat on the edge of her bed.

"She's great." I sighed and shook my head, laughing to myself. "Brand new iPad of her own, she gets to be flower girl at her father's wedding, and she's getting used to me not being around. All good."

"I'm sure she's not." Lisa's sympathetic smile didn't make me feel any better. "I bet if you picked her up right now, she'd jump on you and ask you to take her home. My mom worked long hours and I stayed with my grandmother a lot. I loved Nana, but when my mom came home, she was all I'd see. I'm sure it's the same." She nudged my shoulder.

A pang twisted my chest. We had no home—not one of our own. I'd given up my apartment in Queens, and on Thanksgiving, Victoria and I would be staying with Josh and Brianna. Maybe that's where the sour feelings were coming from. I was in a weird limbo I wasn't used to.

"You, my dear, need a drink." Lisa grabbed clothes out of her dresser and headed toward our bathroom. "Let's freshen up and head to Night Owls, and you are not saying no! You're off tonight and don't have class until noon tomorrow. Time to embrace college life, girlfriend." She lifted an eyebrow before shutting the door.

"I'm trying to save whatever I can. The internship doesn't pay much—"

"Well, tonight is on me, and you can spare a couple of bucks for a drink or a cup of coffee once in a while, I'm sure. You won't be a recluse on my watch!" She scowled before she shut the door.

When was the last time I went out for the simple sake of going out? I'd lost touch with all my friends by the time Victoria was a year old because I had no time to see them. The culinary students varied in age—some were late twenties or early thirties like I was. But this bar would probably be filled with college kids—kids I'd have no clue how to interact with.

I raked my hand through my hair and fell back on the bed. As painful as a bar sounded tonight, staying in my room and stewing over all the ways I came up short as a mother would be torturous. Conversation, drinking, it couldn't be that hard. I did it at one time. I'd met Josh in the bar I worked at when I was a different person in an entirely different life. I managed then, but could I manage now?

I was afraid to find out.

$$\underset{\mathbf{v}}{\mathbf{v}}\, \underset{\mathbf{v}}{\mathbf{v}}\, \underset{\mathbf{v}}{\mathbf{v}}$$

"SEE, THIS IS fun, right?" Lisa whispered as she nudged my shoulder. "Fun" was stretching it a tad too far, but it wasn't bad. I nursed a couple of beers as I chatted with some of Lisa's friends. An odd smile or laugh crossed my lips from time to time. Maybe this was how it felt to relax.

"This place must be boring compared to your old school in the city, right?" Lisa's friend, Emma, asked me with wide eyes. Emma and Michelle were on the young side—mid-twenties, I guessed. They were both tiny and cute, Emma with her blonde pixie cut and Michelle's auburn curls cascading down her back.

Much to my surprise, I didn't feel out of place. No one gave me the "what the hell is this chick in her thirties doing here" once-over or treated me differently.

"Not that much different, really . . ." I drifted off as my eyes landed on a familiar face over Emma's shoulder. His head turned as he leaned over the table to line up his pool shot, but the tiny glimpse was enough to be certain. Drew, the tall, dark, sexy-in-a-way-I-didn't-want-to-notice, poor stranger I crashed into in the hallway on my very first day. I hadn't seen him since and hoped maybe he was a visitor or a part-time student, but no such luck as he was here.

His looks weren't the only thing making it so damn hard to look away, although he really was gorgeous. The cropped yet purposeful mess of ink black hair, chocolate eyes, and olive skin—the whole package—equating to what an old coworker at my last restaurant would've referred to as a dreamboat. It was the fluidity of his movements I found intoxicating. The scraping of the chalk at the end of the stick as he laughed at something his friend had said, the natural grace when he leaned over the table. Even when I slammed into him, he seemed to catch me as if we were dancing. How he told me his name with a cocky confidence I felt in my toes, but he didn't come off as full of himself.

I turned my focus back to Emma, nodding at all the appropriate times and fighting the urge to watch him a little more. Although, I'd passed watching about two minutes ago and was close to full-on ogling.

Emma glanced over her shoulder as her brows pulled together. "What are we missing?"

"Nothing. I thought I saw someone from the restaurant, but false alarm." I forced a tight smile as the relaxed position I enjoyed for the past hour disappeared and I stiffened on my bar stool. Our encounter lasted all of three minutes, so why was I so flustered seeing him again?

"Excuse me." I had the sudden urge for some cool water on the back of my neck and a breather. I'd wanted to ease myself into being social, not jump headfirst into the deep waters. I felt out of place and on display, and when I pushed through the ladies' room swinging door, I glanced at the bathroom window to decipher if I could slip through and escape.

After my minute alone, I forced myself back out there. How pathetic was it that I was probably one of the oldest people there, but on the inside, the most immature by far? I put my head down and trudged back out, only to slam into a familiar hard chest.

"Sorry, hey there." Drew's lips stretched into a megawatt smile. It had been a long time since I liked a guy, but Drew didn't count as I didn't know him enough to like him. He was something pretty to look at, like the coq au vin from class the other day. Rich and decadent, but bad for my health if I indulged.

"We have to stop crashing into each other like this." The corner of his full mouth tipped up. "Sara, right?"

"And you're Drew. I remember." I swayed to move past him, but he moved directly in my path.

"Well, now that the reintroductions are over. Want to join us?" He jerked his chin toward the pool table behind him.

"No, thank you. I'm here with some friends of mine. If you'll excuse me—"

"Oh, I just figured since you kept looking, you wanted to play." He cocked his head to the side and laughed.

"You . . . noticed me looking over here?" I was too flustered to come up with a good denial. And I'd spent the past fifteen minutes with my eyes glued to Drew's ass as he lined up his shots. To lie and say I wasn't would only make it worse.

"I noticed you when you first came in. I was looking, too. Just stealthier about it." He shrugged with an arrogant smile.

"I can't. Like I said, I'm here with my friends. Thanks for the offer." I scooted around him and jetted back to the bar.

I touched my flushed cheeks on the way back to the girls, cringing at how I probably ran away from Drew with a beet-red face. Maybe someday I'd be able to have a coherent conversation with an attractive man.

Today was not that day.

⸙ ⸙ ⸙

"SEE, I KNEW you'd have a great time." Lisa arched a brow as she unlocked our door.

"It was great to leave the room for a night, that's for sure." I agreed as I shrugged off my jacket. "The girls are nice. Don't ask me to go clubbing just yet."

She scoffed as she kicked off her boots. "You were fine. Although, if you wanted to play pool, you could have." She cocked an eyebrow, and I knew I was busted.

"No distractions. No matter how shiny and pretty. After my year is up and I finally graduate, I'm moving back to the city to find a job and an apartment for my daughter and me."

"Shame." She tsked as she fell onto the bed. "Mr. Shiny and Pretty was looking back at you most of the night."

"Was he?" My voice came out in an unfamiliar shriek, causing a bubble of laughter from Lisa.

"But, no distractions, right?" She winked as the corners of

her mouth twitched. "Look, I get it. You want to get back home to Victoria. But, you could still have . . . a little fun. How long has it been?"

"Since what? Fun?" I let out a humorless laugh. "Let's see, my daughter is eight, so add nine months to that. I can't afford to screw up again," I whispered, reminding myself more than Lisa.

"You won't." Lisa's expression turned soft. "You are a great mom. You're always speaking to Victoria, planning for her, saving for her. Is it so bad to plan for yourself, too?"

"I should plan to flirt with the hot stranger in the bar next time?" I rose from the bed and trudged into the bathroom.

"Yes. Plan *something*. For yourself. At this point, I think you're out of excuses."

I didn't answer as I shut the door behind me. I guessed being scared shitless wasn't an excuse.

Five

"I HONESTLY DON'T know what happened . . . I hope I didn't break anything. You better have a look." Sabrina peered at me under batting lashes as her finger drifted up my arm.

Freshmen weren't supposed to practice in the test kitchens and didn't have a reason to. Second-year students were here the most, usually trying to crack a technique, and the third- and fourth-years knew their way around enough to test for the hell of it. This girl, twirling her auburn hair through her fingers with doe eyes fixed on me, wasn't here to practice or test. How she got written permission to be here was beyond me, although I'd bet she used the hair thing for that, too.

"I'm sure you didn't. Point me to the station and I'll fix it." I forced a smile and suppressed an eye roll as I stood from my chair. Manning the test kitchen was supposed to be an easy on-campus job, and since the IT positions were gobbled up so damn fast, I thought this was an easy way to make money without too much aggravation. Usually I just signed people in or out, checked the power at one of the stations if a student had trouble, or passed the time during my allotted hours reading a book or working on a project. This girl wasn't here to learn, as the only thing she studied when she'd come in was me. This was the fourth "I don't know what happened" in two weeks.

She had a petite, curvy body topped off with a cute face, but I never gave in to her attempts at flirting. Sabrina was the kind of girl I'd dated a hundred times. Granted, that's what you were supposed to do in college: date, get laid, repeat, but it became tedious for me. My friends still embraced the cycle, but I wanted a woman who made me work for it, not offered herself on a platter before she even said hello.

After I ambled over and found nothing wrong with the station or the equipment, I made my way back to the front desk. Sabrina muttered something about me being her hero, but I ignored it. I hoped she'd get the hint eventually, but eventually didn't seem to be anytime soon.

I slid back into my seat and opened up my laptop, hoping like hell for a quiet rest of the shift.

"Hey," a throaty voice greeted me, pulling my eyes away from my screen. "I know it's late, but could I sign in for just an hour or so?"

Well, I'll be damned. The beautiful hallway and bar angel stood before me. She was the only woman to back away from me as if I had the Ebola virus the two times I'd met her. Both times, my eyes had stayed glued to the contour of her perfect ass as she rushed off to escape me. I noticed her at Night Owls the other night and caught her checking me out a few times. When I finally managed to slip away from the guys and reintroduce myself, she was even more skittish than when I first met her.

Her whiskey-colored eyes searched mine, and fuck, she was gorgeous. A blush spread across her cheeks, and I couldn't resist calling her on it.

"At least we didn't knock each other over this time." My lips twitched as I leaned back in my chair and crossed my arms.

Her eyes narrowed as if I'd offended her. Forget about my usual game, small talk was like pulling teeth with this girl.

She tucked a chestnut lock of hair behind her ear before glancing at her watch with a frustrated hiss. "I didn't realize it was this late. I'd meant to get down here earlier, but classwork from today took longer than I'd thought, and I really wanted to cook something for myself for once. I'll try back tomorrow."

She turned to leave, and I popped out of my seat and grabbed her elbow.

"Not too late at all, Sara. Station in the front is totally free. Cook your heart out."

"Really?" She squinted as her head cocked to the side.

"I have nowhere to be tonight." I shrugged and leaned against the front of my desk. "It's no trouble at all."

She gave me a small smile, and a little air whooshed out of my lungs. She really was beautiful, if not the most outgoing. She intrigued me even from that first day. So much so, I bought myself an extra hour in the cooking lab for a chance to get to know her a little bit.

"Thank you so much." She rushed over and happily dug out a mixing bowl for whatever she had set out to make. I'd never seen one of the students enjoy what they were doing so much. Her passion was intoxicating. A thought crossed my mind that maybe, when pushed enough, she could be passionate about other things, too—and use those full pink lips to show it.

Screw it. I was stuck here for an extra hour anyway. I'd give small talk another try. Sabrina and most of the other students already left so Sara and I were almost all alone.

"So, what are you making?"

Sara jumped, so engrossed in her task she didn't even register my approach.

"Sorry, I didn't mean to startle you." I raised my hands and took a step back.

"No, it's okay. I'm making cookies actually. I used to make them for my . . . back home, so I wanted to soothe my homesickness I guess." She kneaded the dough with very capable hands, quick, nimble, beautiful. I had never been jealous of flour and water before.

"Where are you from? I'm guessing you transferred here from somewhere."

"New York City. Queens. I did, but I took a little break after my last semester."

"How long?" She stilled at the question before raising her head.

"Oh about, eight years or so." She laughed at my widened eyes.

"Eight years?" I cleared my throat, doing a terrible job of covering my shock. "What made you come back after so long?"

She was silent for a few beats, rolling tiny balls of dough and carefully placing them onto a sheet.

"Long story."

"So, you're . . ." I fumbled, now caught way off guard.

"Thirty-two." She quirked an eyebrow before shoving the trays in the oven.

"No." My hand drifted down my face. "I mean . . . I'm glad you were able to come back." *Get it together, idiot.*

She gave me that little smile again, and my chest swelled. I had the feeling smiles from Sara didn't come easy. My gaze fell on her mouth again, hypnotized by the way she was chewing her bottom lip. Her nervous tic had me hot and bothered. Telling me her age was probably her way of making me back off, but it didn't work. I wanted to know her. I wanted to see who she was beneath all the tentative toughness she pushed to the surface. What I really wanted was to see that smile again, and the cat and mouse staring game we were playing the other night gave me a twinge of hope that maybe I could figure out how.

"I have cousins in Queens. Astoria. The crazy Kostas family, maybe you've met them."

"Can't say that I have." She glanced at the floor before lifting her eyes to mine. "I'm really sorry I kept you here."

I waved my hand. "No bother at all. Although if you're feeling badly about it, you could make it up to me . . ."

"Make it up to you?" She squinted and rested her elbows on the counter.

"Coffee. Just one cup tomorrow afternoon. I'll go easy on you."

She dropped her eyes to the floor and shook her head. "I can't. It's just not a good idea. I need to . . . focus while I'm here."

"And . . . coffee is a distraction? I don't follow." I inched over to her station, close enough for her not to be able to ignore me.

"It could be. I'm sorry." She studied my face with a silent plea, her chest heaving before her wary eyes locked with mine.

"Maybe another time, then."

An unexpected laugh bubbled out of her chest.

"Finish your recipe and whenever you're done, I'll lock up."

"Thanks, Drew," she whispered with that sultry voice.

I did say I loved a challenge.

Six

SARA

"THE COFFEE ON our floor is free. Why are you dragging me here again?" I cocked a brow at Lisa when we arrived at the tiny coffee shop. There was a fall bite in the air, more than I was used to for only early September. Another adjustment I needed to make after relocating all the way upstate from Queens. I shivered in my light denim jacket.

"Well, the free coffee sucks," she scoffed. "I'm used to it, but they make a killer latte here. It won't break the bank, I promise. And I told you I wasn't letting you molt in our room when you're not working or in class." She held the door open for me to walk through.

"Molt? I'm pretty sure I don't have feathers." I smirked as I strode up to the counter to read the menu on the wall.

"Hi, Sara. I guess this means I get my coffee after all." My head swiveled to Drew's voice. For the life of me, I couldn't escape this guy.

"Hi, Drew. Lisa made me come here." The words sounded garbled and defensive as they fell from my lips as I stumbled back when we made eye contact. What was it about this man that had me evaporating IQ points and any semblance of coordination?

"Coffee?" Lisa turned to me, her mouth twisted into a smirk before she looked over at Drew. "Hey, Drew."

"Lisa," he nodded a hello with his dreamy eyes fixed on me. Lisa and I were going to have a talk about forcing me into social situations that terrified me.

I frowned as I looked between them. "Drew let me stay late at the kitchen a few days ago and says I owe him coffee."

"You know what?" Lisa glimpsed at her watch and moved backward toward the door. "I think I forgot something in our room, and coffee will keep me up late anyway. You should pay your debts, Sara." I spied a quick wink before she bolted out the door.

Some friend she was. She forced me here and then ran out. I knew what she was trying to do, and her heart was in the right place—but I was going to kill her anyway.

Great, now what?

"So, you're here, I'm here, why don't you take a seat?" His mouth curved before he motioned to an empty table in the back. I headed over and slid into a wooden seat, sucking in a long breath and letting it out slowly, without any effect on my bobbing leg.

This was pathetic. It was only coffee. I'd be here fifteen, maybe twenty minutes, and leave. Pay my debt to Drew as he phrased it and move along. *It's coffee, Sara. For fuck's sake.*

"Looking to make a break for it?" I turned to Drew's snicker.

"No. I . . ." I allowed myself a glance at his deep brown eyes and lush lips stretched into a smile. He was pretty and shiny, all right.

He raked his hands through his thick hair, still laughing at me, and settled across the table.

"You're either looking to get this over with or casing the place. I don't bite." He raised his arms as he leaned back into the chair, his eyes falling to my bouncing leg. I stilled when his warm hand gave my quivering knee a quick squeeze. "Honest."

My knee shaking ceased thanks to the odd, maybe a little too intimate, gesture. But I wasn't offended or even taken aback, only embarrassed as shit for being once again an awkward basket case in this guy's presence.

"I'm actually surprised you suggested coffee in the first place." My lips pursed as our eyes met.

His brows crinkled as he leaned forward and rested his elbows on the table. "Why would you be surprised?"

I let out a long, humiliated sigh. "Because every interaction we've had up to this point has somehow made me act like an awkward mess. I'm actually afraid to stand from my seat as I'll probably trip and land right in your lap."

His head fell back as his broad and most likely ripped chest rumbled with a laugh. "If that happens, I promise I'll catch you and set you down in your own seat. I'll only make you linger on my lap for maybe . . ." He shrugged with an adorable smirk. "No more than a minute or so."

I fought the smile threatening the corners of my mouth. My eyes drifted from Drew's dreamy chocolate orbs to my fidgeting hands on the table.

Drew tapped my wrist for me to look up, his smile fading as he scooted his chair forward. "You're a beautiful woman. A woman who keeps slipping away from me." His eyes narrowed. "I tried to trick you into coffee, so we could get to know each other a little."

"Trick me?" I crossed my arms.

"I was hoping to make you feel obligated. You can still pretend you're paying back a debt if it makes it easier."

It didn't make it easier, but I wasn't as uncomfortable as when

I first arrived. Drew was smooth, but no bullshit alarms went off in my head. He seemed genuine, and it would be nice to get to know people other than Lisa and her circle of friends. That's as far as it would be able to go, and I'd have to make sure that was crystal clear, but for the first time since he suggested it, spending time together didn't make my body go rigid with panic. Maybe acknowledging how flustered he made me would take the power out of it, although the idea of lingering in his lap made me jumpy in a whole different way.

"What can I get you? Your leg stopped shaking but I'd probably go easy on the caffeine if I were you."

I held in a laugh as I dug out my wallet. "Regular coffee with half-and-half is fine."

Drew grabbed my wrist and shook his head. "On me."

I pushed the money into his hand. "I do still owe you. I kept you at the test kitchen for an hour past your shift."

"You stayed. Consider us even," he whispered in my ear as he placed the money in front of me. *Shit, he smelled good.* I rubbed the back of my neck to get the tiny hairs to lay flat again.

My eyes followed Drew as he ambled up to the counter to give the barista our order. He caught me ogling—again—before heading back to our table with a smile and two cups in his hand.

"So, Sara. Let's see where we left off." He set the coffee in front of me with a handful of sugar packets. "I didn't know which sugar to get you, so I grabbed a couple packets of each. You come from Queens, you transferred here . . ."

"And I'm thirty-two . . . and have an eight-year-old daughter," I blurted as I grabbed two sugars and emptied them into my coffee, blending with the stirrer as I avoided Drew's reaction.

"So that's the reason for the long break." He nodded. "What's her name?"

Another surprised smile stretched my lips. I usually got the "wow, you have a kid, what's that like?" from single friends or younger coworkers that didn't understand the concept of being a parent. Lisa, and now Drew, didn't make me feel awkward or odd because I was a mom. It was a wonderful, if foreign, feeling. Drew asking her name caused a warmth to spread in my chest I couldn't explain. Plus, he was still sitting here and not running for the hills yet.

"Victoria." I wrapped my hands around the cup and took a sip.

"And her father is . . ."

"Taking care of her in Queens with his soon-to-be wife." I held back a smile at the relief washing over Drew's face.

"New stepfamily, huh?" He winced. "She'll get used to it. Took me a little while when I was a kid, but now I don't even think about it. It's just normal."

"You have a stepmother?"

"Stepfather. My mother had me when she was really young. She still gets mistaken for my sister sometimes. She met my stepdad when I was about six."

"Do you see your father?" Drew's mouth strained for a moment before he set his cup down.

"I'm sorry." I grimaced. "I didn't mean to—"

"No, it's okay. Yes and no. I see him once in a while, but he's never been what you'd call a full-time parent. My mom had it pretty hard for a while. I'm glad she found someone like Phil and had it easier when she had my sister."

"How old is your sister?"

"She just turned seven. I was eighteen when she was born."

A quick math equation ran through my head. Drew was

seventeen when I had my daughter and was seven years younger than I was. I was already working two jobs when he was only a kid. The ease I was starting to feel in his presence evaporated.

"Hey, what's wrong? Where'd you go?" He nudged my ankle with the tip of his foot.

"Nowhere, nothing." My coffee cup almost slipped out of my hands as I set it back down.

"I don't care that you're thirty-two and have a daughter. I know that's why you keep mentioning it. Does it bother you that I'm twenty-five?"

"No," I clipped as I lied. Josh was a couple of years younger than me. I didn't realize it the night I met him, and two years is a world of difference away from almost a decade, especially now. Drew was in the prime of his young life, and I had extra years and a load of baggage I couldn't see a man his age wanting anything to do with. But this was only coffee, right? Why was I getting so ahead of myself?

I sucked in a long breath and let it out slowly before I brought my eyes back to his. "I've never been the most social person, at least since Victoria was born. I worked two, sometimes three jobs, and didn't have time for friends or small talk or . . . coffee."

Drew's eyes grew wide. "Three jobs? Wow, you're a warrior."

I shrugged. "My daughter wanted to go to dance school, and her recital costumes cost the same as my utility bills. So, the extra hours and skipping a meal or two paid for a lot of sequins." I laughed but Drew didn't laugh with me.

"Victoria is lucky to have such an amazing mother. I'm glad you found a way to go back to school." He gave me a heart-stopping, but sincere smile.

I nodded. "Me too. I owe her father a lot. He took her in, so I could take the internship at McQuaid's and finish school. I'm in the accelerated program, so I'm only here for a year."

"She's his kid, too. It sounds like you almost killed yourself taking care of her alone. He owes you both."

I silently agreed with a shrug, not wanting to taint a nice afternoon with the whole one-night stand and not telling her father she existed story.

"So, what about you? What are you studying? I thought you lived in Berman Hall, but I never saw you after that day."

"I was helping a friend move in when I almost knocked you over. I was beginning to think you were an illusion until I saw you at Night Owls."

I froze, unable to hide a cringe. "I remember."

"Next time you want in on pool, just say so."

"Anyway," I sighed, rolling my eyes and hoping he didn't notice the blush I knew was creeping on my heated cheeks, "you're not a culinary student, so—"

"No, I'm an IT grad student. I wound up working the test kitchen since all the IT jobs were taken. It's easy work, which is great since this last year is a bitch."

"Until culinary students like me mosey in and ruin your night?"

"You didn't ruin my night. You were the highlight of my day." His eyes found mine as the air in the coffee shop thickened. Or maybe the air just thickened between *us*.

Nope, nope. This was coffee. We could talk and be friendly but that's it.

"Drew, listen . . . I'm . . . still trying to figure things out. I haven't been just Sara in a long time. So long, I don't even know who she is." I chuckled to myself. "I'm not ready for any—"

"Are you ready for a friend?" A soft smile lifted the corners of his lips. His lush, full lips. Any female on campus would kill to be in my seat. It all seemed unfair. What was he doing wasting time with me?

"I'd like that. Although, you've only had a peek at the hot mess I am. I'm still learning basic socialization."

"I can teach you. I convinced you to stay, didn't I?"

I laughed at his cocky smirk. "Are you sure you want to burden yourself with having a friend like that?"

His grin grew wider.

"I can handle you."

My mouth parched at the husky rasp of his voice. I took a long, shaky sip of lukewarm coffee.

But can I handle you?

Seven

SARA

"EXCUSE ME," I clipped at the redheaded bombshell perched on the test kitchen sign in desk. I was already in a pissy mood thanks to my lack of sleep last night and screwing up in class earlier today, most likely because of the aforementioned lack of sleep. Two hours of overtime was hard to resist, especially when I needed every cent. But when you have to wake up for an early class and be ready to learn something, I suppose rest has its importance. Over the past nine years I probably averaged about three to four hours of sleep a night, but the game was different now. Or I was just old and couldn't keep up. My jaw ticked at both the thought and this bimbo who wouldn't move.

She peered at me with wide, mascara-drenched eyes. "What? I'm waiting for Drew."

Of course, she was. I let out a sigh and ignored the urge to push her off the desk and right onto her perfect, young ass. Drew and I were friends and a girl waiting for him in the test kitchen was not my problem or my business, regardless of the rancid taste it left in my mouth. A decade ago, I would've been "waiting" for Drew, too, although not as brazenly or obvious.

"Sabrina," Drew groaned. "I told you before, stop sitting

on the desk." Drew didn't seem happy to see her. He scoffed in irritation as he dropped his bag next to the desk.

"Well, I was here early, and you weren't here."

"There are stools at each station to wait, and you're covering the sign in sheet." He jutted his chin toward the clipboard she was covering.

"Sorry," she whispered as she moved off the desk in a slow and seductive slide, like one of those game show models my grandpa used to love on the *Price is Right* when I was a kid. I remembered how fake and forced it seemed and even while playing with dolls on their living room floor, I would roll my eyes. Maybe I was cynical and salty from birth. Drew seemed as unimpressed as I was as he picked up the board and handed it to me.

"She can't take a hint," he whispered with a half-smile as his gaze slid to mine. "Nice to see you, Sara."

I grabbed the board, letting a smile pull across my lips as I scribbled my name and the time.

"I'm sure it's a hardship," I teased, motioning to where Sabrina scowled at the both of us before setting the board back on the desk.

I settled at one of the stations, pulling out all the ingredients I'd brought with an odd sense of satisfaction from Drew's lack of interest in Sabrina. This was exactly the involvement I didn't want. I shouldn't care where Drew's interests were or weren't. My sole priority was to ensure I knew what I was doing in class, so I could graduate and support my kid. To my dismay, knowing I shouldn't care didn't actually *stop* me from caring.

I got to work, losing myself doing what I loved to do best, and what I was good at. The money I spent on ingredients and the time I spent here tonight was all to prove a point to myself.

The issue in class today wasn't because I didn't know what I was doing; it was from being too tired to focus.

"You really get in the zone, don't you?" Drew noted from behind me as he approached my station. I stole a glance at the sinful dark eyes and thick lashes as I stirred.

"I screwed up in class today, so I came here for extra practice. I guess I need to sleep after all." I sighed and lowered the heat. "Or, maybe I'm just out of practice."

"Yeah, right. Overachiever." Drew crossed his arms and shook his head at me.

"Ha," I scoffed. "I think that's the first time I've been called that."

"Seriously? I could tell in five seconds. You could probably cook with your eyes closed. You don't fumble around like I see most of the students do here." He lowered his voice as he came closer . . . his buttery sweet voice. Something on him had to be unattractive, but hell if I could find it. Again, why attempting a friendship with this guy was a terrible idea.

"Well, my eyes were almost closed in class today and I didn't do such a great job. Soups were always my thing which is why messing up today pissed me off so much. My daughter was sick last week, and her father told me she only wanted my soup. He tried giving her the packaged stuff and she said no." A sad laugh fell from my lips. I hated how I couldn't take care of her while she was sick but loved that she wanted something only from me. Being away from her for so long had my insecurities running haywire.

"At least he's trying to take care of her, finally."

"Well . . ." I shrugged. "That's not really his fault."

"How?" Drew squinted at me. "Were you and her father . . . together for long?"

I lifted my head to Drew, holding in a cringe. There was no good way to tell this story. Getting pregnant by someone you knew for less than twenty-four hours, regardless if it was the only time it happened, didn't say much for your character.

"I'm sorry." His face crumpled in a contrite wince. "I didn't mean to be—"

"No, it's . . . we weren't. I only knew him for one night, but one night was all it took." I offered a nervous laugh. "It's not something I'd ever done before. It just sort of happened."

He held up his hand. "No need to explain. I'm familiar with things that sort of happen."

"I bet." I nodded to Sabrina, who in the time we were all here hadn't really cooked anything. The only heat coming from her station was her sultry glare at Drew.

"Not that. Believe me. I like a little substance, someone who won't offer everything until I've worked for it." His eyes leveled on me, causing me to squirm under his perusal. I blinked and focused on my bisque, ignoring the challenge in his stare.

"Anyway, how is it not his fault he hasn't taken care of her until now?"

I clicked my tongue against my teeth and leaned back in the chair. "He didn't know about her. I knew how to find him but chose not to. I mean, he seemed nice enough, but I had no idea who he really was or how he'd react. Once he found us, he surprised me by actually wanting to be a father."

"He found you? How?"

I bit the inside of my cheek, remembering the worst day of my life.

"He was friends with my daughter's school principal. One day they called me in for a meeting, and as luck would have it, Josh was there for a visit. He had just moved back to New York. He took one look at her and the same weird eye color they shared and had figured it out in seconds."

I left out the part when I ran, scared of how he'd react or if he'd try to take her. My fear, guilt, and wounded pride made us all miserable for quite a long time. Well, made *me* miserable. I was still fighting against all three, and it was exhausting.

Drew's silence was unnerving. His eyes wide and still fixed on me. My life was a bad made-for-TV movie and I hated Drew seeing me differently after hearing all about my lowest point. Something about him made me open up and tell him things I hid from others. I never cared about what people thought, but I cared what *he* thought. Maybe I'd found the one thing to make him back off.

"Josh is a great father," I continued. "I never gave him a chance, and both he and Victoria suffered for it. Aren't you glad you asked?" I poured the soup into a container after it cooled, satisfied with my culinary ability but disgusted with myself for other reasons.

I omitted the horror show of acclimating to Josh's presence in our lives. I had so much to atone for and the path to redemption was long and uphill.

"You had no idea who he was then, and now," Drew finally said, "he may've turned out to be a good dad, but how could you have known that? He could've been the complete opposite." He inched closer and squeezed my shoulder. "Sara, you did what you had to do. You're a great mom. Don't let anyone make you feel otherwise." He gave me a small smile that, for the first time, allowed some of the self-loathing to dissipate and circle the drain.

My throat thickened as he strolled back to the front desk. Why did I tell him everything, and why didn't he back away?

Having real friends took some getting used to.

Eight

DREW

"HEY, JODI." I nodded at the waitress at the counter before I slid onto one of the stools. The diner outside of campus was small, but they had a killer breakfast. After being up for half the night on my group project, I wanted some grease in my stomach before I went back to my apartment and passed out. School was a breeze before I became a graduate student. Now, it sucked, but I could glimpse the light at the end of the tunnel.

"Drew?" My groggy eyes turned to the familiar sultry voice behind me.

"Sara," I croaked as my gaze met hers. "Good morning."

"Good morning to you, too. You look like you've been up all night. Did you party too hard?" She tilted her head as she strolled up to the counter. How could anyone look this good in only a long sleeve T-shirt and leggings? Sara had natural beauty that radiated off of her every time I saw her. But I was only a friend and wasn't supposed to notice. After complaining that so many girls were too open, I set my sights on one so tightly closed I'd need the jaws of life to get her to budge even a little.

"I wish," I answered on a yawn. "Brian, Carlos, and I were finishing up our final project most of the night. I'm here to pick up an egg sandwich before I sleep the rest of the day."

"Oh, okay then. Enjoy and get some sleep." Sara frowned before she backed away.

"Hey," I whispered before I caught her arm. "Why do you look like you were about to ask me something?"

A wave of shyness flashed in her eyes as she motioned to the back tables. "I'm here by myself and was going to ask you to join me." She squinted at me with a cute as hell bashful smile.

"Join you? That sounds like socializing. Sure you're up for it?" I arched an eyebrow, loving the scowl I received in return.

We'd hung out a couple of times after I bribed her into coffee. Usually during or sometimes after my shifts in the lab. I was coaxing her out of her hardened shell little by little. From the small things I'd gotten her to share, I got the feeling she'd been alone with her daughter so long she didn't know how to reach out to anyone else. An insignificant thing like an invite to breakfast was a big deal where she was concerned.

"Very funny." Her eyes rolled. "Go home and get some sleep."

"No, no. I'm not one to refuse such a nice invitation. Lead the way."

Sara fought a smile as she jerked her head toward her table in the back. I followed, willing myself to keep my eyes north of her waist.

"What brings you here alone?" I asked as I slid into the booth across from her.

"I don't know," she shrugged as she leaned her elbows onto the table. "I was up early and didn't feel like a bowl of cereal from our kitchen. You kept saying how good breakfast was here, so . . ."

"You listened to me?" I clutched my chest. "Wow, I'm impressed."

"Surprised me, too." Her lips stretched into a wide smile, making the air whoosh right out of my lungs. When the smile made it to her eyes, she was the definition of breathtaking. Whatever life did to her made that smile hard to come by. It was the second time I'd seen it, but I knew it was as rare as it was beautiful—like a shooting star.

"I used to take Victoria to the diner by us once a month on a Sunday morning. She loved stuffed French toast." She fidgeted with the silverware next to her plate. "That and dance school were my big splurges."

"Think of all the French toast you can buy her when you're a big fancy chef." I tapped her wrist to make her look up. "And I bet she lived for those Sundays. My mom used to take me to the comic book store once a month before she met my stepdad. I still remember those as the best days."

"Comic book store?" She crinkled her nose.

"No self-respecting computer nerd doesn't know his comics." I leveled eyes at her.

"Does your little sister like comics, too?"

"Cassie? She likes girly stuff. Dolls, Hello Kitty; she still sleeps with the Pinkie Pie My Little Pony doll I gave her year ago. Although, I snuck in a Wonder Woman comic book in her stocking last Christmas and she didn't hate it. I took that as progress."

Her eyes welled with tears, but she blinked them away. "Victoria loves Wonder Woman. That's the theme of her room at her father's house."

"Maybe they should meet one day. She could help me convert my sister."

"Maybe," she whispered and offered a smile, but a forced one this time.

"Who knew that I'd have to leave her to give her a good life." She pinched her eyes shut and groaned. "Sorry, Drew. You came in for eggs, not a sad story."

I reached for her hand across the table and gave it a squeeze. "That's not true. And even though I'd never met Victoria, I'm sure she'd agree. You gave her the best life you could, and now you're working your ass off to make it even better. Chin up, Caldwell." I tapped her chin with my knuckle and was rewarded with a real laugh.

"I FaceTimed with her this morning and she told me all about her father's wedding yesterday. The pictures looked beautiful and she looks like she . . . fits with them. I'm afraid after this year is up she'll think she doesn't fit with me anymore."

The defeated look in her eyes made me want to rise from my seat and wrap my arms around her. She came off as cold, but I'd bet that was because no one took the time to see how she was or gave a shit as to how she was feeling.

"You have something they don't. They can give her all the iPads in the world and decorate her room any way they want. They aren't her mom. She'll always fit with you, Sara."

Our food came and brought a welcomed halt to our heavy conversation.

"You're pretty wise," Sara noted as she poked at her scrambled eggs.

My mouth fell open. "Did you just pay me a compliment? Look at you being social AND pleasant."

She gave me a wry grin. "I mean, wise for a comic book geek. Marvel or DC?"

I tapped my chin. "Probably DC. I've always been a huge Batman fan. *The Dark Knight* should have won the Oscar for Best Picture."

"Of course, it should have." She nodded with a hint of a smile. "I'm glad I found you here today." She said it so softly it was almost inaudible.

"I'm glad you did, too. You know, you're pretty when you smile. Beautiful, actually. You should try it more often."

She scoffed and rolled her eyes.

"See, that?" I jutted my chin in her direction. "That, not so much." She laughed around the rim of her coffee cup.

"You can find me here on Saturdays or Sundays usually. Want to make eggs and sad stories a regular thing?"

She peered up at me, showing a hint of the smile I was starting to yearn for.

"I'll try to keep the sad stories to a minimum, but . . . sure, why not?"

I dropped my head, smiling to myself. I'd get through those walls she caged herself in, one tiny crack at a time.

Nine

SARA

"I'M SUCH AN idiot," Emma lamented as we strolled out of class. "This burn is going to make lab suck for the next week." Her mouth twisted as she examined the scaly burn on the side of her hand.

"You aren't an idiot. It happens all the time. I see your burn and raise you my cut." I held up my palm to draw attention to the slice I made down my hand when I was supposed to be carving a chicken. "You should've seen my waitress injuries. I came home looking like I handled a snake in a fire pit." I laughed to myself. I could laugh about those days now; it was anything but funny back then.

"What did you do? I can't miss lab." She cradled her injured hand against her chest.

"A good cream and liquid bandages work wonders." I gave her forearm a reassuring squeeze. "You'll live, I promise."

"How did you work through all of that?" She scoffed and shook her head. "I couldn't."

A humorless laugh fell from my lips. "You'd be surprised what you can do when you have no choice."

My landlord wouldn't have cared that I burned my hand, and

the supermarket didn't allow you to put food on loan, so I worked through the pain. Because I had to.

"Hey, ladies!" Drew waved as he passed us on the way inside. "Good class? Any leftovers?" He gave us a wide smile, but Emma groaned before I could answer.

"No. We're the walking wounded. I got burned and Sara got cut." Still clutching onto her hand, she nodded her chin at me.

"Wounded? What's wrong?' Drew's brow pinched as he squinted his eyes in concern—at me. Emma was forgotten to him, but she was too busy over-nursing her burn to notice.

"A cut, it's no big deal. Occupational hazard. My personal best is ten stitches down my wrist from a serrated knife." I jutted my chin out in mock pride, but Drew didn't laugh.

"I'm going to find some cream and run more cold water over it." Emma backed away from us, regarding her hand as if it were about to fall off. Poor thing. She'd learn soon enough.

Drew grabbed my hand to get a closer look. He shot me a concerned glance as his thumb drifted down the open cut. I gasped, but not in pain. I didn't want to acknowledge the jolt of electricity caused by his skin sliding across mine.

"It's fine, really." I withdrew my hand, wincing at the sting as I wiped the sweat from my palm onto my jeans. "Comes with the territory. All I need is a liquid bandage or even some Krazy Glue." I shrugged, and the flat line of his lips curved into a smile.

"Krazy Glue?"

"You never watched a medical show? Krazy Glue is gold for cuts. You should try it, you know in case you come down too hard on one key and injure yourself." I raised a brow, fighting the urge to rub at the painful sting across my palm. If glue didn't work, it would be a long and painful night.

"Always the warrior." He sighed and crossed his arms. "I bet you were one of those kids who had perfect attendance every year."

"I was raised as long as you didn't have a high fever, you went to school. If you could crawl, you could still go. I guess I still think along those lines." I shrugged. "How long are you here tonight?"

"Tonight is my late night if you want to come by, but you probably want to rest the hand."

I gave him a slow shake of my head. "I work tonight. I'll fix it up and it'll be fine."

The worried pinch of his brows returned. "Are you sure? No need to be a hero, Sara."

I fought a roll of my eyes. "This is nothing, and I could use the extra money." Every cent I could spare went into a new life fund for Victoria and me when my year was finished. I couldn't renege on that even for one night for the sake of a silly cut. I'd get us the best apartment I could find, and she'd love it as much as Josh and Brianna's new place. Not that I was subconsciously competing or anything.

"Promise me you'll cut the night short if it hurts too much." The pleading in his dark eyes almost made me stumble. When was the last time anyone worried about me? My mind rewound to when my grandparents were still alive, meaning decades ago.

"Yes," I lied. "I'll show you my just fine hand tomorrow at breakfast. I believe it's your turn to buy."

The more time I spent with Drew, the more I liked him. He was funny, charming, and as easy to talk to as he was on the eyes. Our comfortable friendship made me feel less alone. The old Sara would be mean enough to make him never want to speak to her ever again, and it only would have taken a couple of tries. This new Sara enjoyed his company and his adorable wisdom beyond his twenty-five years.

His lips spread into a slow smile. "I believe you're right. I'll meet you after my run."

"I miss running," I sighed. "The gym is so boring." I worked out at the free gym in Berman Hall but running on the elliptical was like watching paint dry. I'd wanted to run on campus but didn't feel comfortable alone so early.

"Run with me. Meet me on the campus track at six."

"A.M.?" I gaped, pulling a throaty chuckle out of Drew.

"A.M.," he confirmed with a cheeky grin. "Any later, the track team takes over and it's crowded as hell. Embrace the dawn, Caldwell." He slapped my arm before heading back into the lab.

❦ ❦ ❦

"WHY DON'T YOU take a break?" Loretta, one of the chefs I was assisting for the night, glared at me as she motioned to the break room behind the kitchen.

"I'm fine. It's busy tonight and I'm here to help you." I waved her off, the rush of air hitting my cut and bringing out an involuntary hiss. My usual go-tos didn't work, and three Band-Aids fell off when I had to wash my hands.

"You're working in pain, and you won't learn anything that way. You only have a half an hour left anyway. Why don't you head to the back, clean it up and put a fresh bandage over it? Last thing I need is my best worker getting an infection." She squinted at me and pointed to the door.

I nodded, reluctant and pissed off at myself for not paying attention in the lab today. I couldn't afford injuries or sickness now but agreed with Loretta that I wasn't of any use for the remainder of my shift. I lumbered out of the kitchen and once again rummaged through the first aid kit. I whimpered as I cleaned out the deeper-than-I-thought wound, hoping I could hold the steering wheel on the short ride home.

I fell into one of the chairs and dropped my head back, attempting to will away the self-pity at the number I'd done on my hand. The vibration of my phone in my pocket startled me. Carefully digging it out with my good hand, I couldn't help but smile when I glanced at the unread message on the screen.

Drew: *How's the hand? You took it easy tonight, right?*

My smile grew wider as my heart squeezed. I wasn't used to anyone checking on me. I pictured his dark brow crinkled with worry. This boy was hopeless. Adorable, but hopeless.

Me: *It's fine. Not my first rodeo, I've worked through injuries a ton of times.*

Drew: *Stop distracting me with visions of you as a hot cowgirl. That was a bad cut and looked painful as hell.*

Me: *I told you, I'm fine. And cowgirl? Are you kidding me?*

Drew: *You're the one who started it. Now I'm picturing you in the tight pants and boots.*

I groaned as my head fell back. He was exasperating, but my lips quirked into a smile. Two seconds ago, I was feeling sorry for myself and even though pain still seared across my hand, our ridiculous banter over text made me forget, if only for a moment.

Me: *Okay, stop. I'm not in tight pants or boots. I'm in a filthy assistant chef uniform with sweaty hair and runny makeup.*

Drew: *And now you're telling me you're filthy. If you want us to stay in the friend zone, this isn't helping, Caldwell.*

Me: *Me being filthy is a turn on to you?*

Drew: . . . you have no idea.

My bandage-wrapped palm scrubbed down my heated face.
I peered into the mirror next to the couch and was surprised to
see a smile still stretching my cheeks. He was getting to me—or
had already gotten to me—and I was still dead set on denying it.

Me: You're sweet to check on me. If it makes you feel any better,
I'm done for the night and just put a fresh bandage on it.

Drew: It does. I was worried and knew your stubborn ass wouldn't
rest unless someone told you to.

Drew: Which is what happened, right?

I scowled at the screen.

Me: Maybe.

Drew: You can never admit when I'm right.

Me: Because who wants you more full of yourself?

Drew: I'm letting that golden opportunity slip right by . . . can
you drive, or do you want me to come get you?

Me: I can drive, thank you. See you in the morning at the track?

Drew: 6 a.m. Get home safe, Caldwell.

Me: Thank you for checking on me.

Drew: What are friends for?

Friends didn't give you a case of the butterflies with a text
message. I eyeballed my throbbing hand and let out a long sigh.
In my old life, I would have never allowed a close friendship with
anyone, much less someone I was fighting an attraction to. I was
happy in my solitude—or so I forced myself to believe.

So what if we were spending more and more time together
and he checked on me? It didn't mean anything.

Too bad I didn't believe me, either.

Ten

DREW

"GET THOSE LEGS up, Caldwell!" I chided Sara over my shoulder.

"Seriously?"

I cracked up at her breathless and frustrated reply.

"You said you were a runner." I turned around and jogged backward as she ran toward me. "Gotta say, not so sure now that I've seen you in action." I arched an eyebrow and could've sworn I'd heard a growl erupt from her throat. Wisps from her ponytail licked her damp cheeks as she glared at me.

"I said . . . I liked to run . . ." Her words were stilted as she tried to catch her breath and tell me off at the same time. "I didn't say anything about being a track star . . . jerk."

A laugh rumbled from my chest after she whispered the last word. This was the second time this week I dragged her to the running track on campus. She struggled to keep up last time but refused to admit it. For a second, I thought she would collapse and I'd have to carry her back to her dorm, not that I would've minded—at all. When I asked if she wanted to slow it down next time, she answered with a scowl of death. It was fucking adorable.

The running track used to be my solitude in the early morning hours and a place to clear my head. I gladly traded that peace for breaking Sara's chops.

"Hey, we have two more laps left!" I yelled as she jogged off the track.

"I need a break. I should've known you were a fitness freak." She craned her head and glowered at me before plopping onto a bench.

"Should've known how?" I sat beside Sara and nudged her ribs with my elbow.

Her eyes rolled before she unzipped her hoodie. "Look at you. There isn't an ounce of fat anywhere. You're probably here every morning. I told you I was a *weekend* runner. I'd get a few laps in during Victoria's dance class on a Saturday. I don't have your endurance, Drew."

My mouth slanted into a smirk. "So, you're saying I'm hot?"

She groaned before massaging the back of her neck. "I'm saying it's obvious that I'm not on your level. Next time, I'll go at my own pace and you go at yours."

Sara stood and unzipped her sweatshirt, chasing the teasing smile right off my face. Her body was curvy yet lean, the tight pink tank accentuating every inch of her perfect silhouette. Full breasts and a tiny waist poured into delicious tight thighs and . . . don't get me started on her ass. She had no clue how sexy she really was, which only made her even more irresistible. I wished she could see what I saw. What *everyone* saw. Eyes followed Sara everywhere and she was too deep into her own head to notice.

"Drew?" She snapped her fingers in front of my face. "Are you okay? You just spaced out for a minute."

I spaced out checking you out. I controlled myself around Sara for the most part, but I'd lapse from time to time. If she noticed, she didn't call me on it. She trusted me as a friend, and I wouldn't fuck up the only piece of her she allowed me to have.

"I'm here, you were saying?" I straightened and brought my eyes to hers, no matter how tempted they were to drop lower.

"I don't have to come next time. I'm holding you back." She stood from the bench and I grabbed her wrist to pull her back.

"You are not. It's fun having you here, huffing and puffing behind me."

She slapped my arm. "Not the best coach, are you?"

"Hey, Kostas!" A voice called out behind us. "Still coming here at the butt crack of dawn?" Chase ambled over to us. He was a grad student, too, but I only knew him through a friend of mine. "And you've got a pretty running partner now."

I didn't like or dislike him, but his presence now made me bristle with irritation. I suspected it had something to do with how he brazenly eye fucked Sara as she leaned back on the bench.

"I don't think we've met. I'm Chase. Nice to meet you." He extended a hand to Sara with a huge, shit-eating grin. I gripped the edge of the metal bench to fight the urge to ball my hands into fists and pummel them right in his face.

"Sara." She gripped his hand, and he didn't let go as easily as he should have, or at least as easily as I thought he should have. He settled next to her, again too close for my comfort, and blood boiled in my veins. He was always on the creepy side, but I never wanted to kick the shit out of him for it before.

"Are you one of Drew's friends?" She squinted as she looked between us.

"We were in a few classes last year." I shrugged before standing. "And we were just on our way to breakfast, so if you'll excuse us." I grabbed her hand and yanked her off the bench harder than I'd meant to. Something inside me snapped and needed to get her away from this asshole as soon as possible.

Maybe I didn't accept being just friends with Sara as much as I let on. Maybe I hated that I had no claim or right to tell Chase or guys like him who approached her to back off. Maybe I wanted her to be mine—now. Not maybe at some unsure point in the unforeseeable future.

"Are you all right?" Sara stilled and yanked back.

"Fine," I clipped, still irritated as fuck, and doing a shit job of hiding it. Her brows pinched in confusion, and I didn't blame her. Sometimes, I wondered what the hell was wrong with me, too.

We were supposed to be *only* friends, but I hadn't so much as glanced in another woman's direction since Sara stumbled into the lab that night. I'd go to the bar with the guys and the girls either wouldn't be pretty enough or smart enough or something else enough. The problem, or *my* problem was, they weren't Sara enough.

Silence fell over us as we made our way to the diner on campus. It was only when I reached for the door that I realized I still held her hand in mine. I'd never dropped it, and she never pulled away. Now I was even more pissed at myself for wanting to make that simple gesture mean something between us.

The waitress brought our menus over right after we were seated. The usual playfulness between us wasn't there. The air that surrounded us was thick and uncomfortable. Shaking off what happened with Chase was harder than it should've been. He only shook her hand . . . and leered at her. I raked my hand through my hair as the thought pissed me off all over again. What would I do if a guy tried more than that? I'd end up in jail if I didn't reel myself in.

"Why do you waste your time, Drew?" Sara's voice was small.

I lifted my head to meet her pained stare. Her chocolate brown eyes bore into mine, half questioning, half exposed. I'd never seen her this vulnerable before.

"Waste my time?"

"You could spend time with anyone. *Be* with anyone . . . without issues and a ton of baggage. Someone your age. Someone who could keep up with you." She put her head down and laughed.

"But that someone wouldn't be you." Her eyes brightened right before they squeezed shut. I still wouldn't push, but I was done lying to myself or her.

"Drew, you're a good guy. I'm holding you back, I can tell. I love hanging out with you, but I can't ask you—"'

"You never asked me to do anything. I love hanging out with you, too. I don't know who convinced you that you were some kind of unwanted burden, but you're not. Never. So, you're not blowing me off, Caldwell. Nice try." I let my lips curve up, hoping to draw out a smile.

"You wanted to punch Chase, didn't you?" The corners of her mouth twitched.

"Maybe." I shrugged, pretending to peruse the menu I'd seen a hundred times.

She let out a heavy sigh as she opened the menu. "You're a foolish man, Kostas."

Maybe I was a fool, but she was worth it. Sooner or later, I'd get her to believe that.

Eleven

DREW

"HEY MAN, YOU alive?"

I winced at the light tap on my door. Even the almost muffled sound made my head throb.

"For now," I croaked out a reply before the hacking started. I never got sick, and even on those rare occasions I did, I sucked it up and kept going. A fever of 102 combined with aches and chills knocked me right on my ass. I missed a day of classes and two days in the kitchen lab. It sucked but I felt too much like shit to care. "What's up, Carlos?" My heavy legs lumbered over the side of my bed, the room spinning from my first attempt in the past day to sit upright.

"You have a visitor."

I squinted at my roommate's quirked brow, half hoping my mother didn't listen to me earlier and drove over to the apartment with a quart of chicken soup anyway.

"A visitor?" I shivered as I reached for my hoodie next to the bed.

Carlos nodded. "Yep, waiting for you in the kitchen with a big pot of soup."

"Ugh," I groaned and shook my head. "I told her not to drive here after she got out of work." I trudged out of my room toward the kitchen. I appreciated Mom coming here to take care of me, but it was late, and I didn't like the idea of her driving home by herself. Soup, however, sounded fucking wonderful. I didn't remember the last time I'd eaten. Maybe yesterday afternoon before I took three ibuprofens and passed out.

"Mom, I told you not to—" I scolded before I trailed off. Even being sick with swollen, red eyes, Sara was a vision. I blinked a couple of times to make sure the fever wasn't causing hallucinations.

"Wow." She grimaced as she ambled over to me. "You look like shit, Kostas."

"Thanks for the compliment," I laughed, triggering another coughing fit.

"Easy," she whispered as she tapped and rubbed my back. Even two beats away from death, her soothing touch caused my heart to seize.

"Sit. I snuck in the lab early tonight and made as much as I could." She led me to the table. "It's run-of-the-mill chicken noodle soup, but you have enough for today and tomorrow." She draped her hand over my forehead when I plopped into the chair. "Clammy but not too warm. Hopefully, you're past the worst of it."

I smiled at the concerned furrow of her brow. She breezed around the kitchen in caretaker mode, which I guessed as a parent came as second nature to her. I glanced at the huge pot of soup on the stove, loving the hell out of the fact she came all the way here to take care of me. Even though I was weak, I rose from the chair to where she stood. I kept a safe distance in case I was still contagious, but I was so drawn to her, the kitchen table was too far away.

"I haven't eaten since yesterday. Homemade soup sounds amazing."

Her head jerked in my direction as she gaped at me. "Yesterday? That's not good. I always made Victoria eat a little when she was sick as long as she wasn't throwing up. I'd heard you're supposed to starve a fever, but I think all of that is bullshit." She stirred the soup and adjusted the knob on the stove.

"Old wives' tale, maybe. Is that what your mother used to tell you?" I elbowed her side with a snicker, but she didn't smile back. Her body stiffened as she shook her head.

"No. I just heard it a few times. And most old wives' tales are bullshit." I'd never heard her mention family other than Victoria, and the way she flinched at the mention of her mother confirmed they probably weren't in the picture. The only constant in her life was her daughter, and I hated that for her. I wanted to be her constant. It was a burning urge I wouldn't be able to hold back for much longer.

"You made all that for me?" I rubbed the two-day old scruff on my chin. "You must like me or something."

She rolled her eyes as she fought a smile. "I may have missed having you around. I figured this maybe would get you better faster. And I've made this so many times I could do it with my eyes closed. Now I'm assuming by the coat of dust I had to wipe off the stove, you boys don't cook very much, but do you at least have bowls and spoons for cereal?" She clicked her tongue, and sick and all, I wanted to kiss the hell out of her.

"We do." I crossed my arms and leaned against the counter. "How do you know when it's ready?"

"When it comes up to a simmer, you can eat."

"Simmer? Look at you with the chef words."

She huffed and rolled her eyes. "Simmer isn't a chef word. Everyone knows what it means."

"I don't." I shrugged. "Teach me, Caldwell. What does simmer mean?"

Her eyes darted from where I stood to the pot. Even though I was sick as a dog, we still had that current running between us. We'd made a couple of wimpy acknowledgments, but for the most part skated around it.

She licked her lips and set the spoon down next to the pot. "Simmer is heating through but making sure it doesn't come to a boil."

"What happens if it gets too hot? Like you try to keep the heat down, but it boils over anyway? Is it all ruined?" My froggy voice dipped to a husky tone.

"Depends," she whispered as her gaze slid to mine. I wasn't talking about the soup and neither was she—whether or not she could admit it.

"Hey, is there enough to share?" Carlos came back into the kitchen and pulled two bowls out of the cabinet. "My throat's a little scratchy." He winked at Sara and gave her a tiny smile until he met my pissed off glare. He gave me a tiny nod and held up his hand before digging in the drawer for spoons.

"Enough for everyone. You can keep the pot for now. I swiped it from the lab, but I didn't think you'd tell on me." She smiled as Carlos handed her a ladle with a lot less charm than when he first stepped into the kitchen, having received my message to back the fuck off loud and clear. Not that he would try anything; he'd heard me talk about Sara enough to deduce how I felt about her and wouldn't make a real play. I cupped my forehead and massaged my temples. My feelings for Sara made me want to beat anyone up who noticed her, even one of my best friends.

My head was still stuffy and clouded, but I knew without a doubt how fucked I was.

Sara made me eat two bowls of the best chicken soup I'd ever had before piling me back into bed.

"That was the best soup I ever had in my life." I yawned before downing some cold medicine. I desperately needed a good five decongested hours of sleep.

Sara nodded to the pillow for me to lie down before she put the sheet back over me.

"I'll check on you in the morning. Get some sleep." She brushed the hair off my forehead before she realized it and jerked away. "Carlos said he'd let me out." *And probably stare at your perfect ass as you leave.* The medicine kicked in and made my eyelids heavy. I'd kick the shit out of him for it tomorrow when I woke up.

"You're gorgeous; you know that, right?"

She turned to me with a half-smile. "Sleep it off, Kostas."

I grabbed her hand. "Goodnight, Sara. Thank you."

She smiled, and it made it to her eyes. My chest pinched at how breathtaking that smile still was, and how she only gave it to me. It was a gift, like everything else about her. Unlike this sickness, my crush on Sara was an affliction I wouldn't be able to shake quite so easily—if ever.

"Anytime, Drew." She squeezed my hand back before sauntering out of the room. My hazy vision followed her path out my bedroom door. A wonderful woman with such a huge heart shouldn't have been alone for so long. Sara should be surrounded by people who care about her.

People like me. Sara should be with me.

I drifted off to sleep, dreaming of an angel who was only supposed to be my friend.

Twelve

SARA

"WHAT WAS THE weirdest thing you made as a bartender?" Lisa's eyes lit up before she threw back another shot.

I shook my head at her widened and glassy eyes. "I was a bartender for two days. I filled beer mugs and shot glasses. No fun concoctions, sorry!" I took a long pull of my own beer bottle and eyed my roommate. We both had a long and grueling week of kitchen lab testing, and I was willing to splurge and get some drinks to celebrate. Lisa was already on drink three and shot number four. I didn't mind helping her out of here, but carrying her, as she had a good six inches of height on me, would be a bitch. The bar was close to the dorm but not that close.

"That's so cool!" She shrieked as she stumbled onto the stool beside me. That helping/carrying window was approaching faster than I'd anticipated. "You know so many different techniques and recipes. I wish I had that kind of experience." She sighed before downing the rest of her beer. "I wish I worked in New York City like you."

I sucked in a deep breath and turned away from Lisa. Her comments came from an innocent place. Classmates would sometimes guffaw in class if I knew an odd ingredient or dish from the countless restaurants I'd waitressed at. And there were many: Italian, Turkish, Mexican, Indian. I didn't discriminate and thankfully neither did they when I applied for a job. I was always too busy bussing tables to really observe what went on in the kitchens, but I'd catch things from time to time and even experiment at home with a dish when I had an extra couple of bucks. My quest to keep us fed and sheltered made me a Renaissance woman to my friends. It was funny and sad at the same time.

I motioned to the bartender for two glasses of water and spotted Drew strolling in with a few of his friends. He stopped short when he caught my gaze, his brows shooting up in mock surprise.

"What's going on with you and Drew?" Lisa slurred before I shoved the glass of water in her face.

"We're friends. Nothing beyond that."

She snickered around the rim of the glass. "Riiight. You guys are adorable."

"Keep drinking, Lisa." I nudged the glass of water back into her hand.

"What are we talking about?" Emma squeezed herself between us and motioned for a drink.

"How cute Drew and Sara are." She batted her eyelashes and folded her hands under her chin.

"I know . . . the little glances of longing when they don't think the other is looking." She let out a squee and I groaned into my hands.

"There are no glances of longing. Don't encourage her, Emma."

"Um . . ." She leaned forward to whisper in my ear. "I see one right now. He looks your way every chance he gets." She grabbed her bottle of beer and turned to Lisa. "How hot would they be together? With Sara peaking and all."

"Peaking?" My brow crinkled as my fingers massaged the sudden ache in my temples from these two. "What the hell are you talking about?"

"Well, you're in your thirties, right?" She offered a sheepish smile. "I read an article about how that's when you like, hit your sexual peak. And Drew with all those fuckable inches of lean muscle and the dark bedroom eyes? Holy shit, you guys would combust from all the heat."

"For sure," Lisa agreed, her eyes less cloudy but still fixed on me. "Don't you want to peak with Drew, then come back and tell us all about it in Every. Single. Detail?"

I shot up from my stool, clutching the edge of the bar and shaking my head. "You guys are insane. I'm not peaking with Drew or anyone else." I huffed before dropping a ten on the counter.

"Tell Drew we said hi," Emma mocked as I stalked to the back of the bar with shaky breaths. If I were honest, I thought of "peaking" with Drew quite a bit. A few times when Lisa wasn't in the room I considered a private game of pretend, but I wouldn't allow it. I couldn't. Bad enough the fight to keep things on a friendly level grew harder each day. Sliding my hand between my legs and using thoughts of Drew to . . . as tempting as it was, it would only make things that much worse. My limbs weren't the only parts of my body that ached after our weekly runs together.

"Something wrong?" The velvety timbre I knew all too well made me stop. I turned and couldn't help my smile when my eyes met those deep chocolate ones. He really did have bedroom eyes, but as much as I wanted to, I couldn't test that theory.

"No, just escaping my drunken roommate for a few minutes

and thought I'd say hi. What?" Drew bit his lip to hold in a snicker.

"Out in public again. Look at you!"

I nudged his stomach as it rumbled with a laugh. Despite my best efforts to scowl, my mouth quirked into a smile.

"Ah, that's what I'm talking about," he whispered as he cupped my chin, causing a shiver to run through me.

"What is?" I breathed, forgetting to throw him my usual attitude.

"A real smile. From you, those are pretty damn rare." The sexy curl of his lip made me stumble.

Drew was an adorable contradiction. He was a sweet and funny nerd, his favorite pastime teasing me. He also dripped sex, and my traitorous body wanted nothing more than to lick it up. Sexual peak like Emma said or just the product of a decade long sexual drought? Maybe both? I had no clue what it was like to actually like someone anymore. I didn't have time to, so I never let myself consider it. The more time we spent together, the more I *considered*. The more I *liked*. The more I *wanted*. This wasn't good on so many levels.

"I smile. I'm not a robot or an ice queen. Maybe I just don't giggle like the girls you're used to." This time, I pulled off the scowl perfectly until he pulled me flush to his body.

"I know you're neither of those things. But you're so tense, your smiles are always tight and forced. A real smile?" I stilled as his thumb grazed my bottom lip. "Only I get those. All mine."

My knees liquified as my heart galloped in my chest. He was right. They were all his.

"Want to dance?" He whispered in my ear so close his lips grazed my lobe. It was as if I was being tested every day and getting dangerously closer and closer to failing. Why did he have to be so sexy and nice and stupid? Couldn't he see he was wasting his time?

"Dance?" I huffed out a laugh. "I'm not the dancing type." We were surrounded by the bumping and grinding of some students I knew from around campus. My own bumping and grinding days stopped a long time ago—nine years to be exact.

"I bet you would be if I found the right song." He tapped his chin. "Stay here."

He rushed over to the jukebox. My mind went to the bar I'd met Josh in that night and the jukebox older than me that still played actual records. I didn't dance in that bar either even though I'd been younger than Drew was at the time. Irritation flowed through my veins. I never really got to be a kid, did I? Carefree was never in my vocabulary. Maybe that's why I never danced.

My mouth fell open at the first notes of "Sara" by Starship. I shook my head as he sauntered back over.

"I don't think you can really dance to this—" My words halted as his arm snaked around my waist and brought me closer . . . and closer. My heart thundered in my ears as I froze.

"Yes, you can," he whispered. "Sway with me. Not that hard, Caldwell."

I looped my arms around his neck and moved with him. I saw his friends gawking at us in my peripheral but wouldn't look. Being in his arms felt too good to care what was bad about it—for now.

"I didn't think you knew this song. A little before your time, no?" I raised an eyebrow.

"It suits you." The husky rasp of his voice made butterflies somersault in my belly, never mind flutter. Despite all that heat I was trying so hard to deny, I was about to go up in flames right next to the pool tables.

"Suits me?" I cocked my head to the side. "Because the song is named 'Sara?' That's deep, Kostas."

I laughed until the back of his hand feathered down my cheek, grazing the corner of my mouth. I didn't feel thirty-two in that moment. It was as if I were a teenager, with all these foreign feelings ricocheting all over my body, feelings I had no clue what to do with. Well, maybe I *did* know, but I was too scared. Too terrified to let myself give in to this, to need someone. The lyrics spoke about storms brewing in Sara's eyes. It was more like a hurricane—wild and untamed with the potential for total devastation.

"Fire and ice. You show ice to everyone else, but I see fire. I see . . . I see so much." He swallowed as he searched my face. "I wish you did, too."

"I'm scared," I admitted as our eyes locked. The urge to kiss him was so strong my lips tingled. What was so wrong with giving in?

Everything.

His hand splayed on my lower back, bringing us even closer together. A hint of a smile floated across his lips before he whispered in my ear.

"Don't be. I've got you. Or I will." He pressed a soft, wet kiss behind my ear. Every little hair on the back of my neck stood straight up as goose bumps flared across the spot where his mouth had been. "Once you let me."

Thirteen

DREW

THE LAB WAS dead, but I expected that the Tuesday before Thanksgiving. I was about to close early when Sara rushed through the door. I rose from my seat to greet her but was rooted to my spot by the pained look in her eyes.

"Hey," I whispered as she scribbled her name on the sign-in sheet, still not acknowledging my presence. Something was wrong, and I was about to drag it out of her one way or another. "Talk to me."

"I'm working Thursday. All the other students are off but since I have a paid internship they need me to cover Thursday afternoon." Her voice cracked on the last word. "I don't even know why I'm here. I was going to make bread pudding for Victoria tonight, but I won't see her, so why . . ." Her eyes clenched shut at the first tear she couldn't hold in.

I pulled her into my arms without thinking about it, and she didn't fight me. We were alone, but I wouldn't have given a single fuck if we weren't. She whimpered into my chest as her shoulders shook.

"Did you tell her yet?"

She nodded as she pushed out of my hold. "They promised me

Christmas week off since the restaurant closes but Thanksgiving is their busiest day. And it's time and a half, which I could use," she sniffled as she swiped her cheeks with the back of her hand. "I just . . . I miss her so much. Josh offered to drive her up here, but that's a long way to only see me for a few hours. I go back in on Friday for the whole day."

"Are you going to be alone on Thursday?"

She shrugged. "Lisa invited me over to her parents' house, but I'd get there after six, so I said no. I probably won't be very good company anyway."

"We never eat before six. My stepdad usually has to work. Come to my parents' house."

Her eyes widened as she shook her head. "That's really sweet, Drew. But I can't—"

"Why can't you? They live fifteen minutes from campus. I'll wait until you get out of work and we can go together. And we all love bread pudding, so . . ." I nodded to the empty stations in the back. "Get to work, Caldwell."

"Drew," she whispered as she inched closer. "Are you sure you want me to come to your—"

"You're my friend and I'm inviting you to my family's Thanksgiving dinner. No one, including me, will make it more than that. Thinking of you here alone will twist me up so much you'll ruin my favorite meal of the year. You wouldn't do that to me, right, Sara?" I jutted my lower lip in a pout. She laughed and swatted my arm.

"You play dirty. Okay," she relented with a hint of a smile. "I'll come. With bread pudding. So, if you'll excuse me."

She ambled to one of the stations a little lighter than when she first came in. All she'd been talking about for weeks was seeing

Victoria and I knew she hated waiting another month. Sara never mentioned any family, and I knew they weren't in the picture for holidays. Thanksgiving both away from her daughter and alone would eat away at her, whether or not she admitted it. That wouldn't happen—not as long as she had me. Would things get complicated and even more muddy between us? I didn't doubt it, but I didn't care.

⸱᷍⸱᷍⸱᷍

"YOU'RE SURE THEY'RE okay with this?" Sara winced as I pulled into my parents' driveway. "Bringing some strange woman over for Thanksgiving."

I snickered as I shut the engine off. "The strange woman is my friend. My mom always adopted all the friends I brought over. She's like that, and she'll love you." I slid my palm against hers and laced our fingers together. "Relax."

My eyes held hers for a long minute. I couldn't stop touching her—and she was letting me. Maybe I was getting under her skin as much as she was under mine. What would she do if I kissed her? I shook off the burning inclination. *Baby steps, Kostas.*

I reached for the door and stilled when Sara cupped the back of my neck. She pressed a long kiss to my cheek before resting her forehead on my temple. "Thank you," she sighed into my ear.

My body didn't move as it stiffened—*everywhere*. God, I wanted those lips. This woman turned me into a panting little puppy and I had no shame about it. I turned and kissed the top of her head.

"What are friends for?"

"Andrew!" My mother bellowed from the kitchen window. "Get inside, everything is almost ready!"

Holding in a frustrated groan, I stepped out of the car and led Sara up our front steps.

"Nice to meet you, Sara. I've heard wonderful things about you." Mom smiled at Sara as she held the door open for both of us.

"Nice to meet you, too, Mrs.—"

"Julia." She enveloped Sara in a big hug. "Glad to have you here." Sara glanced over at me with widened eyes before she gave into my mother's embrace with a relieved smile.

Sara would always kid how she was socially inept, but her real issue was accepting kindness. She never expected it, so she didn't know how to react.

"Drew said you liked bread pudding and it's my daughter's favorite, so . . . ." She trailed off when Cassie's voice drifted down the hallway.

"Drew!" My sister raced over to me and tackled me with a hug. I lifted her by the waist and twirled her around until her giggles made her breathless.

"This monster is my sister, Cassie. Cassie, this is my friend, Sara."

"Hi, Sara!" She clung onto my neck as she gave Sara a wave.

"Hi, Cassie. Nice to meet you." She smiled but it was stiff. The sight of Cassie probably made Sara miss Victoria even more.

I spied Mom squeeze Sara's shoulder. "I heard you're a chef. And I'm glad because the gravy is giving me issues today."

Sara's head snapped back to my mother. "Oh, I'm actually pretty good at sauces, if you want me to take a look—"

"Are you kidding? Let's go." She grabbed her hand and pulled her down the hallway. Mom looked back and gave me a nod. My chest heaved a sigh of relief, and I gave thanks for my mother's sixth sense.

"Drew," Cassie whispered as she pulled at the hem of my T-Shirt, "is Sara your girlfriend?"

I knelt in front of her and yanked her messy blonde ponytail. "Well, she's a girl that's my friend."

Her brow crinkled, and I prayed that wimpy explanation satisfied her for the time being. "She's pretty."

I nodded as a smile stretched my lips. "Yes, she is."

"Andrew!" My stepdad traipsed through the door and planted a kiss on my sister's head. "Happy Thanksgiving, son."

"You too, Phil." I stood from the floor to give him a hug.

"Did you bring your friend?" he asked as he scanned the room.

"Yeah, she's in the kitchen with Mom."

"Right." He nodded. "She's a chef."

"Almost. She graduates this year—"

"She's pretty, Daddy. Like *really* pretty."

His lips twisted into a smirk as he caught my gaze. I shrugged and nodded.

"I look forward to meeting her. Let me change and I'll meet you guys in the dining room." He slapped my arm and headed down the hallway.

"Come on, baby sister. Let's see if Mom needs any help." I nudged her toward the dining room.

The table was already set. Sara helped my mother set steaming bowls on the table, seeming a lot more relaxed than she was in the car ride up. Her eyes darted to mine and she gave me a relieved smile.

"Hi, Sara." Phil ambled over and extended his hand. "I'm Phil, Andrew's stepdad. I've heard a lot about you."

Sara grinned and took his hand. "Julia said the same thing. I'm getting a little worried." She quirked an eyebrow at me.

"All good." He raised his hands. "I promise."

Her cheeks flushed as she let out a nervous laugh. "Let me see if Julia needs any more help. It's nice to meet you."

She returned to the kitchen as Phil settled into his usual seat next to me. "Cassie was spot-on. Nice work, son."

"We're friends, Phil," I groaned. I didn't need anyone spewing out any comments to make Sara uncomfortable when she was finally starting to relax.

He nodded and patted me on the back. "I was your mom's friend too, at one time. How it starts."

"She's a little skittish," I whispered while eying the hallway. "Just don't say anything—"

"I won't." He put his hand on my shoulder. "Promise. I'm glad you brought a friend over for dinner. The four of us can only make so much conversation." He winked before rising from his chair to grab a piece of bread.

"Okay, everyone. Let's eat." Mom laughed when her eyes landed on Phil. "Just in time. Sara, this is my husband, Phil."

"We've met." Phil smiled at Sara. "Nice of Andrew to bring a chef home for Thanksgiving."

"Tell me about it. She's great. Next time you come over, you're bringing that shrimp bisque you were telling me about." She squeezed Sara's shoulder and motioned to the table. "Sit anywhere you'd like."

I patted the seat next to me with a crooked grin. An easy smile spread across her cheeks and stole the air out of my lungs. Friends aren't supposed to do that to you. I was running low on denial about my true feelings for this woman. Probably because they grew stronger by the minute. I knew it, my family knew it, and she knew it. But she wasn't running, at least not yet.

"So, Sara, what kind of chef are you? Like, do you bake or cook?" Phil asked her as he scooped sweet potatoes onto his plate.

"I bake, but I'm learning cooking techniques at school. I transferred my credits from my old school, so I only have a year to go until graduation."

"Oh, so you'll graduate the same time as Andrew." Mom noted from the other side of the table. "Do you know where you'd like to work?"

Sara speared a piece of turkey with her fork and nodded. "There are a few restaurants in the city I've been applying to around Midtown Manhattan."

"Only there?" My mother asked. "I used to love the restaurants in the Village downtown."

"Well, my daughter lives in Queens with her father . . . for now. But I'd like to work and live close, so she can stay in her school and stay close to her father. The commute from Queens to Midtown Manhattan is quicker than downtown."

"Oh, for sure! Andrew's father lives in Queens. That's about what, a four-hour drive from here?"

"It is. I'd planned to make the trip before I had to work." She forced another smile and shot me a weary side glance. I wrapped my arm around her before I could help myself.

"But, you'll still have Christmas together." I squeezed her shoulder, lingering long enough for my mother to raise an eyebrow at us.

"I'm sure it's hard to be away from your daughter today. When Andrew was little, I had to work a lot of holidays. I always hated it, but you have to do what you have to do. She appreciates it, even if she grows up to not visit as much as she should when she goes to grad school less than twenty minutes away." Mom narrowed her eyes at me, and Sara and I both laughed.

"This final project is killing a lot of my free time. I'll get better, I promise." I gave her a guilty grin.

Mom scowled at me but couldn't hide her smile. "Bring Sara and some shrimp bisque and I'll forgive you."

Sara sipped from her water glass and didn't acknowledge Mom's request. I'd gladly bring her back if she wanted to come with me. In a few months she'd be back in the city with her daughter, and my time with her would be over. If I had any sense of self-preservation, I'd keep her at a healthy distance but, as Sara liked to point out to me, I was a foolish man—at least when it came to her.

After dinner, I followed Sara into the kitchen. She promised my sister she'd make real hot chocolate from scratch instead of the packets we all grew up on. Mixing bowls and utensils brought her a peace nothing else did.

"I told you they'd love you." I snuck up behind her and snaked my arm around her waist. She leaned into me, forgetting herself for a moment I supposed before taking a half inch step away.

"You have a great family, Drew." She reached for the cocoa powder and sprinkled it into the bowl without meeting my eyes. "Do you see your father for holidays?"

"I may go to Astoria after Christmas. I haven't decided. I'd like to see my grandmother and cousins. Not that I don't want to see him, but he never makes much of an effort. How about you? Do you see any family for Christmas?" I stepped beside her to gauge her reaction. She stopped mixing and placed both hands on my mother's marble top counter before lifting her eyes to mine.

"I haven't spoken to my family in years. Since before Victoria was born. They always thought of me as the screw up, and the whole knocked-up by a one-night stand thing confirmed it. My little sister has been trying to contact me. I don't know how she found my number, but she sent me a Happy Thanksgiving text this morning. I miss her, but I don't know how to respond. It's been such a long time, you know?" Pain washed over her features and squeezed my chest. "I promised I'd find a way to see her, but I was so busy with Victoria and the zillions of jobs I had over the years that I never did. I'm a little afraid to face her." She sniffled as she kept her focus on the bowl in her hand.

"I'm sorry," I whispered into her hair. She stilled, her eyes pinching shut as if she were in pain. "I knew there was something since you've never spoken about them, but I didn't know that."

"None of them have seen Victoria. I've sent pictures, but I don't know if they even bothered to open the cards I sent. You're lucky, Drew. The only unconditional love I've ever known was from my daughter. When she came along, she gave the stupid little life I had some meaning." A humorless laugh passed over her lips. "Being without her, trying to be something without her . . . it's hard, Drew." Her voice cracked again.

"I think you're doing just fine. Amazing, in fact." She rolled her eyes with a groan.

"I've cried to you yesterday, almost just now—I'm a mess. You're too nice, anyone ever tell you that?"

"Sometimes." I shrugged. "You deserve more. You *are* more. I'll convince you one day."

"Yeah, yeah." She waved me off. "Now, let me work. I promised Cassie. Go."

"Yes, ma'am." I smirked before I stepped away, trudging out of the kitchen with a sour pang in my stomach. How could anyone not love Sara? I rubbed at the ache in my chest I wanted to write off as indigestion. Victoria may have been the first to love Sara, but she wasn't the only one. Not anymore.

Fourteen

SARA

"I DON'T BELIEVE you," Drew scoffed as we strolled through the mall.

"I'm serious. When Josh found us, I ran away from him while covering Victoria's face. I was a raving bitch. Mean, cruel, I even tortured my poor kid."

Sure, spending Christmas and New Year's at Josh and Brianna's apartment wouldn't be weird at all. *Right.* I tried to remember a conversation with Brianna that was longer than "hello" and some fact about Victoria either of us had to pass along before leaving her or picking her up. I came up with nothing. I searched for some kind of peace offering to bring to their home, but what do you buy for someone kind enough to let you stay in their house despite the hateful way you behaved from the moment you met? My search was fruitless and frustrating.

Drew squeezed my shoulders as I rummaged through the bath set display. A soft sigh fell from my lips, half frustration, half irritation at the tingles from whenever Drew touched me in such an intimate although innocent way. I guessed I should focus on one hopeless situation at a time.

"It was something new you had to get used to. Anyone would

have reacted that way."

I set down the bundle of gifts in my arms and leveled my eyes at Drew.

Sweet, clueless Drew.

"Would anyone have ripped child support checks in tiny pieces and mailed them back to her daughter's father to prove a point? Would anyone have purposely bought recital tickets a row in front of theirs just so she wouldn't have to see or speak to them during the show? Would anyone have screamed bloody murder at her daughter's almost stepmother for taking her out for a day and buying her a toy and ripped it from her daughter's hands before dragging her back home?"

Drew cringed and peered at me in disbelief.

"You did *all* that?" For the first time since we met, I rendered Drew speechless.

"See, even you can't explain me out of this one." I patted his cheek and laughed before snatching a random cellophane-covered package and praying for the best.

"If you don't mind me asking, if you felt so strongly, why did you leave Victoria with them?"

I lifted my eyes to Drew's. "That's the thing. I didn't hate them. I resented the shit out of them for being so perfect and good for her. They made me feel like the world's worst parent. Granted, I helped that along," I huffed. "For the first time in my life, it was as if I were competing for my daughter's love—and losing. It terrified me." I let out a sigh before I continued. "When Josh offered to take her, I knew I'd never get another opportunity like this. Not taking it and staying in our closet-sized apartment while continuing to struggle . . ." I dragged my hand down my face and shook my head.

"I would've spited the both of us for no reason other than my stupid pride. I'd made my girl suffer enough. She's healthy, happy, and I now have some actual money to spend this Christmas and possible real job offers for the spring. All's well that ends well, it's . . ." I sucked in a breath through my nostrils. "I feel like there will never be enough crow to eat to make up for the awful way I was. They should make me sleep on the terrace." I laughed as I made my way to the register.

I dragged Drew to the mall with me and tried not to think about how much I was going to miss him for two weeks. I'd miss Lisa, too, but I didn't anticipate choking up when I said goodbye to *her*. Drew was the first real best friend I'd had since . . . maybe ever. Someone who really worried about me, who cared, it was something foreign to me—even now. I still didn't know how to handle depending on or needing someone for anything, never mind the attraction between us that pulsed stronger as time went on.

"You're not a bad parent, Sara. Stop beating yourself up. I'm sure it's a weird situation." He leaned on the counter, regarding me with understanding and sympathy I didn't deserve. A laugh escaped me at the sincere crease in his brow.

"You're doing it again." I bumped his shoulder with mine.

"Well, I won't apologize for it. I'll defend you to anyone. Including yourself." He gave me a crooked grin that made my heart skip a beat. It'd been missing a lot of beats thanks to Andrew Kostas lately.

"What would you say about a Christmas dinner on Friday?" Drew asked as we strolled into the parking lot. I hesitated for a beat before continuing onto my car and unlocking the door.

"Yeah . . . sure. I'm off after tomorrow." I fiddled with my keys, not grasping why nerves overtook my body. We'd had countless breakfasts and cups of coffee; why did dinner strike such an internal chord of fear?

"Hey." He squeezed my shoulder. "I said dinner. A *friendly* dinner. Not a date. You can let the blood stop draining out of your face now."

I nodded, unable to even repeat the word "date." The thought of a date with Drew made the air drain from my lungs and dampened my palms, but I couldn't do it. I had my reasons—reasons I struggled to remember when we were together. Lisa and Emma still asked almost daily if I'd "peaked" with Drew yet.

"Sure. Dinner sounds great. I leave on Saturday morning, so we couldn't stay out that long . . ."

"That's fine. Oh, I forgot to tell you. I'm heading to Astoria after all." The smile faded from his lips. "My dad decided to come home for Christmas and asked if I'd come."

"So, you'll be in Queens making uncomfortable conversation, too?"

"You know it," he snickered. "Let's make a pact to call each other if we need an out."

"Deal." Knowing he'd be so close brought me an odd sense of relief, but I felt uneasy introducing him to Victoria. She would love Drew, and I would love for her to meet him, but she didn't need to get unnecessarily attached. Bad enough I was, but I could turn it off if I had to. I thought. I hoped. My real problem was that I didn't want to—but I'd eventually have no choice.

Fifteen

DREW

"GOD, I WISH this hell was over."

Brian, our other roommate, groaned before he slapped his laptop shut. "Of course, this project has to be two fucking semesters long."

"It's grad school, dude. It's supposed to be a bitch. And we got an A on part one. Stop looking. Relax and have some eggnog or some shit when you get home." I slapped him on the back, hoping it would stop the whining. Brian was a good friend and smart as hell, but it was hard to dig him out of the complaining vortex he sometimes fell into.

"Yeah, maybe when we have our own company and women are falling at our feet, I'll remember these past long nights with some sort of fondness," he mused before shoving his computer in his travel bag.

I gave a noncommittal shrug. "Let's get the company first. We can worry about perks later."

"Drew doesn't need the women." Carlos smirked at me as he strolled in the door. "He's got a hot older woman already, isn't that right?" He came over and nudged my arm. "So, more for us, Brian."

My eyes rolled, but I didn't respond. I didn't even believe me when I insisted we were just friends anymore. I let people assume we were together, so any guys would back off if they had any ideas. Even Chase apologized to me when I ran into him for "almost hitting on my girl." I never corrected him and kept walking.

"Good." Brian nodded at me with his chin. "Last thing we need is John Stamos, Jr. over there cutting in on our action anyway."

My brows pulled together as I crossed my arms. "John Stamos, Jr.?"

He shrugged. "My sister watches *Full House* reruns. Only difference is Uncle Jesse had a guitar and you have a laptop." He snickered as he slipped his arms into his jacket.

"Why, because he's the only other Greek you know of?" Carlos cracked up, reaching into our fridge for a beer. "That's not stereotyping at all."

"You can't see the resemblance? The hair, the skin—you never got the 'oh, you're Drew's roommate?!'" Brian clutched his chest and shook his head.

My head fell back as I barked out a laugh. "I didn't know you had such a crush on me. You should thank me for being such a great wingman. I didn't even have to be there, and I was able to get girls to speak to you."

"Whatever, man. I have a train to catch. Happy Holidays, gentlemen. Eat, drink, and don't think of this fucking project until January. I know those are my plans."

Carlos plopped next to me on the couch and took a long pull of his beer.

"Want to go to Night Owls tonight? A couple of the guys said they were heading there later."

"Nah, I have dinner with Sara tonight. I'm headed out in a

few minutes."

"Holy shit, dinner? A date?" His jaw dropped as a shrill whistling sound escaped the side of his mouth.

"It's not a date. It's a dinner. She heads down to Middle Village in the morning and I'm headed to Astoria early."

A smirk tickled the side of his mouth. "Sara also being in Queens for the holidays had nothing to do with agreeing to see the father you can't stand?"

"No," I spat out. "Coincidence, that's all." And that was true. Sort of. I probably would have agreed to go anyway but having Sara close lessoned my usual hesitation when it came to my father. I rose from the couch and grabbed my jacket.

"Hey, Drew. Word of advice," Carlos called out. I stilled before I turned around.

"There's biding your time, and there's wasting your time. I hope you can tell the difference."

A sad laugh rumbled in my chest. "I can tell the difference. Just not sure I can help it."

⋎⋎⋎

"THIS PLACE IS pretty nice." Sara's eyes searched the room as we sat down, a lot more relaxed than I'd expected to see her tonight. It was hard to pick a restaurant. I wanted to take her somewhere nice, but too nice would scream "date" and make her panic. Smith's was an upscale bar and grill fifteen minutes from school and seemed casual enough. When we sat down at a table, she was fine—I was the one struggling. Why did she have to be so damn sexy? Sara wore skinny jeans topped off with a chunky sweater that fell off one sexy shoulder. I couldn't remember when the sight of a woman's collarbone caused a tent to rise in my pants. I wanted to run my lips over it to see if the creamy skin was as silky as it looked. Every day, I wanted her more, and every day I had to hold myself back. I thought I'd gotten used to it, but there was something about her tonight. Maybe it was the ease in her smile or the way her eyes held mine when she spoke. She was comfortable with me, and I was falling hard for her. The word "doomed" echoed through my frazzled brain as I forced my eyes to stay level with hers.

"I wouldn't mind owning a place like this." She took another wistful glance around the room.

"You'd want to own a restaurant?"

She laughed with a shrug. "Maybe. Someday. I got a call back for a restaurant this afternoon and I guess it's making me ambitious. You're right, aim for chef first."

"What do you like about this place that would make you want to own it?"

She folded her arms on the table, making her sweater droop even more on one side. I pretended to adjust my napkin and not my cock.

"I always liked tweaking regular recipes. My daughter used to love to be my guinea pig. Granted, most of the time it was a product of me stretching out the food I had until I could afford to go shopping again, but changing or adding just one thing," she whispered as she held up her index finger, "could change everything. Burgers, mac and cheese, I had my own spin on it all. My restaurant would be traditional but just different enough. And I love these wood walls and floors." She clicked her tongue before lifting her head. "What about you? What do you dream about?"

You. Out of that sweater and on my lap.

"I don't have a definite plan yet. The guys and I may shop the app we're developing around after graduation. I know there are millions out there, but you never know what will catch on."

Sara strummed her fingers on the table after the waiter took our order.

"Merry Christmas." She placed the gift bag she tried to hide since I picked her up on the table.

"For me? Caldwell, I'm touched." I sifted through the white tissue paper and found a laptop bag. The one I used for school had seen better days and I needed a new one to look presentable on an interview. My fingers drifted over an embossed AK. She must've ordered this weeks ago and knowing how she scrimped and saved every penny she made for after graduation, the gesture made my chest pinch.

"Sara, this is great. You didn't have to go through . . ."

"Look inside," she whispered with a shy smile.

I obliged and found vintage Batman comics printed on the inside fabric. My mouth fell open at the most thoughtful gift anyone had ever given me.

"Just because you have to look professional doesn't mean you have to be boring." She offered an unusual nervous laugh. "The size is supposed to fit a Mac, but in case it doesn't—"

"Sara, this is perfect." I picked up her hand and kissed the back of her wrist, my lips lingering for a moment longer than they should've. "The best gift I've ever gotten." My gaze stumbled to hers, overcome with gratitude for two gifts this Christmas, but only one I could actually call mine.

"You," her voice cracked before she bit her bottom lip. "You are the best friend I've had in, maybe ever. I still don't know why you waste your time," she choked out a laugh. "But I'm so thankful you do."

"I'm not wasting my time. It's not a waste if I don't want to be anywhere else." I reached into my jacket pocket for the two envelopes I'd brought. "Merry Christmas to you, too."

A wide grin spread across her cheeks before ripping them open. Her hand draped over her mouth as she shook her head in almost disbelief.

"A gift certificate to Serendipity and Collective Comics," she whispered as she studied the slips in her hand.

"You said you never got to have fun with Victoria. Now you can. When you're in the city this Christmas you both can have all the frozen hot chocolate you want. And Victoria can have all the Wonder Woman comics she wants. Win-win." I winked, hoping I'd get a smile but she threw the certificates on the table.

Sara's head fell into her hands as she pinched the bridge of her nose.

"Why are you so fucking wonderful?" She wailed as her head shook. "How am I supposed to not—"

"To not, what?" I pressed, peeling her hands away from her face.

"To not fall in love with you?" Her words punched me in the stomach. I asked myself that question about her at least once a day. It's what I'd wanted to hear, but the pain in her eyes made it hurt.

"I imagine it's tough." A giggle bubbled out through her tears.

Sara rose from her seat and bolted to my side of the table, flinging her arms around my neck and kissing my cheek. "Thank you."

I had no clue how not to fall in love with her, either.

I stood and pulled her close, smiling at her gasp when I tucked a lock of chestnut hair behind her ear. My eyes held hers as we stood in the middle of the restaurant, neither of us wanting to break contact.

"What do we do now?" she asked, her voice still scratchy and small.

"We eat, we stay friends, and we wait until you're ready for anything else." I swiped at her tears with my thumbs. "And I'll be right here." My lips found her forehead. "*Not* wasting my time."

Sixteen

SARA

I CLIMBED THE slushy outside steps to Josh and Brianna's apartment, trying to balance my suitcase and bags of gifts and groceries. Managing to press the outside buzzer with my knuckle, I waited for one of them to answer the door. My eyes clenched shut as I prayed for the first time since . . . well, since the last time I was here. Regaling all those awful stories to Drew about how I'd acted when they first came into our lives made the shame already twisting my gut coil tighter. I asked for patience and acceptance, especially when I'd learn all I'd missed and they'd enjoyed with Victoria. I hoped for a way for us to be friends, or at least *friendly*.

The lock clicked, and I straightened the best I could with what felt like fifty pounds of packages. All my irritation dissipated when my eyes met my daughter's forest green ones. They lit up before she tackled me.

"Mommy! I've been waiting all day! I missed you so much!" She squealed into my shoulder as she still had my neck in a death grip. I laughed, hoping she wouldn't see the tears welling in my eyes. My body almost collapsed onto hers as I tried to wrap my package filled arms around her, and I already dreaded having to leave her again.

"Sweets, let your mom come in," Josh instructed from behind her before rushing over to me to take the bags out of my hands. "And she has. Vic hasn't moved from the window for the past two hours." He laughed before heading back inside.

"Dad blew up an air mattress, so you can sleep in my room! Just like the summer!"

I could only afford one air conditioner in our old apartment, so on hot days Victoria would sleep in my bed at night. She'd cuddle into my back and never complain.

Wheeling my suitcase into the apartment and shutting the door behind me, I craned my head around and took in all the Christmas in every corner and crevice. I suspected that was my daughter's doing. She loved to decorate every single thing for the holidays. One year, she even drew snowmen on our bathroom mirror. It took hours to scrub it off, but I couldn't find it in me to yell.

"Hi, Sara," Brianna greeted me with a warm smile I did my best to return. "How was the drive?" I noted how she kept a comfortable distance away from me and Victoria, who hadn't let go of me and was hanging on my hip. She was welcoming but trying not to interfere. If this were reversed, and Brianna visited Victoria at my home, I probably would have stroked her hair or did something to show my claim and connection to her. Unlike me, or at least how I *used* to be, she was free of any jealousy or pettiness. Josh hit the jackpot with his wife.

"Not bad. Long, but not too much traffic." I looked between Josh and Brianna. He slipped his hand around her waist and drew her to his side. They were one of those sickeningly in love couples even just at a quick glance, but the gesture seemed more for comfort than closeness. Her gaze had no resentment, but I could sense sorrow. Before I had a moment to ponder anything, my daughter pulled at my down coat.

"Take off your coat! It's almost Christmas Eve, and I have a surprise!"

I gasped, drawing out a giggle. God, I missed my daughter's laugh. FaceTime wasn't the same as hearing it in person. No matter what kind of shitty, depressing day I'd have, hearing her laugh would turn it all around and remind me the daily bullshit I endured to keep things going would be worth it—because she was.

"Well, tell me!" I unzipped my coat and hung it on the rack by the door.

"I'm an angel in the school pageant tomorrow night! Bri helped me with the wings."

"But, you should probably take a look," Brianna noted. "Victoria said that you used to fix her dance costumes every year, so you can make sure I didn't completely screw anything up." She huffed out a laugh.

"I'm sure it's fine, but I'll take a look." I brushed Victoria's hair away from her forehead. "I wanted to talk to you guys about something. I'd like to cook dinner for you. I stopped at the supermarket on the way here. Do you guys like lasagna?"

"Do you really think we're going to refuse having a chef cook for us?" Josh's chest rumbled with a laugh.

"Not quite a chef yet. But Victoria always liked my lasagna, and I learned a few other dishes I thought I'd try if that's okay with you." I lifted my eyes to Brianna's.

"Very okay." She nodded. "It's just us for Christmas anyway."

"Thank you. Both of you." I dropped my head and studied Victoria. She'd grown and thinned out a bit since August, and my heart broke at the loss of her baby face. She was obviously well cared for and happy. My throat thickened as I lifted my gaze. My own family had no interest in me or Victoria, but Josh and Brianna cared enough about the both of us to allow me this chance—a chance to have a better life.

"All right, let's see those wings and you can catch me up on everything." Victoria nodded before yanking me down the hall. I was back with my girl, and I couldn't remember ever feeling so happy or content. Probably because I never was.

⸙ ⸙ ⸙

THE DAY BEFORE Christmas Eve, I took Victoria everywhere—a luxury I'd never had. Galivanting around New York City without worrying about what time my next shift had to start was a whole new world for us. I never even took her to a movie. Josh and Brianna were cool about letting us come and go as we pleased.

Victoria couldn't keep her eyes open, nodding off after a long but great day, yet still insisting to help me bake.

"Baby, why don't you go to bed? You can help me put the frosting on it tomorrow."

I cracked up when her head crashed into her folded arms on the table.

"Who's Drew?" she mumbled on a yawn.

My spatula stilled in my hand. "Drew?"

"You texted him our picture at Serendipity." She turned and buried her head in her elbow.

"You noticed that, little spy?" I pursed my lips but fought a smile.

"Mm-hmm." Her eyelids fluttered as they got heavier. "I

saw his name on your phone screen before that, too. Is he your boyfriend?"

Jesus. How do I answer that when I don't even know myself?

"He's my friend. He's actually the friend who bought us the gift certificates we used today. Maybe you could call him and thank him tomorrow."

I lifted my gaze to my now sleeping daughter. Poor thing couldn't take it anymore.

"She is a fighter until the end." Josh shook his head as he sauntered into the kitchen. He gingerly lifted her out of the chair and cradled her limp body in his arms before he carried her down the hall. An odd warmth washed over me at the sight. He had no idea she existed until she was eight years old, but he loved her fiercely.

"Hey, sorry to interrupt. Just making some tea." Brianna fluttered in and grabbed the tea kettle. "I guess you guys had a great day."

"We did. I never got to have fun with her like that." I sighed as I leaned back in my chair. "I owe you both a lot."

She waved me off. "She's a joy. We love having her here and are happy to help you out." Brianna fiddled with the stove until the burner came on.

"I never told you congratulations."

She offered a wistful smile. "Thank you. Not exactly sudden, but it was time."

"Josh said the same thing, exactly." I rolled my eyes but smiled. "You guys are like two peas in a pod."

"We were always like that. For the most part, anyway. I don't know if Josh told you, but we met in kindergarten." She sat across from me and rested her elbows on the table. "What are you making?"

"Chocolate cupcakes stuffed with cream. You know, like the Hostess ones. Victoria said those were your favorite. I'm guessing as much since Josh calls you 'cupcake'."

Her jaw went slack as her eyes went saucer-wide. "You know how to bake Hostess cupcakes? This is the best Christmas *ever*."

I laughed at the wonder in her expression. "Seriously, thank you for taking such good care of Victoria. I bet you guys can't wait to give her a brother or sister."

The smile drained from Brianna's face as the tea kettle whistled behind her. She took a sharp breath through her nostrils as if she was fighting off a sob.

"Your tea is ready, Cupcake." I jumped at Josh's voice behind me. I didn't hear his approach or know how long he'd been standing there. Their eyes locked and had the same pained stare.

"I . . . um . . . don't think I want it anymore. I'm kinda tired. Thanks for the cupcakes, Sara." She shot up from her chair to shut the burner off before Josh pulled her into his chest, whispering something in her ear. She nodded before giving him a long peck and rushing out of the kitchen.

"Josh, did I say something wrong?" My brow furrowed as he fell into the seat Brianna had bolted from.

"Brianna can't have children. We found out a few months ago. Most days she's okay with it or does a good job of pretending to be. I think seeing Victoria get all excited about Christmas and the fun you guys are having—" He jerked his head toward me. "Not that she's mad at that. She's happy you're here for Victoria and that you guys are having such an awesome time together. It's just making her think and remember more than she'd like."

"I'm so sorry, Josh. I didn't know—" I stiffened, feeling the blood drain from my face and praying I was wrong about a sudden realization. "The day I came to get Victoria after they went to the mall . . ." I left out 'and screamed bloody murder and told Brianna she'd never be Victoria's mother.' "Did she know?"

Josh didn't look up as he gave me a slow nod.

"Oh, God." I clutched my chest in horror. "Josh, I'm . . ." My flour covered hands raked through my hair as panic seeped into my veins. How could I be so cruel? Victoria was the light of my life, and it saddened me to know Brianna couldn't have children of her own. "I didn't know, I never would have—"

"Water under the bridge, Sara." He reached over and squeezed my wrist. "She's not mad at that and neither am I. Well, I'm not mad anymore." He quirked an eyebrow and we shared a laugh.

"Have you . . . looked into other ways?"

He cocked his head back and forth. "Trying to. She doesn't like to look into it because she's afraid she'll be disappointed." He let out a long sigh. "Breaks my fucking heart. You don't know how good she is. How much love she has to give."

"I know," I agreed. "I hated her for it at the beginning, but I'm so grateful now. She's too good of a mother for the universe not to come through. Even deep in my cold heart, I believe that."

He snickered. "You aren't cold. Tough. I admire that, believe it or not."

"Right," I scoffed. "I wish there was something I could do."

He rose from his seat. "Cupcakes are heading in the right direction. I'm going to head to bed. I don't want her to be alone too long when she's like this. I'm excited for our Christmas Eve dinner! I'll make sure to save my appetite." He rubbed his stomach with his inked hand. "Goodnight, Sara."

"Goodnight, Josh." I wiped my hand on a dish towel as my phone buzzed across the table.

Drew: How's it going? Have you moved out of their kitchen at all?

Me: How do you know I'm in the kitchen?

Drew: . . . really?

Me: Okay, so I am. Smart ass.

Drew: You love my ass, I catch you staring on the track.

Me: Right. Thanks for today. Victoria had a ball.

Drew: I'm glad. She's beautiful. You both are in that picture. Maybe I can meet up with you when I get there. I leave in the morning.

Me: Maybe. I'd like that. Let me get back to my cupcakes.

Drew: Ooh, does that mean something else? What's on your cupcakes, baby?

Me: You have a long drive tomorrow. Get some sleep.

Drew: Fine. You're no fun. I miss you.

Me: Goodnight, Drew.

Drew: Say you miss me.

Me: You miss me.

Drew: Now who's a smart ass?

Me: My ass is great.

Drew: Sure is. Goodnight, Gorgeous.

I threw the phone across the table, my cheeks sore from smiling. When it buzzed again, I was about to call him and yell when the air stilled in my lungs.

Denise: Merry almost Christmas, sis.

I missed my sister, but I couldn't bring myself to text her back. She was only a kid, and it was wrong to make her suffer for my mother's actions, but I was too terrified to reach back out to her. The fear and guilt mingled in my system and turned my stomach.

It was a holiday full of surprises. Some I welcomed, some I was warming up to, and some that threatened to pull me into a past I couldn't handle.

Seventeen

SARA

BY THE TIME the sun rose on Christmas Eve, I was already awake for two hours. Baking was done, lasagna was finished and ready for the oven, French Toast Casserole prepped and ready for tomorrow morning. The kitchen was the only place I ever found peace, but my turbulent mind wouldn't give me any.

My parents and I never got along, even before I became pregnant with Victoria. My father worked long hours and couldn't be bothered with any of us, and my mother took her frustrations out on me. Nothing was good enough; my grades, my hair, my choice of school—nothing. I was happy to live in a dirt-cheap studio apartment and dine on Ramen noodles every night when I first started culinary school. Still, I came back once in a while, mainly for my sister. And, as pathetic as it was, even though my parents starved me for love my entire life, I still craved it. I'd think, maybe they'll see my grades and be proud or maybe be impressed with all I was learning—learning on my own dime, too, thank you very much. It was never any use. I'd leave their house close to tears but would will them back in my eyes. I would never let them make me cry.

When I had my own daughter, I vowed she'd only get the best

from me. My best for the first eight years of her life was less than stellar, but I gave her all I had and always thought of her first. I praised everything she did and told her I loved her multiple times per day. As someone in her thirties and all kinds of fucked up from being denied something so simple from my family, I made sure that even though my daughter had to go without on many things, she never had to question whether or not she was loved.

Denise ran through my mind a lot. I pictured what she looked like now, if she still had that crazy, curly hair that she could never tame. When I told my family I was pregnant, they threw me out and told me I was never welcome back or allowed to speak to my sister. She was too young to have a cell phone to text, and I knew better than to try to call the house. She was about twenty now— an adult. Maybe that's why she was reaching out? I shrugged to myself as I made a pot of coffee.

The buzz of my phone across the counter snatched me from my tortured musings.

"I could be sleeping," I snapped as I leaned against the sink, smiling despite myself.

"But I knew you wouldn't be. Talk to me. It's been a long and lonely drive." Drew's voice made me almost forget. Having him close by soothed me even if I wouldn't admit it out loud.

"I know, I made the same drive a couple of days ago. Is your dad there already?"

"I doubt it," he snickered. "It's always a crap shoot if he'll show up at all. I have other family that I want to see. Either way, it'll be worth it."

"You never talk about him much. That's probably because my issues monopolize all our conversations."

"That's not true. There's not much to say, Sara. My dad never grew up. I spent a lot of time as a kid disappointed over some broken promise he'd made. As I got older, the disappointment became resentment which graduated to indifference. The end. See? Short story."

"You can't be that indifferent if you're driving four hours to see him." I was met with a long silence, unusual for Drew.

"Well, I guess the kid in me is hopeful. Like this will be the time he'll come through and show he gives a shit about me. I suppose I'll never lose that completely."

I nodded but stayed silent. I was familiar with wasted hope. Each year I'd hope my parents would see Victoria's Christmas picture and contact me. I'd allow myself until New Year's before I'd give up. Unlike Drew, I couldn't say I was indifferent. The resentment was fresh and never faded.

"Yeah, I hear you," I sighed into the phone.

"Did you text your sister?"

"No, and she texted again last night. I feel horrible because she has nothing to do with how my parents treated me, but . . ." I couldn't complete that thought. I wanted to see her so badly it ached, but the fear over another rejection from my parents paralyzed me. "Makes me awful, doesn't it?"

"No, Caldwell. You aren't the awful person in this situation. They are."

I smiled and shook my head. "You always know the right thing to say."

"I just speak the truth. Things going okay with Josh and his wife?"

"Yes, and no." I exhaled a long breath and cupped my forehead. "I found out I was even meaner than I thought. And they're way too fucking nice about it."

"You aren't mean. Don't make me come there and straighten you out."

I coughed out a laugh. "I think you'd even agree with me on this one."

"No, I wouldn't." His tone hardened. "Because I see you for who you are. And you're so much more than you ever give yourself credit for." I fought the urge to melt against the counter from the resolute sincerity of his words.

"Drive safe, okay?"

"I will. Merry Christmas Eve, Caldwell."

A large grin split my mouth. "You too, Kostas." I ended the call and drifted my thumb down the screen. Foolish, wonderful Drew. I fought hard to not let myself fall in love with him, but I feared I already lost that battle.

"Good morning," Brianna yawned from behind me.

"Good morning," I replied, a little wary. She was hurting, and I, although unknowingly, poured a fresh stream of salt on her open wound twice. How did this woman not despise me? She had countless reasons. Not only for the way I acted, but who I was—the woman who had a child with her husband, a child she couldn't have.

"Wow," she mused as she scanned the kitchen. "Look at all of this. What time did you wake up?"

"Nerves prevent me from sleeping late. I guess heading from shift to shift, I still have the inclination I have to be somewhere." I let out a nervous laugh. "Everything is done for tonight."

I offered a tense smile, studying her reaction as she slid into a seat at the table.

"You are a life saver. Thank you for making dinner for us. Cupcakes are done, right?" She gave me a genuine smile, but her eyes clouded with sadness.

"I'm . . . sorry." I swallowed as Brianna regarded me with puzzled eyes.

Once she realized what I meant, her gaze fell to the coffee cup in her hand as she nodded. "You didn't know. And I need to deal with this better than I do sometimes." She exhaled a long breath as she shook her head. "Nothing to be sorry for."

"Yes, there is. There's a shit ton to be sorry for. You've shown my daughter nothing but love and I was too bitter and resentful to appreciate it. And if I had known . . ." I trailed off, scrambling to find the right words.

Brianna adjusted her long, blonde ponytail before turning to me with a raised brow. "You wouldn't have pointed out how I wasn't Victoria's mother . . . if you knew I couldn't be *anyone's* mother."

"How do you not hate me?" I couldn't hold in my grimace.

"Again, you didn't know. We came along and although we never meant to get in between you and Victoria, I could see why you resented us. I don't know how you did it alone for so long."

"I wonder that myself." A real laugh fell from my lips.

"And, if I'm honest, I *am* a little jealous of you. You have something I don't with Josh, and never will. Even if we try another way and succeed, it won't be the same." She bit her lip and looked away. "It's a bitter pill to swallow sometimes."

I took the chair next to her at the table. "It would be a tragedy for you not to be anyone's mother. Victoria loves you. Why I used to kind of hate you."

Her head jerked up and we shared a chuckle. "I don't hate you, Sara. Not then, and not now. It makes me happy we're able to be friends and give Victoria a great Christmas."

"Me too." My lips curved into a smile. "Thanks for not making me sleep on the porch."

She giggled and dropped her hand to my forearm. "Thanks for making us dinner."

"Morning," Josh muttered as he stumbled into the kitchen, pressing a kiss to the back of Brianna's head before making his way to the coffeepot.

"Isn't it like the butt crack of dawn? I know why *I'm* up this early." He squinted at us as he took a sip of coffee. "No clue why the two of you are."

"I had nervous energy, so I finished prepping dinner for later and finished baking. Well, I'll be finished when Victoria wakes up and ices the cupcakes."

"She needs to be in bed early tonight." Josh nodded to her room down the hallway. "I have that bike to put together. It's too big to hide."

"Are you going to be able to do that in one night?"

Josh answered me with a cocky grin. "I can do it in an hour. It's what I do all day. This one doesn't have an engine so maybe forty minutes." He snickered before putting the empty mug in the sink.

"I have some last-minute gifts to get." Brianna downed the rest of her coffee. "I want to get to the mall when it opens."

"On Christmas Eve?" I shrieked.

"Some things I can't hide either." She winked at me before rising from the chair. She gave Josh a quick kiss on the lips before rushing out of the kitchen.

I leaned my elbows on the table and swiveled my head. "You got really lucky finding someone like Brianna."

"And fuck, don't I know it." He chuckled as he ambled over to the table.

"She's so damn understanding. She's almost not even—"

"Real? That crossed my mind more times than I could ever count, and you don't even know the half of it. All I put her through when we were kids." His eyes went vacant for a quick moment. "Anyway, I'm glad you guys are getting along. And we can all make Christmas nice for our kid this year."

I smiled until my eyes landed on my phone. I stared at Denise's text most of the morning but still hadn't decided if I was texting her back. "This is definitely shaping up to be her best Christmas so far."

"I better get going. Shop is closing early, but we have some deliveries and pickups."

"People really buy motorcycles as Christmas presents?" I squinted at Josh.

"You'd be surprised. See you guys tonight." He left the kitchen, and I was alone once again, tapping my finger, trying not to stare at the phone.

Denise had nothing to do with my parents cutting me off, as she was only a kid. I needed to move past the fear and get back the family I had left.

Snatching my phone before I lost my nerve, I pulled up Denise's text and punched out a reply.

Me: Merry Christmas to you, too. I miss you. I'm in Queens until January 3. If you'd like to see me and meet your niece, let me know.

I meant it, all of it. I missed her so much and wanted her to finally meet Victoria. Maybe this was the holiday season for miracles.

Eighteen

SARA

"SO, WHAT IF I just open one . . ." Victoria shook one of the smaller presents under the tree as she pouted her lip at all three of us. Josh was ready to acquiesce before I held up my hand.

"Tomorrow. Josh and Brianna don't know your Christmas M.O. One turns into two, then you want to wait up for Santa." I crouched on the floor and kissed her forehead before I took it back.

"That was the best lasagna I've ever had in my whole life. Seriously, best Christmas Eve dinner I've ever had." Brianna gushed from behind us. "And dessert."

"Santa has like ten different cookies this year, too!" Victoria's eyes widened. She forgot about the present, as I predicted she would.

"And he's got cupcakes." Brianna gave Victoria a big smile.

Victoria stood from the floor and shook her head. "No, he's got cookies. The cupcakes are for you, Bri."

She laughed and came over to my daughter, enveloping her in a hug and kissing the top of her head. "Thanks, Vic," she whispered.

A smile ghosted my lips, my sister's text a heavy reminder of how I was short on parental love, but my daughter had it in overabundance. Only the hugest asshole would begrudge her child of that. I decided this holiday that asshole would stop being me.

My phone buzzed in my pocket. Every alert made my heart gallop a couple of beats until I forced myself to glance at the screen.

Drew: Guess who showed up?

Me: Wow, and you said he probably wouldn't.

Drew: I guess it's the season for miracles. How are things there? Getting along?

Me: Actually, yes. It's nice.

Drew: I told you so.

Me: They're both forgiving people. I'm glad they were extra charitable this holiday.

Drew: I'm close enough to spank you if you start in on yourself again.

My cheeks heated before Victoria tapped me on the shoulder. "Is that Drew?"

"Who's Drew?" Josh asked from the couch.

"Mommy's boyfriend," my daughter answered for me. "He bought us the gift cards to Serendipity and to the comic book store."

"He's not my boyfriend," I blurted and spied Brianna hold in a laugh.

"That's a pretty fierce denial. And you know what that means." Josh wiggled his eyebrows and I popped off the floor on an exasperated sigh.

"What does it mean, Mommy?" Her brow crinkled.

"It means your dad is a troublemaker. Excuse me."

Scowling at Josh, I stalked in the kitchen just as the phone vibrated in my hand with a call. I glanced at the screen, thinking it was Drew again, but my stomach dropped when I recognized the same number my sister texted me from. This was it. My feet rooted to the tiles on the floor as I clutched the back of one of the dining room chairs. My teeth sank into my shaking bottom lip before I pressed accept.

"Hello?"

"Sara?" Denise's voice cracked. My chest pinched at the flood of memories. She sounded like the baby sister I was forced to leave almost a decade ago. My nose burned as I struggled to find the air in my lungs to answer.

"Hi, Denise. Merry Christmas."

"I've missed you so much," she whispered. "And I'd love to meet my niece. Does she know about me?"

Whenever Victoria would ask about my family, I would respond with an abrupt change in subject. Telling her I had a sister and answering questions was too painful for me to even attempt.

"No, but I'd like her to. Maybe Saturday we could find somewhere to meet up."

"Why don't you come here? It's been so long, Sara," she pleaded.

"That's because I'm not welcome there. I'm surprised they opened my cards."

"Well, they didn't, I did . . . but I show them her picture every year. Please, Sara."

"Denise, I'm not bringing my daughter into that . . . horror I grew up in. She's sweet and innocent and I don't want her tainted by grandparents who don't want to love her." My fingers white-knuckled the chair now in anger. I couldn't and wouldn't set foot in that house with Victoria.

"They do . . . hold on." Denise muffled the phone, and garbled words came through the receiver. I fell into a chair, my legs quivering and my breathing shallow. For years, I'd been completely on my own, no one to depend on, no one in my life other than my daughter. How could I ever forgive them for that?

"Mom, take the phone." My heart thundered then stopped in my chest.

"Talk to her." My sister's distant whisper was followed by more mumbling I couldn't decipher.

"Hello?" My body folded, my head crashing into my knees at the recognition of my mother's voice. It's what I heard on the days I came up short, when I'd play Tetris with my bank account and the one credit card I was allowed to manage the bills and keep a roof over our heads, and the nights I'd curl up in my bed alone, wondering how I'd do it the next day.

Can't you do anything right?

Cooking school? Wow, that's a big future.

You don't even know your baby's father? What kind of a whore doesn't know her baby's father? Get out!

Even without the usual malice in her tone, her voice cut through me like a knife.

"Mom," I finally squawked out. "Merry Chris—"

The call disconnected, and I froze with the phone still attached to my ear. My mother hung up on me, refusing to speak . . . on Christmas Eve. My hands shook as a plethora of emotions rushed through me. Again. I put myself out there, right on the cutting slab, knowing the response I'd get but hoping for something different.

Your mother is supposed to love you or at least wish you a happy holiday. What was so wrong with me that she couldn't? My hands shook as the walls seemed as if they were closing in on me. I had a good life now, or I was heading toward one. I even opened up to having friends, a . . . whatever Drew was, accepting Josh and Brianna as family. But the one thing I wanted, the one thing I yearned for my entire life, I'd never have. This wasn't news but speaking to them brought it all to the surface and gave it an overwhelming permanence. Why did I reply to my sister's text? Why did I put myself in this position? A full-blown panic attack filtered through my system and I needed to run. Where, I had no clue, but I needed to go somewhere. Victoria couldn't see me upset, and even with the truce I'd made with Josh and Brianna, I couldn't confide in them about this.

I raced to Victoria's room and shoved my feet into my sneakers, moving so fast I almost tripped on the air mattress next to her bed.

"I need to run out," I muttered, making no eye contact with anyone as I reached for my coat and scarf on the rack by the door.

"But Mommy, we still need to set cookies for Santa. Where are you going?" I winced at my daughter's panicked voice but couldn't turn around.

"I'll be back." I almost made it out the door when Josh's hand gripped my bicep.

"What's going on?" he whispered.

"Nothing. I'm fine," I clipped, resisting the urge to shake his grasp and call more attention to the awful state I was in.

He huffed and let go. "Be careful; it's late. Victoria's already worried about you."

Staring straight ahead, I replied with a curt nod.

The sting from the frigid bite in the night air chilled me to the bone as I rushed to my car. I unlocked the doors and turned on the engine, cranking up the heat but unsure of where the hell to go. Then it happened, wetness streaked my cheeks as a new coating of snow gathered on the windshield. A hysterical laugh bubbled out of my chest, as this night was turning out to be some kind of bizarro Hallmark movie, one where the happy ending *didn't* happen. A white Christmas where the family didn't take back their long-lost daughter with open arms. Instead, they shunned her and made sure she felt alone, because that's exactly what she'd been her entire life. I touched my cheeks and glared at the tears on my fingers I could taste as they dripped down my face. She made me cry—with a phone call. I was that weak.

My body went on autopilot as I fumbled in my purse for my phone, pressing Drew's number with a shaky finger.

"Hey, Caldwell. Happy almost Chris—"

"Drew," my voice was gone, now just a barely audible whisper. If I spoke, I was terrified the sobs would rake through me and not stop. A lifetime of rejection barreled over me like a cannon and I couldn't breathe.

"What's wrong? What happened? Is Victoria okay?"

"Yeah, she's fine. I . . ." I gulped, desperately trying to find the air to get this out without collapsing. What the hell was happening to me? "I spoke to my sister. She put my mother on the phone and she . . . she hung up, Drew. She wouldn't even say Merry Christmas."

"Where are you?"

"In my car in front of Josh and Brianna's apartment. I can't let Victoria see me like this, but I can't move. Nine fucking years, Drew. Why does this still hurt so much? Why do I care? What's so wrong with me that my own mother hates me?"

"Don't you believe that for a second. Not one thing is wrong with you. What's their address?" A door slammed followed by the revving of an engine.

"The corner of Fifty-Eighth Avenue, next to the highway. Drew, you don't have to come—"

"I'm on my way. Stay in the car. I'll be there soon." He hung up, and more tears fell from my eyes. I didn't fight him that hard because I wanted him here. After all this time of flying solo, I finally had someone to call. Drew was my someone—denying it any longer was pointless.

My head fell on my steering wheel as the first sob finally broke free. Josh admired me because I was tough? No, I was well-versed at ignoring. Tonight, I came face-to-face with my demons and they destroyed me.

I lifted my aching head to the tapping on my driver's side window. I pushed the door open and climbed out. Drew was next to the car, his dark locks full of snow and big eyes peering at me as if I were about to explode before him. He wasn't far off.

"Where did you park?" Resisting the urge to leap into his arms was almost impossible. Drew was a balm to my shattered soul tonight, but even now I still fought the blinding pull.

"On the corner." He nodded with his chin behind him.

"You should be with your family. Even your dad. At least he cared enough to ask you to come for Christmas." My chest heaved as the words fumbled out of my mouth. "Plus, you have cousins you like, right? I think you said an aunt, too? Family is good. It's important."

Drew didn't reply as he inched toward me and opened his arms. It took me five seconds to collapse onto his chest in sobs.

"Shh," he crooned as he tightened his embrace around me. "It's okay." He pressed a kiss to the top of my head. "I told you, I've got you."

"I don't understand." I lifted my head off the wet spot of pooled tears on his jacket. "What did I do that was so awful? Why do I still want them to love me and be proud of me? Why am I letting them get to me? I swore she'd never make me cry." I sniffed and shook my head.

"Listen to me," he growled as he cradled my face and swiped my tears with his thumbs. "You're amazing and smart and brave and beautiful. Don't waste your tears on awful people like that. You're raising a daughter and working your ass off to make a future for both of you." He kissed my closed eyelids and rested his forehead against mine. "*I'm* proud of you, Sara. I'll tell you more when you're ready to hear it."

I stepped closer and brushed my lips against his. It was quick and light, but we both shuddered at the contact. He pulled back, pausing to study my face as if he didn't believe what just happened.

"I couldn't not kiss you after you said that." I feathered my hand down his cheek, breathing him in, my heart now racing with passion instead of despair.

"Once we cross this line, that's it. I won't be able to go back," he rasped against my lips. "I need you to be sure."

"You don't want to kiss me?"

"Are you kidding?" His eyes narrowed into slits. "I want you so bad it's killing me. But you're upset, and I won't take advantage—"

I kissed him again, this time letting my lips linger. Drew hissed as I nibbled his bottom lip when I pulled away.

"Just do it, Kostas," I begged as I ached for him to make a move. All the resistance I'd built up all this time evaporated in a rush.

Drew covered my mouth with his, gliding his tongue across

my bottom lip, sensual but careful. His body was rigid and shaking from holding back.

"God, Sara." My name fell from his lips like a tortured prayer before our mouths crashed together in a hungry, bruising kiss. He groaned as his tongue tangled with mine with deliberate and knee-buckling strokes. It was too much and not enough all at once. His soft, plump lips devoured mine as all the heat simmering between us for the past few months finally boiled over on a quiet, snowy street.

Was this still a bad idea? Probably, but I needed him too much to care. Drew made me feel loved and whole and wanted. I fisted the cropped hair at his neck, and he moved faster, drinking me in with fervor as if he was terrified I'd change my mind and tell him to stop. We weren't stopping. Not anymore.

A whimper escaped me when he pulled away, both of us panting white clouds into the winter air.

"Those lips . . ." Drew drifted his thumb over my bottom lip. "You're shivering." He ran his hands up and down my wool-covered arms.

"Maybe, but I'm not cold."

"No, you're not." He kissed the tip of my nose. "You're warm and sweet and I need to get you inside before we start attracting an audience."

I laughed and wiped my damp cheeks with the back of my hand. "Thank you for . . . coming here."

"A blizzard wouldn't have stopped me. Not when it comes to you." He pecked my lips.

I took his hand and led him toward the apartment. "Come meet my daughter."

"Yeah?" His dark eyes, now almost black, widened. "I'd love

to, but you're sure?"

"Yeah." I nodded. I still felt as if I'd been punched in the stomach, but Drew made me want to stand back up. I took one last look back tonight, but I wouldn't let it keep me from moving forward—and I was starting with the man I'd been afraid to want.

That's how I wouldn't let them beat me.

Nineteen

DREW

WHEN SARA CALLED me, her voice full of anguish and devastation, I bolted out of my aunt's house without giving anyone a goodbye or an explanation. I'd get shit for that later, but I didn't care. Sara didn't know how to ask anyone for help. She never trusted anyone enough. But she called *me*. She sobbed in my arms and then she kissed me and let me kiss her. My mind was reeling as I followed her into the apartment, her hand still clutching mine like a lifeline.

I hated that she felt so unlovable when she was the complete opposite. I remembered the brittle and withdrawn beautiful woman I'd met all those months ago, and the little pieces of herself she gave me as she slowly let me in. She had the purest heart behind all those walls she barricaded it with. Now that I had a taste of her, pretending to only be her friend would be impossible. I'd been dreaming of those soft lips on mine since that first day in the hallway, and I wanted more. I wanted *her*.

She turned to me with those deep brown eyes, still bloodshot from crying. She gave me a sweet smile before pulling me all the way inside and locking the door.

"You're a foolish man, Kostas. Crazy and foolish." She let out a long sigh and buried her head in my chest. I cinched my arms around her and kissed the top of her head.

"I'm crazy about *you*, Caldwell," I whispered into her hair.

"Mommy!" A little girl barreled into us, hanging onto Sara's leg as she cried into her hip. "I thought you left; I thought you'd miss Christmas."

Sara grimaced as she crouched down in front of her. "I'm so sorry, Victoria." She took Victoria's face in her hands and kissed her cheek. "I would never leave you at Christmas. I . . ." She winced before her pained gaze slid to mine. "I heard some bad news and I didn't want you to see me upset. But I never meant to worry you. Forgive me?" She pouted her lip at her daughter, drawing out a giggle.

I'd known Sara was a mother from the beginning, but seeing her *be* a mother knocked the wind out of me. The soft way she spoke and the pure love in her eyes caught me right in the chest and made it real. Loving was who she was and thinking of what she'd gone through at the hands of her own mother made my blood boil.

"Everything all right?" A man's voice asked from behind us. His eyes bore into us as he crossed his inked arms, raising a brow as he looked between us.

"Drew." I extended my hand. "I'm a friend of Sara's. You must be Josh." His mouth flattened as he took it, still eyeing me as if he was sizing me up.

"Drew?" Victoria's head shot up with a gasp. "You're the one who gave us the gift certificates. I got *two* Wonder Woman comics."

"Two, wow!" I knelt down before her. "I love a girl who loves comics. You must be Victoria. I've heard so much about you, I feel like I should get your autograph."

She laughed. "I don't know much about you. I know I saw your name on Mommy's phone screen a lot."

I turned my head to Sara's apologetic shrug. "Well, we should get to know each other then. Can I see the comics you bought?"

"Yes! Stay here, I'll be right back." She scrambled down the hall, her brunette ponytail bobbing behind her.

"She's lovable," Sara whispered.

"I normally wouldn't pry." Josh ambled over to me, his jaw still tight. "But with the way Sara ran out, and now you're here making friends with my daughter, I need to know if there's going to be any more trouble."

"He didn't cause the trouble." Sara stepped in between us before letting out a long sigh. "I spoke to my family for the first time in nine years and . . . it didn't go very well. I ran out so Victoria wouldn't see me upset, and I called Drew from the car." She slid her hand into mine and laced our fingers together.

Josh grimaced as his shoulders relaxed. "I'm sorry, Sara. I wish you would have said something. You had us all worried."

"I'm so sorry." A woman with long blonde hair wearing a red bathrobe came up to Sara and squeezed her shoulder. "That's awful."

Sara nodded but kept her gaze on the floor. "It's something I should be used to. My own fault."

"No," I growled and gripped her hand tighter. "It's not."

"Drew is right," she agreed before turning toward me. "I'm Brianna. Nice to meet you."

I nodded a hello before Victoria rushed back in, holding her comics against her chest.

"This one's my favorite." She pulled at the sleeve of my jacket before poking the cover. "Her hair looks so awesome. I want my hair long like that, so I can wear a tiara." Her gushing was adorable. Sara was right, she was lovable as hell.

"I guess every girl wants to be a princess, right?" I winked.

She folded her arms and glared at me. "I want to be a princess with a sword who kicks ass."

"Victoria!" Sara scolded.

"Not a nice word, Sweets." Josh agreed but let a snicker slip out. "And this princess needs to get into bed, so Santa can come. Cookies are out, say goodnight." He kissed the back of her head and pointed to her room.

"But Drew just got here!" She yanked my hand and pulled me toward her.

Sara smoothed the loose hairs around her face. "You'll see him again soon, I promise."

"It's pretty bad out there." Brianna pulled back the curtains and made a whistling sound. "Why don't you stay, Drew? I'll make up the couch."

I held up my hands and shook my head. "I don't want to impose on Christmas."

"Yes, stay! I have so many more comics to show you. And Mommy is making French Toast Casserole tomorrow morning. Please!" Victoria bounced up and down and looked between her parents.

"It's up to you guys. You're more than welcome." Josh came over to his wife but kept his gaze on us.

"I'd hate to think of you driving in this when I dragged you out in the first place. Stay." Sara's eyes held mine, and she didn't have to ask me twice.

"Sure. I'll stay." Victoria hissed a "yes" as Sara's lips curved into a slow grin.

"Time for bed. Go get your pajamas on. I'll be right in." Sara kissed Victoria's cheek and pointed down the hall.

"Okay." She grunted before turning to trudge to her bedroom. "Goodnight, Drew." She tackled my legs with a hug. "See you tomorrow."

"Sweet dreams, kiddo." I bent to return the hug, wishing her mother took to me this easily from the beginning.

"How about us?" Josh pulled her back by the waist and kissed her cheek as she giggled. "Merry Christmas, Sweets. Get some sleep."

Brianna knelt to kiss her other cheek. "See you in the morning after Santa comes."

She grinned at them both before scurrying down the hall to her room.

"I'll go get you a pillow and some blankets." Brianna smiled as she looked between us.

"Thank you. This is nice of you to let me stay."

"No problem at all." I cast a side glance to Sara before she followed Josh out of the living room.

"They're *really* nice." I smirked and laughed when she jabbed me in the arm.

"Sure, rub it in." She leveled her eyes at me as she stepped closer.

I cupped her neck and inched toward her. She stilled but relaxed before looping her arms around my neck.

"You're sure you want me here?" I dipped my chin until my eyes were level with hers. "I didn't think we were up to sleepovers yet."

She nudged my shoulder. "I don't want you to drive in this,

and . . . it feels nice to have you here. I want you here. There, I said it." Her lips pursed as she fought the twitching at the corners of her mouth—the same sweet mouth I'd tasted twenty minutes ago and wanted to again. The urge to pull her back to her car and drag her into the back seat was so powerful it was fucking blinding, but was our kiss a fluke? The last thing I wanted to do was push her and set us back.

"I'll be honest," I whispered, our lips so close they brushed again. After starving for this woman all these months, I had a ravenous appetite but had to hold myself back. "I'm a little afraid that was some kind of spell," I nodded outside, "and if I try to kiss you now, it'll be broken."

"One way to find out." Sara closed the distance between us, flicking the seam of my lips with her tongue. I let out a growl before I covered her mouth with mine. She tasted so damn good, she *felt* so good. My fingers threaded in her hair as I swallowed the soft moans traveling straight to my dick. I smiled against her lips when her body sagged against mine.

"Did I just make you weak in the knees, Caldwell?"

"Why are you such a damn good kisser?" she whined as I painted kisses along her jaw.

How the hell was I going to sleep knowing she was close enough to touch—and that she'd let me? I'd have to summon that pain in the ass self-control I'd been exhausting all these months.

"No going back now." My thumb drifted along her swollen bottom lip, swollen from me. My chest swelled. "You know that, right?"

"I hope not." She pecked my lips and drifted her hands down my chest. "Merry Christmas, Drew."

I grazed my thumb across her lips and kissed her forehead.

"Merry Christmas, Fire and Ice."

A sad smile lifted her cheeks. "Thank you, Drew. I don't know what I would have done if you didn't come—"

"There was nowhere else for me to be." I grabbed her hand, smiling at her gasp when my lips found the top of her wrist.

She kissed my cheek before turning down the hall. "You wear me out, Kostas."

"And I think I'm in love with you, Caldwell," I confessed when I was sure she was out of earshot.

⋎ ⋎ ⋎

THE COUCH WAS comfortable, but I couldn't sleep a wink. The temptation to coax Sara out of her daughter's room to finish what we started earlier consumed me. But I kept reminding myself that moving forward didn't mean at warp speed. I still had the nagging feeling our kiss was the product of her heartbreak tonight, but there was no way for either of us to deny that constant undercurrent between us—not anymore. I couldn't and wouldn't push her, but she felt so damn good in my arms. I smiled to myself thinking of her slumped against me after I kissed her senseless. Now that I had a taste of Sara on the opposite side of the friend zone, I wanted her even more. Tossing and turning on the sea of blankets Brianna left out for me, I willed my mind and keyed up body to slow the fuck down before I squinted at a sudden flood of light.

"Hey, sorry!" Josh whispered before setting down a toolbox in front of the couch. "I wanted to make sure Vic was in a dead sleep before I came out." He tiptoed over to the love seat and slid a box out from behind it.

"I thought this was the perfect place to hide this until the damn blanket kept sliding." Josh laid all the metal pieces inside along the carpet.

"New bike for Christmas?" I rolled up to sitting.

"Yeah, this has been . . . well, it's been a long year for her. A lot of adjustment. We came into her life, and her mom went away to school. I went overboard this Christmas, I guess." He shrugged as he settled onto the floor and with a quick precision, had half the bike assembled before he even turned back to me.

"You're pretty quick," I noted on a yawn. The day was catching up to me, the adrenaline pumping through my system finally subsiding and giving way to exhaustion.

He snorted as he tightened one of the wheels. "I should be. I do this for a living. I run a custom motorcycle shop. When I get bored doing office crap I hang out in the garage and get my hands dirty." His eyes darted to mine a couple of times, his mouth twisting with each glance as if a question was on the tip of his tongue.

"How long have you and Sara been together?"

"Oh, about . . ." I took a dramatic glimpse at my watch. "Four hours, maybe?" I laughed until he leveled his eyes at me. "We've been . . . good friends for a while. I didn't expect that to change when I ran over here tonight, but—"

"I'm glad you did," Josh interrupted, still fixed on the almost finished bike. "She flew out of here and none of us knew what to think."

"Yeah." I nodded, resting my elbows on my knees. "The second she called me, I grabbed my jacket and my keys and flew out of my aunt's house. She . . . doesn't usually ask for help—"

"No shit," Josh snickered, and I couldn't help laughing with him.

"For her to actually call me, it had to be pretty damn awful. I hate this for her. She's . . . she doesn't deserve it. Any of it. I know you all had your issues, but Sara is . . . so much more than what her parents made her believe. I didn't know the half of it before tonight, but she's had it pretty hard."

"We know that. She took care of Vic all alone all that time. I admire the shit out of her for it. I'm glad we moved past all of . . . well, I'm sure she filled you in. They both deserve a good Christmas, you know?"

"Absolutely." I offered a smile, still noting Josh's intense stare, another unspoken question dangling between us.

"You love her, don't you?"

"Yeah," I admitted for the first time.

"I thought so. Good. I'm happy I don't have to have the 'if you hurt either of them I'll twist you like this bike' speech."

I laughed and answered with a slow shake of my head. "Nope. You never have to worry about that. If she gave me a chance, I would—"

"You have a chance right now." He planted a bow on one of the handle bars before rising from the floor and lifting an eyebrow at me.

"Now, the rest is up to you."

Twenty

SARA

THERE WAS NOTHING like waking up more exhausted than when you went to sleep. Christmas Eve drained me in every way possible. I laid on top of the air mattress, eyes wide open, since four o'clock. My weary mind replayed everything in full detail on a torturous repeat reel: my sister's voice, my mother's rejection, my kiss with Drew, my second kiss with Drew. I fought the urge to head into the living room and cuddle next to him on the couch for most of the night. I needed him and called for him. I never called for anyone, and my lack of hesitation scared the shit out of me.

I shouldn't have given into my feelings for Drew for so many reasons. He said he didn't care about our age difference, and I knew he meant it. Maybe it's just seven years, but right now at this point in our lives, it was a pretty damn significant amount of time. He was in grad school, starting his life with a clean slate and bright future. I was in a much better place than I was and would graduate with a lot more options, but I had a past and baggage that put us in completely different places in life. I hated referring to my daughter as baggage, but she would always come first. I would never be as free as other women because I came as a package.

But, despite still feeling it was wrong, I didn't regret kissing Drew. During all those hours awake, I tried to reason away my loss of inhibitions as a knee-jerk reaction of digging up old family wounds. Maybe that pushed me, but I wasn't simply seeking comfort. I'd denied myself love for so many years because they made me believe I didn't deserve it. I missed out on so much in life, partially because of being a parent, but more because I never felt lovable. Drew made me feel lovable and sexy and wanted. Standing in the street in the middle of a snowstorm, I gave in with a kiss—and I didn't want to stop.

Careful not to wake Victoria, even though she'd be up any minute now, I crept out of bed and tiptoed into the hallway. I made my way into the kitchen, inching the refrigerator door open to grab the French Toast Casserole and pop it into the oven. I winced at the creak of the oven door as I shoved it in. As I waited for the oven to beep before I set the timer, I peered out the window behind the sink. Flurries still blew over the mounds of fresh snow, still white and pretty before the air got to it and it turned gray and dirty. Maybe it was a magical white Christmas after all.

I jumped when a strong hand splayed across my stomach and pulled me back.

"Merry Christmas," Drew whispered in my ear before smoothing my hair to the side. He feathered soft kisses over the nape of my neck, my body going limp against him like a rag doll.

"Merry Christmas to you, too," I replied in a hoarse whisper. I felt his smile against my skin as he looped his arms around me.

"How long do we have until everyone wakes up?" His lips dove into my neck, and it took everything I had not to loll my head to the side to give him more access.

"Not long enough." I elbowed his stomach and he dropped

his head to my shoulder with a groan.

I laughed as I craned my head. "I'm glad you're here." A slow grin stretched my cheeks as I took in the sight of him. His dark hair spiked in all different directions, his dark eyes still heavy with sleep. He was the most beautiful thing I'd ever seen.

"Me too." He kissed my cheek. "The couch was pretty comfortable. I'll deal with my family later."

"They're mad?" I winced as I turned around. "I'm so sorry—"

"Stop." He pressed a finger to my lips. "I called my aunt last night just to let her know I was staying over and I'd see them later. There was no way I wasn't coming here last night. They aren't mad, but I wouldn't give a shit if they were." He shrugged and pulled me closer. "You're sexy in the morning."

I huffed out a laugh. "Yeah, right." I smoothed down the wisps of hair from my matted ponytail, now self-conscious under the weight of his stare. "I'm a mess in the morning."

He shook his head as he slipped the rubber band out of my hair. My eyelids fluttered as his fingers threaded through the tangled strands. Drew's lips curved into a small smile as his eyes locked with mine.

"Fucking gorgeous," he rasped. "Always gorgeous." My eyes zeroed in on his lips, now tempered with another day's worth of stubble. We inched toward each other like magnets, my lips aching for his. I couldn't stop this if I wanted to. And I didn't—and wasn't. Was this being brave or reckless?

"Mommy!" A frustrated groan fell from my lips as Victoria charged into the kitchen. Drew's shoulders slumped as he laughed, mouthing "next time" to me before he stepped aside and let Victoria tackle me with a hug.

"I don't ever remember you sleeping this late on Christmas

morning." I kissed her forehead and pulled her to me. "Merry Christmas, baby."

"This is late?" Drew scoffed as his eyes widened.

"The sun is up. Or almost. Usually Victoria first tries to check if Santa came around three or so."

She lifted her head and giggled. "Can I look now? Please?" She folded her hands under her chin and bounced. Her excitement caused a pang I couldn't identify deep in my gut. I always made sure she had a pile under the tree, but it was a small pile. I was able to afford a little more this year with all the overtime I'd worked at the restaurant, but now that she had Josh and Brianna, I was sure she had a mountain of gifts awaiting her. Ever since Josh mentioned he bought her a bike, I'd been prepping myself to look thrilled for her when she saw it, not jealous as all hell he beat me to it.

"There's a big stack of presents in the living room," Josh's voice drifted in from the hallway. He raised an eyebrow at Victoria with Brianna beaming behind him. Victoria let go of my waist and gasped.

"A big stack?"

"Huge." Josh nodded slowly. "Unless you want to eat breakfast first, because we can if—"

Victoria dashed out of the kitchen and almost made it past her father. He lifted her up and planted a loud kiss on her cheek. "Merry Christmas, Sweets. Santa left you a lot, but there's one big present from all three of us."

My head whipped to Josh as he put Victoria down and she raced into the living room.

"The bike is from all of us. I guess I forgot to mention that." He smiled as he took in the confused slack in my jaw.

"Josh . . ." Now, instead of resentful, I was embarrassed. Again, had it been the other way around, I never would have put all our names on a big gift if it was just from me. Since I dropped Victoria off, I always felt like I had something to prove—to them, to her, and to myself. Keeping her clothed and fed didn't have the same impact to a child as a new bike on Christmas morning—and Josh knew that. A shame-filled lump formed in my throat.

"You didn't need to do that—" Josh lifted his hand up, cutting me off.

"The big stuff should come from both of us, since she has both of us now."

I took in a quick breath through my nostrils and nodded. Last night's emotional roller coaster made the tears all too eager to come back. "She has all three of us." My eyes drifted to Brianna.

"Thank you, Sara." A slow smile lifted her cheeks and almost made it to her eyes. Life wasn't as easy for her as I'd always assumed, and this Christmas she had her own disappointments to deal with. We both shared a bright spot in Victoria today.

"Yes, she does." Josh pulled her by the hand toward the living room.

"I'm going to go." Drew kissed my shoulder as he shrugged on his jacket.

"Why? It's still snowing, and we didn't even have breakfast yet." My pleading sounded foreign to my own ears, but I didn't want him to go yet.

He shook his head and snaked his arms around my waist. "You should have Christmas alone with her—with them. Get used to the new dynamic without the layer of anger." I jabbed him in the side as he snickered. "How about lunch tomorrow, and my cousin's party on New Year's Eve? They have some kids

Victoria's age. Think about it." His lips found my forehead and lingered for a long kiss.

"I don't have to think about it. Yes, we'd love to." He replied with a wide smile. I agreed to more than just lunch and a New Year's party, and the gleam in Drew's eyes confirmed he knew what I meant. No more denying and no more stalling. I wanted Drew enough to push the what ifs and insecurities aside and try. "Victoria is going to be mad you gave her the slip."

"I'll wave goodbye. She'll be knee-deep in presents, so I'm sure she won't notice." Drew's hand cupped my neck before he pulled me in for a quick but savage kiss. Drew was always gentle, but his kisses were rough. He had me panting and wet from just his mouth on mine. I shivered imagining what else he could do to me when he had more time.

"Merry Christmas, Drew," I breathed as he pulled away, nipping my bottom lip before stepping back.

"Merry Christmas, Sara. And I take back what I said last week." His hand feathered down my cheek. "You . . . like this . . . *this* is my best Christmas gift."

I fought the twitch of a smile and rolled my eyes. "You're relentless."

He pulled me flush to his body and shook his head. "Baby, you haven't seen *anything* yet. When I get you alone . . ." His voice dipped low as he backed away. "Then you'll know what relentless is."

Twenty-One

"I GET TO stay up past midnight? You never let me stay up that late." Victoria's lips twisted in confusion as she took a seat next to me in the kitchen. I held in a laugh at her skeptical gaze as I frosted the cake Drew asked me to bring. I'd spent the past half hour eyeballing it for icing gaps.

I was rigid with her bedtime, as if we didn't stay on a routine I was screwed in getting to work and school and wherever else I had to drop her in between. On New Year's Eve, I'd let her see the ball drop and usher her into bed before the TV started playing "Auld Lang Syne."

"Consider it a special case." I smiled when her eyes met mine. We'd spent two days with Drew since Christmas Day, and it unnerved me how natural it was. We ate lunch the day after Christmas and saw a kids' movie the day after that. Keeping our lips off each other was proving to be tough, but we managed. Or managed so far. I'd gotten a bit too brazen on Christmas with our desperate kisses in the hallway and kitchen, and I didn't want to confuse my daughter or get her hopes up. Drew and I were close, but I had no clue how this would play out. Right now, I loved his company and stopped pretending to only like him as a friend. What the future held, I wasn't sure, but I was hopeful. Of course, I was also terrified—but hopeful all the same.

"Your first New Year's Eve party, huh?" Josh threw us a smirk as he strolled into the kitchen and grabbed a bottle of water from the fridge.

"Yeah. Drew said he had boy cousins my age."

Josh stilled as he chugged the bottle.

"Remember what I told you if a boy tries to kiss you. Where I told you to kick." He jerked his knee up and then pointed at Victoria.

"Ugh . . . Josh, she just turned nine," Brianna sighed as she leaned against the refrigerator.

"You forget, Cupcake. I was a nine-year-old boy once, too. Trust me, I know how they all think when they see a pretty girl."

She crossed her arms as her eyes narrowed at Josh. "So, if there are boys like you at the party, if they like her, they'll let her know they like her when they're . . . oh, around twenty-eight or so."

Josh huffed out a laugh as he looped his arm around her shoulder.

"Why don't you go change, Victoria? Drew is picking us up in twenty minutes." I motioned to the hallway.

"Okay, can I wear my new DC shirt? Drew hasn't seen it yet!"

I smiled at her saucer-wide eyes. "Sure." I didn't even get the whole syllable out before she raced out of the kitchen.

"So, things with you and Drew are going well?" Brianna took a seat next to me, but I didn't turn around, as I was still focused on the cake.

I nodded, trying my best to look noncommittal. "He's a nice guy. A good friend."

"When I came back into the living room to give him some

sheets, you looked pretty *not friendly* to me."

My head shot up to Brianna's devious smile. "You saw?" *Shit.* It was one thing to have a private indiscretion you could will yourself to forget, quite another to have people see and confirm it as true. I threw down the icing covered spatula and dropped my head into my hands.

"Well, I walked back into the kitchen on Christmas Day and . . ." I cringed at what Josh was about to say next. His nose crinkled as he leaned his elbows onto the kitchen island counter.

"Seriously? Oh my God." My head fell back into my hands as I groaned.

"Sara, I'd never begrudge you . . . friends, and Drew seems like a decent guy. But Vic may start asking questions if she sees. I don't know how far into it you guys are. I mean, feel free to tell me to mind my own fucking business, but I just don't want either of you hurt."

"No, you're right." I exhaled a long breath and leaned back in the chair. "Drew has been the best friend I've had in . . . ever, probably. I'd been fighting the 'more than friends' feeling for months." Opening up to Josh and Brianna was strange, but oddly easy. "I don't know why. This is probably all kinds of wrong. He's younger, too."

"He's a nice, great-looking guy. Why is it so wrong to like him? Don't beat yourself up for being human."

"You had to throw in the 'great,' didn't you, Bri?" Josh teased as he came up behind her.

Her eyes rolled. "All I'm saying is you shouldn't be so set against depriving yourself. Anyone would be tempted."

"Keep digging the hole, Cupcake," Josh growled as Brianna waved him off.

"But Josh has a point. If you're unsure, spending so much time with him and Victoria is only going to cloud things more. But for tonight, just have fun. Both of you." She threw Josh a scowl before leaving the room.

"You're right." I let out a defeated sigh. "I need to stop acting like a horny teenager around my daughter."

"No, that's not what we were saying. Look," he dropped a hand on my forearm. "Just have fun tonight. Victoria is excited, and you've been icing the same spot of cake for the past ten minutes, so I'm guessing you are too." I met his gaze and had to laugh. "You deserve some fun."

Josh left me alone with my over-frosted cake. I hoped my fun wasn't going to be at everyone's expense.

"MY FAMILY IS a little nuts. A nice nuts, but nuts all the same," Drew warned as he led us up the icy front steps. "My cousin has twin nine-year-old boys, Alex and Aiden. They love comics so you'll all get along fine." He gave Victoria a wink and squeeze on the shoulder before ringing the doorbell.

"Hey, man!" An older replica of Drew greeted us at the door. "Glad you could make it. The boys are excited to have someone here their age." He glanced at Victoria over Drew's shoulder.

"Jesse, this is Sara and Victoria." Drew wrapped his arm around me as he made introductions. "I told them we're all crazy, but harmless."

"More or less," Jesse agreed with a nod. "My mother may not be harmless, so tread lightly with that one. Especially since my baby cousin over here is her pet." He motioned to Drew with a smirk.

"Please, Aunt Maria is all bark no bite. Now could we come inside? It's arctic out here."

Jesse ushered us in and shut the door behind us, his eyes still focused on Victoria and me. "Drew told me so much about you. All good, I promise. Food is set up in the kitchen."

I grabbed Drew's hand and laced our fingers together. Holding hands was new between us, but I reached for him more out of fear than attraction. He locked his eyes with mine and squeezed. Maybe I was older than Drew, but the measly life experience I'd had made me more of a kid than mature adult in a situation like this. I wet my parched lips and followed him inside the living room.

"Everyone, this is Sara and Victoria." Drew draped his arm around me and squeezed Victoria's shoulder. She searched the room with wide eyes. She'd come out of her shell a lot more in the past year, but like her mother, overly social situations weren't her favorite.

It was hard to miss the identical twin boys on the couch. They both focused on the TV screen with blank expressions, only glancing our way for a moment.

"Hey guys," Drew called out to them. "Why don't you let Victoria play, too? Or at least blink once in a while."

"Do you know how?" One of the boys scrunched his face as he studied Victoria. She stepped away from us and turned her head toward the oversized TV screen hanging on the wall.

"I have this game. My dad and I play. We got past this level two weeks ago." Both boys' heads whipped in her direction and one offered her his controller.

Drew gave me a side smirk and pulled me down the hallway.

"She'll be just fine," he whispered in my ear before kissing the top of my head. Every inch of wall in Jesse's house was covered with either something sports related or a family photo. The sight of all those pictures made my chest squeeze.

They don't open them, but I show them.

Denise called back late Christmas Eve, and as much as I hated myself for it, I didn't pick up. I still wanted my sister, but I couldn't acknowledge being rejected yet again by a mother who hated me. It was almost worse than when she originally threw me out. I would have thought the years had mellowed her feelings or that maybe she'd even miss me a little or be curious about her granddaughter. None of that was true, and I was still acclimating to the permanence of it all.

I'd bet none of the photos I sent my parents of their granddaughter made it to a frame. I felt pity for both myself and my daughter in that moment. Love of extended family radiated off every crevice of this house upon entry, and it was foreign to both of us.

"Where's your dad?" I questioned as I took in all the different faces. Faces focused on me, the scrutiny making me uneasy. I clutched on to my cake and hoped his family served alcohol before the ball dropped.

"He took my grandmother back to her assisted living apartment; she's not one for New Year's. And I would bet he's on his way back to Jersey right about now." Drew shrugged. "At least he stayed around for Christmas."

I was introduced to so many aunts and uncles, forgetting the onslaught of so many names to remember. They were all kind and welcoming, except for one. His aunt Maria greeted me with a half-smile and a weak handshake, and I could swear she mumbled something to Drew about not running out this time.

I guessed Drew leaving them on Christmas didn't allow me the best chance to make a good first impression.

"Don't worry about it," Drew assured me after we dropped the cake off in the kitchen. "I see those wheels turning behind those big eyes." He kissed my forehead.

"You think you know me so well." I wrapped my arms around his neck.

"Better than you know yourself, Caldwell." Our eyes locked until his drifted to my lips. He groaned when I gave him a slow shake of my head. Last thing I needed was someone in Drew's family to catch us the way Josh and Brianna had.

Victoria's laughter drifting from the living room brought me a little relief. I pointed to the living room before stealing a quick look to make sure she was having fun.

"The boys don't know whether to be impressed or mad that Victoria is beating them so badly," a blonde woman noted from behind me. "I'm Angie, Jesse's wife. I'm sure all our names are swimming around in your head from that whirlwind introduction." Angie smiled and seemed about my age. Her features were light, her pale hair brushing her shoulders as she laughed at the kids on the couch. "I'm glad Drew brought you guys over. He said you met at school, but you're a culinary student. "

"Yes, I baked a cake for tonight." I cringed at my clipped response. It was as if we were both on display tonight but, thankfully, Victoria was too engrossed in playing to feel it.

"Drew needs to bring you around more. I bet you make all kinds of awesome things at school. I only know the basics, but the guys, even the big one, only eat five things." We shared a genuine laugh. "There's Sangria in the kitchen if you'd like to help yourself to a glass. I know I'd need something if I met us all at once."

"You know, I'd love some. Thank you." I tried to give her a more relaxed smile before I made my way into the kitchen. Drew was speaking with his aunt in loud whispers when I approached, and the tension made me stop in my tracks.

"You don't know what you're getting into, Andrew. She has a child. That's a double obligation I don't think you're ready for." My blood chilled at the accusation in her voice. As much as I hated it, I had to agree with her. Drew was too good to realize it.

"She's not an obligation, Aunt Maria. I care about Sara . . . a lot, and her daughter is a great kid if you bothered to get to know her." Hearing him so irritated unnerved me. I never heard him be cross with anyone, other than Chase that one time on the track. He was upset and fighting with his favorite aunt—because of me.

"You need to be careful. These women . . . they see a young guy like you with a bright future and—"

"So, after meeting her for two minutes you think Sara sees me as a meal ticket?" He scoffed. "She is the most hard-working, brave person I've ever met. You have no right to—"

"Did you find it?" Angie asked behind me and startled all three of us. Drew turned and grimaced at the sight of me standing there.

"No. But it's all right. Victoria and I are going to go." My eyes locked with Drew's. His jaw clenched as he took a step toward me.

"It's fine." I held up my hand. "I'll let her finish this game, and we'll take a cab back to Josh's. I'll see you back at school. No big deal."

His aunt's expression softened when her gaze stumbled on mine. I nodded with a slight shrug. I couldn't blame her for her opinion, especially since there was so much painful truth to it.

I'd never use Drew, but we *were* an obligation he wasn't ready for. My feelings for him clouded my judgment, but friendship was all I had the right to offer him. I slowed my breathing to ward away the burning in my nose, the weight of disappointment heavy on my chest.

"You guys aren't going anywhere. Excuse us." Drew pulled me by the wrist into a small storage closet by the kitchen. He turned the light on and shut the door, caging me against the wall with his arms on either side of me.

I grasped his arm and pushed, but he wouldn't budge. "You should be with your family anyway. Don't worry about us, please." His angry eyes rooted me to the floor. I couldn't move or lie. Hiding anything from Drew was impossible, and I'd never resented it more than at that moment.

His eyes narrowed as he inched closer. "Five minutes ago, you had no problem staying and were excited about our plans for tomorrow. You aren't running, Caldwell."

I exhaled a defeated gust of air. Why did he have to make this so damn difficult?

"I heard you and your aunt just now. She's right. You don't need an older woman with a kid dragging you down. I thought that . . ." I trailed off as his dark eyes heated through me.

"You thought what? My aunt doesn't know anything. Don't use her ignorance as an excuse to bail on us."

I let out a long sigh and shook my head. I framed his face, my thumbs running over the stubble tempering his cheeks. He was chiseled perfection, even while pissed off. Maybe especially.

"You know how I feel about you. That's why I can't let you—"

He cut me off with a kiss. A deep, determined kiss that took everything. Drew possessed me with his mouth and his hands as he pinned me to the wall. I whimpered into his mouth as his tongue tangled with mine, our teeth scraping as the two of us couldn't get close enough.

"You were saying?" He panted as he leaned his forehead against mine. I was dizzy and confused and so turned on my hands shook as I pressed them into Drew's chest.

"I want you," I whispered, "but we can't—"

Drew's hand fisted in my hair as our lips crashed back together. My mouth was sore and bruised but I still wanted more. With Drew's family—and my daughter—only on the other side of the door, we were lost in each other. He looped my leg over his hip, pushing his erection between my thighs. His aunt had just warned him away from me, and here I was dry humping him against the wall in his family's house, but the realization didn't make me stop. There was no running or walking away. My body wouldn't let me. It needed him too much. *I* needed him too much. My teeth sank into his bottom lip as our kiss slowed, pulling a groan out of his throat.

"Did I get through yet?" he whispered against my lips. "I'll do this all night long until I do."

I dropped my head into his chest, breathless. He tightened his arms around me and kissed the top of my head.

"Look at me." His voice was husky and rough.

I raised my head to Drew's flushed face and widened nostrils.

"Foolish. So foolish." My hand drifted across the strong plane of his jaw. I always called him foolish, but this time, I meant the both of us.

"Do you want to walk away from me?" He grazed a finger down my cheek.

"No," I admitted in a barely audible whisper.

"Good, because I'm not letting you. She'll get used to it. And if she doesn't . . ." He shrugged as he trailed off.

I smoothed my palms over my hair, wishing I had a mirror to fix my most likely smeared lipstick. "Do we look like we've been in here making out all this time?"

A smirk tickled the side of his mouth as he brushed my hair off my shoulder. "Maybe. Your lips are a little red and swollen." He cupped my chin and feathered kisses over my raw bottom lip. I clutched his biceps to keep from pooling into a puddle. "Another thing I don't care about. You're mine. People should either accept it or get out of our way."

"Yours?" I choked out. Heat flashed in Drew's eyes as he nodded.

"Damn right," he whispered. "Mine. Now get something to drink and make yourself comfortable." His fingers twisted around my hair and pulled, forcing me to look up. "Because you aren't going anywhere."

Twenty-Two

SARA

AFTER A TEARFUL goodbye with Victoria, I headed back to school. Tearful because I already missed her, not that I was jealous of her new family or terrified I'd made the right decision as when I originally left her in Josh and Brianna's care. I started my last semester lighter, dare I say even happier. The couple of weeks I had with Victoria made my end game even clearer. I'd get us a great apartment and enjoy our life without being preoccupied with the daily struggle of making ends meet by the skin of my teeth—paycheck to shitty paycheck.

I breezed into the diner, smiling at people I didn't even know for fuck's sake and made my way to our usual table. Drew and I had taken a turn this holiday, too. We couldn't pretend to be friends now that I knew what he tasted like. I shivered thinking of the growl erupting from his throat whenever his tongue brushed mine. He said I was his, and I didn't argue, but often wondered what the hell that all meant. After graduation, I was headed back to Middle Village in Queens to find a place close to Josh and Brianna. Drew was based here, and we weren't—well, at least I wasn't—in a place yet to be talking about what we expected for the future. I was playing a dangerous game, as every day in this wonderful man's presence, I fell even harder for him. He saved me on Christmas Eve and saved me when I first arrived here. I'd gone from wanting him to needing him, and lately craving every single little thing about him. I painted myself in quite the corner, but I loved being with him too much to think beyond today. One day at a time was all I could handle.

"Hey, beautiful." Drew slid into the booth next to me and planted a long kiss on my lips.

"Um, why are you sitting on this side?" I glanced at the empty seat across from us as I squinted back at Drew.

He shrugged as he opened his menu. "I get to touch you whenever I want now, so why would I sit all the way over there?" His hand drifted up my thigh under the table and squeezed.

"You sound whipped, Kostas." My lips curled into a smirk. Drew pinched the sensitive skin on the inside of my leg, making me yelp and draw an odd look from our waitress.

"And I'm embracing the shit out of it, Caldwell. Don't pretend you don't love it." He winked and draped his arm around my shoulder.

"That brings me to my next question." Drew turned to face me. "The guys are out tonight, that stupid January kick-off party at Night Owls they forget sucks every year."

I nodded. "Lisa's been after me to go with her. I'm not feeling it. I'll go to the bar once in a while, but parties—yeah . . . no. What's your question?"

"Well . . ." A sheepish grin tilted his mouth. "I thought maybe you could come over to the apartment. We could order in, watch TV, maybe make out a little."

I smiled and inched closer. "Sure, but one exception. I want to cook for you. Has the kitchen been used since I brought you soup?"

"Hell, no. Well, other than the toaster. You cook all day long. I don't want you to have to cook just for me."

I snaked my arms around his neck. "What if I want to cook just for you? It won't be anything fancy on a morning's notice, but . . ." I shrugged. "I want to."

Drew cupped my cheek and tucked a lock of hair behind my ear. "You sound a little whipped, too."

I elbowed his side and twisted my lips into a scowl. I was enjoying the shit out of it too, but wouldn't admit it.

⋎ ⋎ ⋎

"THAT WAS THE greatest dinner ever." Drew rubbed his stomach with one hand while the other sifted through my hair in lazy strokes. I cuddled into his chest, my eyelids fluttering every time Drew's fingers grazed my scalp.

"Homemade macaroni and cheese was your best dinner ever?" I scoffed as I held back a yawn. "I feel sorry for you, Kostas." His laugh rumbled against my cheek. I was so relaxed and contented, I forgot for a moment that we were alone. Sure, we went a lot of places together, just us, but we'd never been anywhere—*only* us. Carlos and Brian were out, so it was Drew, me, and the flicker of the TV I wasn't paying attention to.

"I've never had it that good. Honestly." He rested his chin on the top of my head. "Having a chef for a girlfriend is awesome."

I pushed off Drew's chest and shook my head. "No, I'm not."

He held my gaze with a smirk before sliding his hands under my arms and pulling me on top of him. "You're not what? You're not a chef or you're not my girlfriend?"

"I'm a student," I whispered so close to his lips, they almost brushed. "Nowhere near being a chef, yet."

My breathing hitched as he cupped my neck. I stilled at the heady realization that once his lips touched mine, there was nothing or no one to stop us. Excitement and terror pulsed through my veins and made the room spin around me.

"But you're mine, Sara. All . . ." He kissed my chin and dragged his lips down my neck. "Fucking . . ." My body sagged from the wet, open-mouthed trail of kisses across my collarbone. My fingers threaded into Drew's hair as his lips and his tongue continued their pursuit, devouring every inch of skin before reaching my earlobe. A whimper escaped me when he clutched my hips and pulled me even closer. He was warm, beautiful, and hard—everywhere. I rocked back and forth, savoring the friction of his pulsing erection against my clit. He growled and lifted his hips to meet the movements of mine. It'd been so long, and I wanted him so much. Every cell in my body buzzed with want.

"Mine. All mine, baby." His hands drifted down my back and landed on my ass, grabbing both cheeks and slowing the rhythm down to an aching pace.

"Kiss me," he hissed, his eyes dark and hooded.

I crashed my lips into his, still writhing on top of him and moaning into his mouth. Heat pooled between my legs and seeped through my leggings. Before I knew it, my back fell onto the couch cushions and Drew leaned over me, his breaths heavy and quick. "We don't have to do anything you aren't ready for." He gave me a slow, sensual kiss as he settled between my legs. "I just want to make you feel good." His hand drifted up my shirt, cupping my breasts and making soft circles around the outline of my nipple, now rigid and piercing through the lace of my bra. He brought his lips back to mine, delving his tongue across the seam of my lips before sliding it inside with deep strokes. A throbbing grew in my core and rippled up my spine. Drew was about to make me come by only kissing me.

"Drew," I groaned his name. My hips bucked off the couch, searching for the release my soaked and swollen core cried out for. He smiled against my lips before tracing the waistband of my pants, slipping one finger inside the stretchy fabric and gliding it along my stomach. I gasped into his mouth as his fingers moved lower, inching inside with a tentative touch as if waiting for the point I'd tell him to stop.

I broke away from the kiss, my cheeks hot and damp. "Touch me. Please, Drew . . . touch . . . oh, God . . ."

His hand glided over my slick flesh, his thumb drawing sweet and slow circles around my clit.

"Sara," he grunted as his calloused fingers slid inside me. "You're so fucking wet . . ."

"Harder, Drew. All of it, harder." A guttural moan escaped him before he pushed the hem of my shirt up to my neck and pulled at the lace of my bra until I spilled over the cups. He sucked one nipple into his mouth, pulling at the bud with his teeth.

"So beautiful," he murmured as his tongue trailed to my other breast, tracing circles around that nipple before closing his lips over it. The silk of his tongue, combined with the bristles of stubble around his lips, was an overwhelming but delicious contradiction. I wanted his mouth all over me. My hips bucked off the couch, urging him lower, but he wouldn't budge. Drew rained open-mouthed kisses down my chest and over my stomach as his hand moved between my legs, drifting back and forth over my soaked folds. My clit was hard and swollen under his thumb, and one more little circle would make me fall apart underneath him. Was this what it was like to be worshipped? To have your body glorified by a man's touch? My sex life was a fuzzy memory, and from what I could recall it was . . . nice. Drew's lips and tongue tracing every crevice of my body wasn't *nice*—it was mind-blowing. My legs didn't quiver, and I didn't ache to the point of torture before Drew put his hands on my body. Sex with this man would ruin me—as if he didn't ruin me enough already.

"All right, Gorgeous. I'll give you what you want." He hooked his thumbs on the sides of my panties and inched them down my legs, over my knees, torturing me with his mouth all the way to my ankles until he pulled them off and threw them on the floor. I peered down at Drew's grin as he flattened his tongue and gave me one long lick. Sounds I didn't know I was capable of fell from my lips as ripples started up again in my spine.

I sat up on my elbows and watched as Drew's tongue zigzagged along my core, touching a different sweet spot each time. My eyes blurred at the hot as hell sight in front of me. I grabbed a fistful of his hair as I cried out his name. I was right there, so close it hurt, but as much as I squirmed, he never upped the friction. He ate me like a delicacy, but I wanted to be devoured. I wanted lips, teeth, and punishing tongue as he possessed me. Sweat poured down my face as the fucker gave me a smile. His hooded eyes locked with mine as he wrapped his lips around my clit and sucked hard.

"Jesus, Drew . . ." My head fell back as he inched it out of his mouth and then latched onto it again—only harder.

"I always knew you'd be sweet like this." He twisted two fingers inside me and pulled them out, my body jerking at the loss. He grinned, his lips and chin soaked with what he did to me. "You love my mouth, don't you, baby?" he whispered against my core, peppering kisses all over me before sliding his tongue all the way inside. I mewled, unsure of how much more of this I could take. *Holy shit,* I was about to split in half.

Drew's fingers dug into my thighs as he thrusted in and out, the muscles in his arms tense and bulging as he held my body in place.

"Tell me, do you like this?" He swirled his tongue around my clit, drawing out a desperate whimper as any words I had were gone. "Or this?" His tongue once again plunged inside me as he pressed his thumb onto my clit. My whole body went stiff as I shattered into a thousand pieces.

"That's it, baby. Give it to me. All of it." His lips found my clit again, licking and sucking until my legs flailed back and forth, my body limp and spent. His throaty chuckle rumbled against my stomach before he crawled up to give me a slow kiss. I always avoided kissing after a man did that to me but tasting myself on Drew's tongue sparked tingles between my legs.

"You're gorgeous when you come. I can't wait to be inside you." His words fanned against my neck, making every little hair stand straight up.

Once I could open my eyes, I dove right for his belt buckle, unable to open it with my quivering, impatient hands.

He caught my wrist and shook his head. "Not tonight." My hands dropped to my sides. *Not tonight?* Drew was so hard he wasn't only tenting his jeans, the inside of the zipper jutted out of his fly and seemed ready to burst open.

"This was about you." He flipped us over, bringing me back on top of him. "When we . . . get there, I'll own you, and you'll own me." He tapped my chin and brushed my lips, peering at me with more adoration than desire this time. "And there'll *really* be no going back."

Twenty-Three

SARA

"THIS IS GOING to be the longest semester ever," Valerie, one of the other internship students at the restaurant, lamented as she took a long pull of her beer. She somehow convinced me to have a drink at the bar next door after our shift was over. I thought it would be just us, but she invited our boss, Aaron, on the way out. He sat beside us, quietly sipping from his beer mug. The hairs on the back of my neck stood up when I felt his focus turn to me for most of the night, but I did my best to ignore it.

"It's going to be harder, that's for sure." I nodded while playing with the label on my own bottle of beer. "I like that we're finally getting to the good stuff. All the dishes we made tonight, we're finally doing more than just observing. It's exciting." My mouth split into a wide grin before taking a quick swig. I meant every word. I was still assisting but getting a real feel of what it would be like to be a chef. The fast pace, the intensity, I loved it all.

My intention was to nurse one beer for a little while and head out. Instead of making excuses when one of my friends or class-mates asked me to come out anywhere, I tried to oblige, within reason. I was exhausted and only wanted to hang out with my bed tonight, but thought making a quick appearance wouldn't hurt.

I never felt socially obligated before, but I liked having friends, or at least people I was friendly with.

"I like the excitement, Sara." Aaron smiled at me, and again, something about the way his eyes lingered made me uncomfortable. His father officially owned the restaurant, but Aaron managed the employees. He was a sweet guy, slightly shorter than me and on the stocky side. I'd noticed as of late he was overly attentive to me. He'd taken to lingering in the back when I was working, attempting uncomfortable small talk. I could have killed Valerie for asking him to join us. I'd lost count of the managers who'd hit on me during all the waitressing jobs I'd had, and I always set them straight right away. Sometimes they backed off, but many times they made my life hell to the point I had to look for something else. *Something else* wasn't an option for me. I needed this internship and job for the next few months, and I hoped ignoring Aaron's staring and the skin crawl it caused would work for the time being.

I offered a stiff smile back and diverted my attention toward the back of the bar. It was different than Night Owls, more sport than student-oriented with giant TV screens covering most of the walls. My eyes scanned the room and widened when they landed on something familiar. Or someone. Drew sat at one of the tables in the back with what looked like Carlos and Brian next to him, and a blonde girl on his lap. She threw her head back in laughter at something he said and nudged his chest. I reached for my beer and downed almost half as I glared at the awful scene unfolding in front of me. The air stilled in my lungs, but I couldn't look away. She was gorgeous and cozy as she snuggled against him, her arm draped over his neck, as if they'd done this a million times before. *How could he do this?*

"Sara, something wrong?" Aaron dropped his hand to my forearm and squeezed. I mumbled a no before my eyes darted back to the bar counter in front of me.

Drew never laughed like that with me. Stiff, older, single parent me. The thought made me want to curl up in a ball and cry. But, how could he? After . . . everything? After all these months of close friendship and the last few weeks of more than friendship? After all the "this is for you . . . I want to make you feel good . . . you're all mine" bullshit. He couldn't have been playing me all along, could he? I didn't know what to think. I should've shot off my stool, marched over to where he sat and punched the cheating asshole in the stomach. But I was frozen and refused to let him hurt me even more. If he wanted to date around, fine, he could have at it. No skin off my nose. Maybe a broken and devastated heart, but hell if I was going to try to stop him.

"So, Sara. I'd like to make Valentine's Day a big deal this year. My dad never put much thought into it, but maybe you could help me think of some his and hers dishes or something. He doesn't get that people eat that shit up and guys look to score extra points to . . . you know."

"Score?" I huffed before motioning to the bartender for a second beer. I wouldn't go past two drinks, but I needed something to dull the pain and humiliation. Not that two beers would do it, but maybe it would calm me down enough to quell the shaking in my hands. Even my breaths were uneven and jumpy. Maybe Drew would *score* tonight. So much for him being honorable and patient. He was getting it from somewhere else already. No wonder he wasn't in a rush to have sex with me. My nose burned as I took my first sip of the second bottle, but I sucked in a sharp breath to ward it off. No. I wouldn't cry. Whatever I'd thought we had was all an illusion.

"I think that could be cool. We could all talk about it tomorrow night, maybe brainstorm a little." My voice was dry and dull as I forced all the emotion I was feeling deep inside. My gut twisted, and bile threatened to rise in my throat, but I wouldn't let it show. Pissed off, bitchy Sara could cover this up. She always did.

But she wasn't in love before.

You can't be in love with someone you don't know. And I didn't know Drew. Not like I thought. My breathing accelerated for a moment as I pretended to be interested in what Aaron was saying.

"So, what do you think?" When my eyes met his, he sat closer to me than when we first sat down. I inched to the other side of the stool in an attempt to put some distance between us.

"I'm sorry, what?"

"Well, what if you stayed later tomorrow and just you and I could work on the menu. You have the restaurant experience they don't."

"I was a waitress," I scoffed. "I'm sure most of them have been waiters or waitresses at some point. Is that a dig at me being older than they all are?"

"No, no." He waved his hand back and forth before rubbing his forehead. "I'm not doing a great job of this. I'd like to spend time with you. Alone. I think we could be good together." He leaned closer, brushing my hair off my shoulder. Now, I was nauseous for a whole other reason. My shoulder stiffened, hoping he'd get the hint, but it was no use. So much for ignoring this until it went away on its own. *Fuck, this was all I needed tonight.*

I searched the bar for Valerie, but she vacated her seat at some point around the time my love life imploded and was fluttering around the bar making small talk. We were all alone. *Great.*

"You're stunning. I noticed you from the moment you walked in back in August. What do you say, Sara? Want to give me a shot?"

"Yeah, Sara. What do you say?" A gruff, but familiar voice behind me answered Aaron before I could.

My head swiveled to Drew's furious glare. *What fucking nerve*. After what I'd just witnessed, the anger radiating off him didn't make any sense, and I didn't understand the sneer curling his lips. I returned his angry glower for a moment before turning my attention to my other problem.

"I say no, Aaron. I don't date people I work with, especially not my manager. And . . . I don't think of you that way. I'm sorry." It was already out in the open so if I was fucked at work, there was nothing I could do about it. I needed to extinguish any hope he had of him being more than the man who signed my check and forms for school. "I need this job and don't want it to be awkward. But no. A hard, non-negotiable no." Aaron's face fell, but he nodded, looking between Drew and me with narrowed eyes. He probably assumed I had something going on with the leering man behind me—hell, so did I—but I didn't correct him otherwise. He seemed like an overall nice guy, and I prayed that wouldn't change when I went back to work tomorrow.

Drew's eyes seared into the back of my neck, but I forced myself not to turn around. I reached into my purse and threw a twenty dollar bill I really couldn't afford to waste on the counter, but my frazzled state of mind prevented me from caring. "I'm going to call it a night. See you tomorrow." I waved at Valerie at the other end of the bar, chatting up the bartender and having a blast. I'd never felt older or more beaten.

I rose from my seat and made my way over to the door, still not acknowledging Drew standing there. I bolted right past him and out of the bar, rushing to my car through the slush covered parking lot, not bothering to acknowledge that he was trailing me.

"You can't work there anymore."

I froze, turning to gape at Drew and seeing red. His jaw ticked as he stalked over to me. "I don't want you within ten feet of that douchebag."

"I can't . . ." My eyes grew saucer wide, incredulous at this guy attempting to order me around like some caveman after what I'd seen him doing tonight. I massaged my throbbing temples before I continued. "First of all, that's my job and my internship. I can't quit in the middle of my last semester. He isn't the first manager to hit on me, so I know how to deal with it. And second, it's none of your goddamn business!"

"None of my goddamn business?" he yelled before he grabbed my wrist as I again attempted to get into the car. "My girl working for a guy who thinks they'd be *good together* isn't my business? Not that you mentioned me when you blew him off," Drew spat before he let go of my arm.

"Why should I? You were having such a nice night with some blonde bitch draped over your lap. I saw you, laughing and having a grand ol' fucking time. What an idiot I've been." I muttered, more to myself than him.

Drew exhaled slowly as his shoulders relaxed. "That's what this is about? Sara, nothing is going on. Sam is an old friend of ours. I've mentioned her to you before."

"I don't straddle *old friends* of mine in a bar. Drew, just leave me alone." Our eyes locked, and the heartbreak I'd been stifling for the past fifteen minutes bubbled to the surface. "How could you do this? Why did you make me believe . . . ?"

"She called us tonight to come out and celebrate her getting engaged. There was never anything going on with us—ever. Trust me when I say I'm not her type."

His mouth curved in a little smile, and I lost it. I hit his chest once, then again until I reneged what little control I had left and pounded his torso until he caught my hands.

"What the hell does that even mean? You expect me to believe that? Let me go!"

"Sara, stop!" He wrapped his hand around both my wrists like a handcuff, and as much as I twisted and kicked, I couldn't get out of his hold.

"Sam is getting married next week. To a woman. She prides herself on being a gold star lesbian and never being with a man. *Ever*. She was on Brian and Carlos's lap earlier tonight, too. She's playful but harmless. We aren't turning her anytime soon."

I relaxed my wrists and he let them go.

"Sam is the womanizing friend who Carlos said he couldn't keep up with?" I raked my hand through my hair and fell back against my car door.

Drew exhaled before he answered with a slow nod. All this time I'd assumed Sam was a guy.

"She still shouldn't be on top of you, lesbian or not."

Jesus, what was happening to me? I was losing my mind, that's what. Instead of infuriated and heartbroken, I was humiliated.

"Noted, and I'm sorry, Sara. Instead of assuming the worst, why didn't you approach me, try to kick Sam's ass, something?" His face softened into a frown. "Why did you just run?"

I pulled at the roots of my hair before lifting my eyes.

"I hate that you turned me into this. Made me *that* girl, the insecure idiot that jumps to the wrong conclusion like a bad fucking sitcom. I never needed anyone before I met you. I hate that you made me need you so much." I shook my head and scoffed, so pissed at myself for being such a damn fool. "This isn't me. Falling in love made me stupid."

"What did you say?" Drew stepped closer, but I was too ashamed to look him in the eye. To say I'd made a fool out of myself tonight was an understatement.

"Answer me. What did you say just now?" He clutched my shoulders and squeezed.

"I said that I assumed the worst and made an ass out of myself. I watched you with her and it made me so angry how easy she could make you laugh, that you looked like you were having more fun with her than you ever did with me. I hated it. It hurt. A lot. This is what happens when I let myself have feelings. Can we just drop this? Please?" I begged.

"After that. You're in love with me?"

"I . . ." I met Drew's widened eyes and trailed off. "Yes," I admitted. May as well put it all out there. "And believe it or not, you're my first. Funny thing to say in your thirties." I huffed out a laugh. "I have no clue what I'm doing or how to not act like a psycho. Let's just forget tonight. You go back to your friends and I'll go home. Pretend you didn't see me and I'll do the same. Goodnight, Drew."

Drew grabbed the back of my head and crashed his lips to mine. I grunted in protest before I melted into his arms. His hands roamed my body, drifting down my thighs and grabbing my ass to pull me closer. I would never win an argument if he kept kissing me stupid and senseless. There was something in this kiss making it different than our others. It was passionate, but desperate. As if he was holding back all the other times, and now he was letting it all go. I fisted the collar of his T-shirt, dizzy from the intensity and lack of oxygen. I broke the kiss, gasping for air and limp against Drew's chest. This man made me feel so much it was terrifying.

"I love you," he whispered as he rested his forehead against mine. "I love you so much. I even love how pissed off you got tonight." I shoved his chest as I bit my lip, willing the tears burning my eyelids to stay put. Loving someone and accepting their love in return was something I never thought I'd be able to do. But as much as I'd fought it the past few months, it was impossible not to love Drew. He made me feel loved, protected, and worth it. It was a heady feeling I was still too frightened to fully embrace, but damn it felt wonderful.

He laughed as his lips found my forehead. "And you know what, you're my first, too." The corners of his mouth twitched into a smile. "Now, let's get out of here. Give me your keys." He delved his fingers deeper into my hair and pulled so I'd look up. "You're coming home with me."

Twenty-Four

SARA

MY KNEE BOBBED as Drew drove my car to his apartment. I didn't even protest as nerves, excitement, and exhaustion from the last half hour filtered through my system. I thought I'd witnessed Drew cheating right before my boss hit on me, then after a ridiculous misunderstanding on my part, I blurted, "I love you." It was as if I morphed into someone else tonight, someone without any semblance of control wearing her heart on her sleeve, and that sure as shit wasn't me. But with Drew, I wasn't myself. He brought out a side of me I never knew existed—and didn't know how to handle. I'd always hid my insecurities with snark but being in love was a totally different ball game. I couldn't hide how I felt or how vulnerable it made me.

Drew stayed silent the entire ride to his place, throwing a smirk in my direction a couple of times but not saying a word. He pulled into the spot in front of his apartment and palmed my still shaking knee after he shut the engine off.

"Stop being nervous. It's me. And I love you. Relax, Gorgeous." He grabbed my hand and kissed the top of my wrist before opening the driver's side door and stepping out of the car. I sucked in a breath and opened my door. Drew was the only person on this planet that didn't make me nervous . . . well, not anymore. When I first started spending time with him, sure, my knee bobbed all over the place then, too. But at some point along the way, he became my calming center. It's when he *wasn't* around that I felt anxious and uneasy. As I followed Drew into his apartment, I did a quick calculation in my head of how long it'd been since I had sex. Almost ten years? *Shit.* I was a thirty-two-year-old born-again virgin, and Drew was a gorgeous man in the prime of his life. Hairstyles and music were more or less the same the last time *he'd* had sex.

He led me into his room, shutting the door and locking it. I plopped down on the bed, peeling my down jacket off but so awkwardly unsure what the hell to do next.

"Hey, what did I tell you in the car?" Drew whispered as he grabbed my hand and pulled me up to stand. "It's me. And we don't have to do anything you don't want to do. I just want to sleep next to you tonight. So, if you aren't ready—"

"I am," I cut him off as my hands drifted down the soft cotton of his T-shirt. "It's . . . it's been a really long time." I shrugged as my fingers flirted with the hem of his shirt and inched it over the waistband of his jeans. I traced the smooth skin over the hard muscle, and the corners of Drew's mouth lifted in a carnal smile as I brought the soft cotton higher.

"How long?" Drew's voice dipped to a husky rasp as our eyes locked. My fingertips traced over every muscle and ridge, pressing deeper into his smooth skin as I continued to explore. My heart hammered in my chest as the air thinned between us.

"Nine years. And eleven months. Full decade, Kostas. I hardly remember the last time, to be honest."

Drew stepped back and peeled his shirt off, flinging it on the floor behind him. *My God, he was breathtaking.* I'd glimpsed parts of his hard, muscular body but, I salivated as I took in every detail.

"Sara," he whispered, his eyes almost black. "I don't want to think about you and . . . anyone. Makes me a little crazy." I licked my parched lips, checking the corner of my mouth for drool.

His fingers tangled into my hair as he took my mouth in a fierce kiss. The intensity made my knees buckle. It was rough and hot and somehow still sweet. Shivers drifted up the fibers of my spine as he fisted the bottom of my shirt before pulling it over my head. His hooded eyes glossed over my half-naked body, but I wasn't embarrassed or scared, only impatient we still had clothes on.

His hands glided over my chest, my nipples puckering at his light touch. He kissed down my shoulders, sliding the bra straps to my elbows before unhooking the back and slipping it down my arms.

"You are beautiful. So fucking beautiful." He cupped my breasts on a tortured sigh before dipping his head to suck one of my nipples into his mouth. My body responded by almost collapsing at his feet. "And you have no idea. No clue how amazing you are. I've never wanted anyone this much." Our lips crashed in a searing, breathless kiss. "Tell me to stop," he murmured, his mouth still moving against mine.

"No," the word fell from my lips in a guttural plea. "Please don't stop."

My head was still spinning when he dropped to his knees.

Drew lifted his head, holding my gaze as he unbuttoned my pants and inched them down my thighs, dragging kisses down my leg with each new inch of exposed flesh. I stepped out of them once they pooled at my feet.

His tongue dragged down my stomach before his thumbs hooked into my panties and yanked them down, kissing a path down my legs until they were at my ankles. I was so wet, a cool draft chilled the inside of my thighs. Drew hadn't even been inside me yet, and this was already the best sex of my life.

I latched on to Drew's shoulder in an effort to stay upright, as now I was quivering for a whole different reason. I whimpered when his tongue glided across the damp flesh of my inner thigh, almost where I wanted it. He was the worst kind of tease. He'd get closer and closer, and then back away. My cheeks heated as a sheen of sweat broke out across my skin.

"Drew, please," I begged as I bucked my hips against his face.

He grabbed my leg and hooked it over his shoulder. "Well, you did say please." He glanced up at me with a half-smile before he buried his head at the apex of my thighs. My knees gave out as his tongue and lips worked me over, sucking then biting my clit while twisting two fingers deep inside me. My mouth fell open in a silent scream as the first wave of tremors hit me. My legs shook around Drew's face as I came hard, gushing into his mouth and writhing and twisting against his lips.

"That was the hottest thing I've ever seen. So fucking sexy, and so fucking *mine*," Drew panted as he stood from the floor and kissed me. His lips and chin were once again soaked with me and I loved it.

I reached inside the waistband of his jeans and pulled on his hard, pulsating cock. "Inside me. Please," I pleaded as he laughed against my lips.

"My pleasure, Gorgeous. Lay back." He gave me a gentle shove onto the mattress, playful yet possessive. He fished his wallet from his back pocket and threw it onto the bed before kicking off his pants. He pulled out a condom, rolling it on quickly before climbing on top of me.

He grabbed my wrists and pinned them over my head. "Hands don't move until I say. Now, tell me you're mine." He slid inside me in one thrust and I cried out from the fullness. He stilled for a long moment before moving, slow at first then letting go of my hands as he picked up the pace. "Tell me, Sara."

"I love you." My voice was reduced to a croak as Drew moved deeper. "I'm yours." My head burrowed into his chest. I was so full and already sore, but I didn't care. I wanted more and *never* wanted to stop.

"Eyes on me when I'm inside you," he grabbed the back of my neck and threaded his fingers into my hair. "I need to see you." My eyes locked with his, his features rigid yet reverent. As we moved together in perfect sync, I realized I had another first. I'd never been in love, or actually *made* love before. Sure, I'd had sex, but this was the polar opposite—and I was certain I'd never recover. Throbbing started in my spine and exploded over me in waves. Drew stiffened in my arms as he slowed inside me. He dropped his head into the crook of my shoulder, panting, sweaty, and perfect—and mine.

"We should go into jealous tailspins more often." I giggled in his ear.

"I'll always be jealous when it comes to you." He lifted his head and smiled, causing my knees, and the rest of me, to melt into a puddle. "And if this jerk tries—"

I pressed my finger to his lip. "I know how to handle it, caveman. Now *you* relax." I kissed the damp hair on his forehead. "No going back," I whispered. "I own you, remember?"

"How could I forget? You've owned me for months." He kissed

my shoulder and drew me into his chest. "Don't forget that, okay?"

I nodded into his neck, nuzzling into his side before I let my heavy eyelids shut. I may have owned him, but I wished I could figure out how to keep him.

Twenty-Five

DREW

I FUMBLED IN the early morning darkness for my phone. My alarm was blaring, but unlike most mornings, I shut the damn thing off and stuffed it under my pillow—the same pillow Sara's chestnut hair spilled across. I tightened my hold around her tiny waist and buried my head into her neck. It was our day to run, but fuck it, we weren't going anywhere. I finally got her exactly where I wanted her—naked and in my bed, and mine.

For once in her life, she looked relaxed, even peaceful. She turned to cuddle into my chest with the sexiest groan.

"Five more minutes," she mumbled before pressing a light kiss to my throat.

"I think we can skip the track this morning," I whispered into her hair and kissed the top of her head. "We had plenty of exercise last night, don't you think?" She giggled into my neck and my chest swelled with . . . I wasn't sure. Maybe pride—that after all this time she was finally mine, and I doubted she giggled for anyone else like that. Or that here, with me, she was the woman I always knew she was: sweet, happy, and full of love. She also spent most of last night full of *me*. My chest puffed out a little at that, too.

"I think you're right. Just this once I'll admit it." She rolled over and snuggled into the pillow.

"See how easy that was?" I snaked my arm around her waist and pulled her back, right on my typical morning wood now twice as hard thanks to the hot as hell woman next to me.

She whimpered into the mattress as she grazed her naked ass against my cock. "Don't get a big head, Kostas."

"Too late for that, don't you think?" My hand drifted over her stomach, my fingers splayed wide as I pressed her against my throbbing hard-on. My palm grazed over the silky skin of her thighs, goose bumps puckering her flesh along the trail of my touch. I smoothed her hair to the side and trailed a wet, open-mouthed kiss to the nape of her neck. Her body jerked in my arms as my hand inched lower.

"So wet already . . . were you dreaming about me, Caldwell?"

"Maybe. Ahh . . ." Her hips swayed to the rhythm of my fingers and the big and small circles I made around her already swollen clit.

"Maybe? Oh, I think definitely." Two fingers slid inside her with an ease that made my dick throb.

"What was your dream about? If you tell me, I could make it come true." My tongue traced the shell of her ear as my fingers pumped in and out.

"I can hear how soaked you are . . . so sexy and you have no fucking clue," I growled, my head dropping to her shoulder. I wanted to come inside her, not shoot across her hip like a god-damn teenager. My eyes clenched shut as I tried to calm myself. It was impossible to hold on to any control with Sara. She consumed me, even all those months ago.

"I need to come, Drew," she pleaded. "Please." She reached

back and tried to guide me inside her.

I reached into my nightstand and felt for a condom. Since I met Sara, I hadn't been with anyone else so I never had a reason to buy any. I sighed in relief as I palmed my last one.

Quickly rolling it on, I slid inside her. "Your wish is my command." I kept my hand between her legs, starting the slow circles again while I inched in and out. I cupped her chin and turned her face toward me, covering her mouth with a rough, desperate kiss. Sara brought out an animal in me I never knew existed. Sweat dripped off my brow and rolled down her shoulder.

"Good?" I asked as our lips kept moving. "Better than the dream?" I swallowed her sweet whimper as I moved faster and deeper. Nothing was ever enough with this woman, and I doubted I'd ever have my fill.

"You're always better than the dream." My hand tangled into her hair as I crashed my lips back into hers. She broke the kiss when she came, constricting around me and crying out so loud I had to cover her mouth with mine to muffle the screams. I followed her, sinking my teeth into her neck as I found my release.

"I love you," Sara whispered as she swiveled her head to give me a soft kiss.

"That's a good thing." My finger traced the imprint of teeth marks on her skin. "Because that may leave a mark."

She burst out laughing and rolled over to face me. "Then it'll match the one on the inside of my thigh. You, Andrew, are an insatiable animal." She turned, running her hand through my damp hair, and shaking her head.

"You bring it out in me." I settled next to her and pulled her into my side.

"This is nice." Her index finger glided up and down my

stomach.

"Nice? That's all I get?"

She rested her chin on my chest, her swollen lips stretching into a sleepy smile. "Actually, it was pretty damn wonderful. I was trying to be careful about feeding your ego."

I laughed and gave her a light but long kiss. Her smile faded when I pulled away.

"It was never like this," she whispered as she cuddled into my side.

"Nope, sure wasn't." I dropped my chin to the top of her head. "I love you, too, Gorgeous."

She met my eyes with a wistful smile. "I haven't heard that too much in my life. Other than my daughter. And my grandparents when they were alive." My hand made lazy strokes on her back to get her to continue. "I figured I was just unlovable."

"You aren't. I hate that you think that. You're . . . you have no idea. I watch you in the lab and at the restaurant, working your ass off and never asking anyone for help. You put yourself last all the time. It's time you let someone put you first."

She shrugged and let out a long sigh.

"No one's ever taken care of you, have they?" I brushed the damp strands of hair from her forehead.

"I learned to only count on myself early on. Even before my daughter. Makes it easier." The sad resolve on her face made my blood boil. No one caring was her normal, but not anymore. Not if I could help it.

I cinched my arms around her as she peered up at me with glossy eyes. "I loved you right away, even though I tried to hide it. I'll make sure you never feel that way again."

She sniffled against my chest and wiped at her cheeks with the back of her hand. "Stop being so damn poetic." A laugh bubbled out through her tears. "I'm still not used to having feelings."

"My fire and ice." My hand drifted down her cheek. "I'm only getting started."

Twenty-Six

SARA

"I NEED MORE mushroom croquettes!" Loretta called to me without looking over. I raced to the oven to retrieve the last batch and shove the next one in. I'd thought Thanksgiving was tough, but Valentine's Day was the worst. The prix fixe menu didn't help, as we were running out of the cute little appetizers faster than the starry-eyed couples could order them. We still had two more hours to go, and while I usually loved a fast-paced night like this, not having two seconds to take a break made it miserable.

"Guys, you have to see this!" Corinne, a new waitress who started last week, gushed to us as she beckoned us to the door.

"We're kinda busy, Corinne, and so are you," I clipped as I helped Loretta plate the croquettes over the polenta.

"There is the hottest gay couple having dinner. And I mean hot." She fanned herself with her order pad. "I can't describe them and do them justice."

I finished the last plate and glanced at the timer. I had five more minutes before I had to repeat the process and decided to appease Corinne. She was a sweet kid, if easily distracted.

Peeking out of the glass circle on the door, I spotted one of two male couples in the dining room. The man facing me had smooth olive skin, and a black, button-down shirt stretching across his torso. He was hot, yet a little familiar. His date turned as if in search of their waitress, and I burst out laughing. I'd know those big dark eyes anywhere.

"Sorry to disappoint you, but those two aren't gay," I whispered to Corinne as I nodded toward the two admittedly beautiful men. I couldn't speak with the same certainty for Carlos, but I knew which side of the coin Drew preferred.

"Are you sure?" she whined. "Picturing what they had planned for later was getting me through this long, shitty night."

I couldn't help but laugh as I gazed at them. They did look like a couple if you didn't know them. Drew felt so awful about not being with me on Valentine's Day, but for me it was just a busy day at work as it always had been. Carlos told me he stayed purposely noncommittal on this day, as even a casual date could send a misconstrued message. Drew dragged him here to see me, even if he couldn't be *with* me. Was he for real? I needed to sneak out to see him and somehow douse the burning desire to climb on his lap and thank him for being so thoughtful in front of the entire restaurant. No one would think he was gay after that.

"Loretta, can I take a two-minute break?"

"Sure, last thing I need you to do is collapse. Mushrooms will be here when you get back." She winked.

I smoothed my matted hair and snuck out to the dining room. Drew still had his back to me as I approached.

"Good evening." Drew's head swiveled in my direction as a slow grin spread across his lips. He was mouth-watering in a charcoal button-down shirt and gray pants. This was the first time I'd seen him out of jeans and pullovers. "You guys are a popular couple tonight."

"I know," Carlos huffed. "I had a feeling people would think that when he dragged me here. Not that I mind, but it kinda ruins any game with the single girls over at the bar for me. They'll think I'm cheating."

"I think your game will be just fine, Carlos." I dropped a hand on his shoulder. "Flash them the dimples and they'll forget all about it."

"Hmm." He nodded in agreement. "Your girl has a point."

"My girl shouldn't be looking at your dimples," Drew growled at the both of us.

"I don't know if my dimples could save me. They all think I can't do any better than this loser." He pointed his beer bottle at Drew before taking a long pull.

"That's because you can't." Drew narrowed his eyes at Carlos before turning his attention back to me. "I didn't know the chef here was such a knockout. I should eat here more often." His eyes glossed over my body, and although I was in a stained uniform, heat spread over my cheeks as if I were naked before him. I took a small step back trying to resist taking a big leap on top of him.

"You should take your girlfriend here." My lips tipped up into a smirk.

"Ah, she's working this Valentine's Day. I miss the hell out of her, but I'll be waiting outside her job when she gets out."

"What if it's late?"

"Oh, for her, I'd wait all night." His husky timbre sent shivers up my spine as he grabbed my hand and pressed a soft kiss on the top of my wrist. I needed to get back into the kitchen before the heat between us turned up any higher.

"Ugh, can you wait until I'm out of earshot before you start foreplay?" Carlos groaned. "You're a shitty date, Kostas."

"Sara!" Aaron's shrill whisper came behind me. "What are you doing out here?" He glowered at Drew and me. "You know the rules."

I exhaled and nodded. Aaron and I acclimated into a mostly professional relationship after I shot him down, but I was usually the first person he snapped at.

"Loretta made me take a break and I—"

"Aren't supposed to be out here. Socialize on your own time."

Drew shot up from his chair and took a step toward Aaron. I pushed against his chest and gave him a silent shake of my head.

"That asshole is giving you trouble, isn't he?" He asked in an angry whisper.

"Nothing I can't handle. You guys enjoy your dinner, and I'll see you later." I planted a quick peck on his lips, now flattened into a hard line as he glared at Aaron over my shoulder before I rushed back into the kitchen. The internship was over in April; I could handle Aaron's pissy mood for a couple of months.

Instead of annoyed, I arrived back at my station deflated. Only two more months of Aaron, and school . . . and Drew. I wouldn't ruin today with it, but eventually I'd have to face what that meant. Right now, I was happily in love and blissfully clueless. As great as things were between us, I couldn't ask him to relocate to the city and there was no way I could move up here and take Victoria away from her father again.

I plated more croquettes and tried to get lost in my work, but my lousy predicament weighed on my heart and mind. I was trapped between a rock and a hard place until I had the guts to figure something out.

❦ ❦ ❦

"I THINK I'M going to soak in a tub and stay there until Easter." Corinne groaned as she plopped into a chair in the corner of the kitchen and massaged the ball of her foot. I nodded with a sigh, remembering how much Epsom salt I used to keep on hand at my old apartment. I'd dump it into a large old Tupperware container with some hot water and soak my feet for at least an hour after a grueling night of double shifts. I was on my feet cooking all night, but as a waitress, my toes suffered much more.

"Have a good night." I hoisted my bag on my shoulder and gave everyone a wave before strolling into the parking lot.

"Hey, Sara," Aaron called from behind me once I opened the door. "Where's your car?" I turned to his sheepish smile and hands stuffed into his pockets.

"I'm being picked up. Have a good night." The frigid night air chilled me to the bone, and I shivered even in my heaviest down jacket as I searched the empty parking lot for Drew's car.

"That guy from before . . ." His face fell as he inched closer. With each step he took toward me, I took one back. The last thing I needed was Drew pulling up and witnessing Aaron try to touch me or whatever he was trying to do.

"The one you reprimanded me in front of? His name is Drew. I wasn't the only one taking their break on the dining room floor tonight, so I'm guessing he's got something to do with it."

"He looks young."

My mouth fell open. "How old he is, is none of your business."

"Sara, I'm in my thirties, like you." He let out a nervous laugh. "I'm stable, established. As a parent, I thought that would appeal to you."

I sucked in a breath of chilled air and stalked up to Aaron, not giving a shit about what the repercussions were.

"There's a lot more to him than his age, the same as there's more to me than my age and the fact I have a daughter. I need this job and don't want to leave so late in the semester, but if this continues, I'll speak to my professor about finding something else until graduation."

"No, no, that won't be necessary." He backed away with a sour frown. "If this is what you want, there's nothing I can say."

"Drew is who I want, and I'm stable and established on my own. No one needs to rescue me."

As if on cue, tires rustled on the gravel behind me. I glanced over my shoulder as Drew's car pulled into a spot. The headlights dimmed, and Drew strolled out of the car toward us.

"Hey, Gorgeous, everything all right?" he asked me while glaring at Aaron. I grabbed onto his shoulders and stepped in front of him.

"All fine. Goodnight, Aaron." I nodded as I guided Drew back to the car, almost shoving him against the driver's side for him to get in.

"I will wipe the parking lot with that motherfucker if he touched you," he growled as he leveled his eyes at me. "Did he?"

"No," I groaned and slid my hand around the nape of his neck. "The alpha thing is cute, but I need you to calm down."

"Alpha?" His eyes widened as he looped his arm around my waist. "I'll show you alpha. Get in the car." He swatted my ass with a loud smack before heading to the passenger side and holding the door open.

"Did you just spank me?" I rubbed the stinging cheek while my mouth twisted in a scowl. His possessive side was hot and now so was I, but I refused to admit it.

He fisted my hair before crushing his lips to mine and backing me into the car door.

"I have plans for you," he growled against my lips. "So, get. In. The. Fucking. Car."

Heat pooled between my legs despite the subzero temperature. I needed to have a talk with my jealous boyfriend, but I had plans, too. I was going to enjoy every inch of him.

Until I couldn't.

Twenty-Seven

DREW

WE SPENT MOST of the ride to my apartment in silence. I caught a couple of glances from Sara in my peripheral, but she wouldn't utter a peep.

"I think you scared Aaron." Her shoulders jerked with a chuckle. "I never saw anyone back up so fast."

"Good. You'd tell me if he touched you, right?" I white-knuckled the steering wheel as the thought of that prick touching my girl sparked a rage in my gut. Bad enough he was making work difficult for her. When I pulled up in the parking lot, bad intentions were written all over his pudgy face.

"Why? So, you could choke him like the steering wheel?" She folded her arms with an icy glare. "I don't need a protector, Drew. I've dealt with way worse than him on my own—"

"But you shouldn't have had to. You aren't alone anymore, and if he doesn't cut all that shit out, he's dealing with me." I parked in front of my apartment and shut the engine off. If my stubborn girlfriend didn't want protection, that was too damn bad. I'd make sure he didn't come near her, and if he didn't stop being a dick to her at work, I was all too happy to pay him a visit.

"I didn't take you as the jealous type, Kostas." The corners of her mouth lifted. "Is this how you are with all the girls?"

"Nope." I leaned over the console and inched toward her. "I'm actually a pretty easy-going guy. But when it comes to you . . ." I gave her a quick peck on the lips. "I'm not rational. I'm unreasonable, possessive, alpha. Whatever." I shrugged. "You may not need a protector, but you have one anyway." I kissed her again, flicking the seam of her lips with my tongue. "Deal with it," I whispered against her lips.

She cupped my cheek and let out a long sigh. "What am I going to do with you?"

"Come inside and find out." I buried my head in her neck and nipped her earlobe before she jumped out of the car.

"Where are the guys?" Sara asked as she scanned the empty apartment. Usually, Brian or Carlos left a trail of something when they were around, even this late.

"They both went home." I threw my keys in the bowl and slid my arms around her waist, pulling her back flush to my front. "Carlos headed out right after we got back from McQuaid's. Winter break next week, remember?" I whispered in her ear as I splayed my hands on her thighs and drew her closer. Even in the baggy chef pants she had to wear, her perfect ass beckoned to me. "Why? Am I not enough?" I brushed her hair to the side and grazed the nape of her neck with the tip of my tongue. I smiled against her skin when she slumped against me. "Plus, now you can scream as loud as you want," I taunted as I cupped her ass, pressing my thickening cock into her back.

"I don't scream." Her voice dipped to that throaty rasp I loved as she tried to argue.

"Oh, you scream, all right." My hand drifted up her leg, brushing her core just enough to make her shiver in my arms. I wanted to take my time tonight, but after the buildup at the restaurant earlier and feeling her so pliable to my touch, I forgot any romantic plans I had. Fucking her hard against the wall and proving how loud she really did scream was all I wanted.

"Wait," she half groaned as she stepped away from me. "I need to clean up." She grabbed her duffel bag and headed toward my bathroom.

"You're only going to get dirty anyway, and I love you filthy, remember?" I grabbed her arm and pressed a light kiss to her lips.

"Give me a few minutes." She kissed my chin before squirming out of my hold.

I laughed as I trudged back to my room. Our apartment was empty and clean, ready for part two of my Valentine's Day surprise for Sara. Part one was in the small box on my nightstand. Sometimes, it felt like the age difference was reversed and I was the one showing *her* things for the first time. I'd never understand how I was the first man to love Sara, but I would fight like hell to make sure I was the last.

"Hey, Caldwell!" I called as I peeled my shirt off and lay back on my bed. "Did you fall in? You couldn't have been that dirty—"

My jaw went slack as all the blood in my body redirected to my dick. Sara stood in the doorway of my bedroom with cherry red lips and a matching red nightgown that fell so short, I could make out the red, see-through thong underneath. Her chestnut hair cascaded down her back and shoulders, grazing the top of her breasts that almost spilled over the neckline. Drool pooled at the corner of my mouth as she came closer, my heart hammering in my chest as my cock swelled to the point of pain.

She climbed on top of me, her hair tickling my chest as she painted featherlight kisses up my stomach. I fisted the silky strands as she inched lower, lipstick prints making a trail down my hips until she yanked down my boxers and swallowed me whole.

"Sara," I growled as my hips bucked off the bed. She dug her palm into my stomach to push me back as her head bobbed up and down, swirling her tongue over the tip and inching up and down my length. My cock pulsed as I grabbed the back of her head, tortured whimpers falling from my lips. This woman was going to kill me tonight, and I didn't care if she did. She was my heaven and I'd die a happy man.

I fell out of her mouth with a wet pop. Peering down at her as I chased my breath, I crooked my finger.

"Get up here. Now."

She leaned her elbow on my stomach and rested her head on her hand, a wry grin splitting her lips.

"Or what?"

I sat up and grabbed her by the arms, pulling her up toward me and flipping us over so I was on top.

Taking her mouth in a ravenous kiss, I pinned her wrists above her head. She writhed beneath me, moaning as she fought to wriggle out of my hold, but I wasn't budging.

"You're ruining my plans." I ran my nose along the delicate curve of her jaw and down her neck, biting the skin behind her ear then soothing it with my tongue. "I was going to be romantic and slow and sweet." I nudged her legs apart with my knee.

"Why?" She squirmed against me, my erection jerking against her when I realized how wet she already was. Yep, she was going to kill me.

"Valentine's Day. I wanted to give you romance."

"We can be slow and sweet later. Can't you just fuck me?"

A sharp gasp escaped her as I let go of her arms, yanked off her panties, and granted her wish. My eyes fluttered as I moved in and out of her tight pussy, already clenching around me like a vise. I tried to keep my thrusts easy and light, but I lost control and pounded into her. Her breasts spilled all the way out of the nightgown and I dipped my head to suck on one of her nipples. Sara cried out, her fingernails digging into my back and cutting into my skin as I picked up the speed.

"I love you. I love you so much," she croaked as a layer of sweat draped over us. I exhaled a breath of relief when she pulsed around me. Hearing her say "I love you" with so much need and want tipped me right over the edge. She'd been on the pill a few weeks and feeling her bare already had me close to coming the second I was inside her.

She giggled as I collapsed on top of her and dropped my head on her shoulder.

"I didn't give you your gift yet." I lifted my head and wiped the damp hair off her forehead.

"This wasn't it?" She peered at me with tired eyes.

"Nope. What kind of guy do you think I am?" I reached over her and grabbed the box on my nightstand.

"Drew, what did you do?" She gathered the sheets around her and sat up. Her breath hitched when she opened the velvet box.

"This is . . ." she trailed off as her finger glided down the white gold chain and the charm in the middle.

"It's a diamond spoon. Well, a couple of diamonds anyway. Wait until we sell this app and I'll add some more." I kissed her forehead. "This is only part one. Part two comes tomorrow."

"I didn't get you anything." She sniffled and wiped her cheeks with the back of her hand. "Why do you have to be so damn wonderful, Kostas?"

"Didn't get me anything?" I lay back on the bed and pulled her toward me. "You in that nightgown? Crawling on top of me? When I'm an old man on my deathbed, that will be my last thought, and I'll go with a smile on my face."

A laugh slipped out through her sniffles, but her eyes wouldn't meet mine.

"I have you. I'm covered for every holiday until the end of time."

Sara buried her head in my chest and hiccupped a sob.

"Hey." I tapped her shoulder to make her look up. This wasn't the first time Sara cried without a reason. Usually she tried to hide it from me, but I could always tell. I suspected it had something to do with graduation approaching, but I already had a plan. School may be over then, but we wouldn't be. My intention was to keep it close to the chest until I found out for sure but seeing her this upset almost made me spill.

"I. Love. You. Anything else, we'll figure out. Okay?" I jutted my bottom lip in a pout to make her laugh, but only got a half smile.

"It's late." I cradled her cheek but couldn't make her look at me. "You need sleep, and I need time to shower off all the lipstick below the waist."

She nodded, pecking my lips before coming back to my chest. I ran my fingers through her tangled hair until she fell asleep. Her brow crinkled even in her dreams. I sent up a silent prayer that this would all work out. I wouldn't lose her . . . I couldn't.

Twenty-Eight

SARA

"GET UP, CALDWELL," Drew sang in my ear as he fought me for the covers.

"Go away!" I draped the pillow over my head and groaned. Even after a long, dreamless sleep I was still exhausted. Anything that required getting out of bed or putting on clothes didn't interest me.

"Your other present should be here in less than an hour. You have a head full of sex hair and need a shower. Get up before I carry you in there myself." A loud smack filled the silence, my ass having a delayed reaction and stinging from the contact.

"Ow! Are you going to slap my ass every day now?" I lifted my head to glare at Drew. "Once was cute—all the time, not really." I huffed before sitting up and throwing off the covers.

"Aw, did I hurt you, baby?" Drew lay on his stomach next to me and rolled me to my side, peppering wet kisses up my thigh over the raw soreness left by his hand print. I grumbled, half turned on, half pissed off. Letting myself enjoy his way of making it better for one more minute, I pulled away before rising from the bed and sifting through my bag for some clothes.

"I'm going, I'm going." I lumbered toward the bathroom

when he stopped me and pulled me back.

"Good, since last night you were coming, and *coming*," he growled in my ear. I pushed him away as a laugh rumbled out of his chest.

"You're out of control. And what time did you get up?"

"About an hour ago. Showered, straightened up, tried not to take advantage of the naked, sexy as hell woman sleeping in my bed." He jutted his chin to the hallway. "Go!"

I couldn't help but laugh as I sauntered into the bathroom. I loved that pain in the neck so much.

So much my heart was beginning to break.

¥ ¥ ¥

"ALL RIGHT. I'M dressed and showered." I stalked over to where Drew was sitting on the couch with his laptop pounding on the keys. My boyfriend was such a hot nerd. Watching him in his element gave me a chill. "Where are we going?"

"We aren't going anywhere. Your surprise is coming here." The doorbell chimed in perfect timing. "And here it is." Drew grabbed my hand and dragged me toward the door. "Now close your eyes, no peeking."

"Seriously? Fine," I huffed, even though I was loving this little game Drew was playing.

With one hand draped over my eyes, he reached across my waist and clicked the locks on the door.

"Surprise!"

My eyes took a minute to focus before they grew saucer-wide.

"Hi, Mommy!" Victoria squealed before she barreled into my waist.

"Victoria!" I wrapped my arms around her and squeezed. Did she get taller since Christmas? "Oh my God, what are you . . . how did you . . ." I lifted my watery gaze to Josh standing behind her.

"Drew's idea. He even found somewhere for Brianna and me to stay for the next couple of days not too far away. It's a vacation for all of us."

"It's a breakfast bed!" Victoria chirped.

"Bed and breakfast, I think," I whispered, trying to hold back tears of joy this time. I turned to Drew, beaming like the cat who ate the canary. "This is my part two?"

He nodded. "Yep. Guys are gone until Wednesday, and Brian is the neat one of the three of us, so I have her all set up in his room. Freshly cleaned, new sheets, he's even got comics in there, but try to put them back exactly how you found them," he said to Victoria in a loud whisper. "So, it's the three of us for the long weekend. Good surprise?"

I flung my arms around his neck so tight he choked out a cough. "The best surprise ever," I whispered in his ear. "I missed her so much."

"I know," he whispered back.

I craned my head to Josh. "Thank you for bringing her here."

"Sure. And the 'breakfast bed' looks pretty sweet. Brianna could use a break." His smile faded before he gave me a shrug. My heart broke for what they were going through. The last time I'd spoken to Josh they had seen a fertility specialist who was optimistic, but Brianna was still resisting.

"I never loved President's Day so much!" I pulled Victoria in for another hug and my heart leaped at her giggle. "We're going to have the best weekend ever!"

She replied with a stern nod. "We have a ton of plans."

"We?" I squinted at Drew.

"Yeah! We've been talking about it for weeks." Victoria bounced with excitement. "I almost messed up and told you a few times."

Victoria asked Drew for his cell number before I left Queens, so they could "talk about comics on her iPad." I'd caught them going back and forth quite a bit and loved that they formed such a nice friendship, but I had no clue they were plotting a surprise.

"I didn't realize I was this out of the loop."

"Drew is pretty persistent." Josh handed Drew Victoria's backpack. "You guys have fun. I'll see you Wednesday morning, Sweets." He kissed her forehead and headed back to the car.

"Bye, Dad." Victoria waved at Brianna in the front seat and she waved back to both of us with a sad smile. I'd gotten to know her a little over Christmas and could see her infertility was affecting her in a big way. I hoped the weekend away would be good for them both.

"All right." Drew rubbed his hands together. "First things first. Did you eat breakfast yet?"

"No." My daughter clicked her tongue in irritation. "We left when it was still dark, in the middle of the night. I'm starving!"

"Okay, then. Sara, get your jacket. We're going to the pancake house!"

Her nose scrunched up at Drew. "But it's noon. Are they open?"

"Pancake house serves all day long, pretty girl!"

"Wow! Okay, Mommy. Get your jacket on!" She grabbed my wrist and pulled me toward the door.

Drew handed me my jacket and planted a quick kiss on my cheek. "Happy Valentine's Day, Gorgeous."

I took in a sharp breath to stop a tear from sneaking down my cheek and mouthed "I love you" before Victoria dragged me outside. When we stepped in the car, I called McQuaid's and called out for three days. The restaurant would be slow this week, and I was allowed five days of paid time off I'd never dreamed of taking until now. Spending three days with Drew and Victoria was well worth the few hours of overtime I'd lose.

Until that moment, I didn't know there were levels of falling in love. Granted, I'd never actually been in love before Drew, but what he did for me and my daughter, sacrificing his winter break and his apartment to entertain a nine-year-old because he would know how much it meant to me, it was too much. I pictured the Grinch cartoon Victoria loved and the part at the end when his heart grew three sizes and burst off the screen. My heart swelled so much, it really did feel like it burst. The Grinch and I had a lot in common before I'd met Drew. I saw things differently. I felt things other than anger and frustration. He showed me a different kind of life.

A life I wanted more than anything, but wasn't sure how to keep.

Twenty-Nine

DREW

"WHAT ARE WE doing today?" I set my plate of pancakes and bacon on the table and took a seat next to Victoria. Since she arrived a couple of days ago, the three of us had been nonstop. Sara was shocked there was so much for a kid to do this far upstate, and when I'd first researched places to take a nine-year-old, so was I.

Her nose crinkled as she leaned back and crossed her arms. "Can we just hang out here? Get a movie. I'm tired, Drew." Her lips pursed as she speared the last piece of pancake.

"Tired?" I laughed and nudged her sock-covered foot under the table. "You're the kid, pretty girl. You're supposed to have a ton of energy."

"I ran out of it." Victoria scrunched her nose at me. "Can't we stay here?"

"Did I ever tell you," Sara whispered as she draped her arm around me from behind and kissed my cheek, "when you're not here, he makes me run on the track at six o'clock in the morning."

Victoria gulped her glass of milk and set it down, gaping at the both of us. "Six o'clock? That's too early!"

I craned my head to plant a quick kiss to Sara's lips. "I'm guessing you want to be lazy, too?"

"Lunch and home for a movie isn't lazy." Sara tilted her head with her sexy lips twisted in a smirk. If we were alone, being home all day would have been fine with me.

"Yes, it is! It's a beautiful, sunny day. I'm dragging you ladies out."

"It's supposed to be freezing today anyway." Sara's hair was piled on the top of her head and she wore my T-shirt over her leggings as pajamas. So beautiful and so *mine*—in my clothes and in my apartment. I wasn't looking forward to letting either of them leave on Wednesday. "It's not who you are, but let's be lazy."

"Yay!" Victoria lifted her arms in victory. "Netflix and chill."

I sputtered on my coffee before I lifted my gaze to Sara's. She bit her lip, holding in the same laugh as I was.

"You know what that means?" She giggled at the crinkle in my brow.

"It means watching movies and vegging on the couch. Why? Does it mean something else?"

"Not to you." I snickered at the gruff tone in Sara's voice.

"All right, lunch and movies for your next to last day with us." I couldn't peer into those innocent green eyes and say, "Netflix and chill," although it meant something totally different to her. "Sound good?"

"Sounds great!" Victoria popped out of her seat and scurried back into the living room. I loved how easy she made herself at home here. She didn't complain about sleeping in a strange room, not even searching for her mother after the lights went out. Sara and I made quick and quiet love behind a locked door while her daughter was in the next room in case she wandered out. I guessed if we shared an apartment, this was how it would be.

Maybe most guys my age would see it as an inconvenience—a

chance wasted to have your girl all to yourself, having your way with her anytime you wanted versus inviting her young daughter to stay with you. But I loved every moment I spent with them. I loved the private jokes Victoria and I shared from texting back and forth since Christmas, and I loved how purely happy Sara was when she had both of us in the room. With her daughter so far away, Sara always had a glint of sadness in her eyes because of how much she missed her. This week, she had both Victoria and me, the two people in this world who saw her for the amazing person that she was and loved the hell out of her for it.

The more time the three of us were together, the more I wished it was always like this. If my post-graduation plans came to fruition, it very well could be.

Sara leaned over to pick up Victoria's plate, and I took that opportunity to pull her onto my lap.

"You'll still be here Wednesday afternoon, right? I wouldn't mind a little Netflix and chill then—*naked*," I whispered in her ear before biting the lobe.

"How are you not sick of me yet?" She giggled as she turned and flung her arm around my neck.

"Sick of you?" I huffed. "I may hide your clothes, so you can't leave, and change the locks so those tools can't get back in." I cupped her neck and pulled her in for kiss.

"Mommy." I held in a groan and dropped my head to Sara's shoulder when Victoria burst in from the living room. My frustration was my own fault, but it was hard to be around Sara without my hands all over her. Victoria's visit was an exercise in restraint.

"Your phone is ringing." She handed the phone to her mother before turning back into the living room. Sara stayed on my lap as she grabbed it and accepted the call.

"Hello? Oh . . . hi, Aaron." She glanced at me with a wince. Tension seized my body at the mention of that fucker's name. I didn't trust him as far as I could throw him, but I was certain he had no good reason to call her at ten o'clock in the morning on her day off.

"My daughter is here, I can't work the whole day." Her eyes clenched shut before she lifted them to the ceiling. "If you're in a jam, fine. Only four hours though. I'll come in at twelve and leave at four. I'm sorry, but she's only here for a couple days. I cleared this with your father."

I leaned in but couldn't hear anything cohesive from the babbling on his side. He knew she was off and was with me. This was graduating from an annoying crush to a growing obsession. I'd waited for her after work plenty of nights that he kept her late for some bullshit reason.

"Hold on," she blurted into the phone before turning to me. "Can you stay with her for a few hours? I'm not staying a minute past four. I promise."

"Sure, baby. We'll come pick you up at four," I answered much louder than I had to and kissed her lips with a loud smack. Sara's mouth flattened at my attempt to piss around her over the phone.

"All right. See you at noon." She ended the call and threw the phone onto the table.

"If I didn't love this internship so much, and need it, I'd tell that big baby to screw himself," Sara scoffed before standing. "Are you sure you don't mind taking her for the afternoon?"

"Not at all. Hey, Victoria!" I called into the living room. "Want to visit my comic book store?"

She came barreling back toward me. "You have a comic book store?"

"Well, it's not mine. But it's where we go to pick up stuff. We'll stop by while your mom has to work. Deal?"

"Deal!" She launched herself at me and tackled my neck with a choking hug. I hugged her back just as tight.

"And I could show you the rest of that story!"

"What story?" Sara asked as she studied us with a perplexed gaze.

"I wrote a superhero story for the writer's program at school. I let Drew see the first part. I would show you, but you wouldn't get it."

Sara's eyebrows shot up as she glared at the both of us. I offered a shrug, holding back the twitch of my lips.

"So, you guys have what, your own comic club?"

"Well, not exactly our own," I tapped my chin. "If you learn, we could let you in. Right, Victoria?"

"Yeah . . . we could." I burst out laughing at Victoria's reluctance.

Sara shook her head before backing away. "I better get ready for work, wouldn't want to get in your way or anything."

"Thanks, we appreciate it." I winked, loving the glower on Sara's face before she made her way down the hallway.

"Okay, pretty girl. You got your wish. You can watch a movie for a little bit before we go out."

"We can show Mommy the story. I wouldn't want her to feel bad. You can read first and tell me if it's good." She leaned against the table, fidgeting with the drawstring on her pajama pants.

"If you wrote it, it's always good." I kissed her forehead. "Go."

She rewarded me with an ear-splitting grin and settled herself back in the living room on the couch.

The strangest thing about Victoria's visit, or about how well we all fit together, was that . . . it wasn't strange at all.

.ᵛ.ᵛ.ᵛ.

I SPENT DOUBLE what I would normally spend on comics for an afternoon, but I couldn't help myself. Victoria was so excited it was infectious, and the bewilderment on her face made me buy anything she looked at for more than two minutes. She was easy to spoil, never asking for a single thing but so thankful for everything. That along with her beauty was a trait passed down directly from her mother.

"Hi, there!" One of the McQuaid's waitresses greeted us at the door. I vaguely remembered her from Valentine's Day. She was nice, if over-attentive. "You must be Victoria. I'm so honored to meet you. My name is Corinne." She held out her hand to Victoria.

"Hi." Victoria took her hand with a sheepish smile. "How do you know my name?"

"Your mom talks about you all the time. And what a pretty girl you are! How about two loaded brownies for both of you? The kitchen is quiet, so it'll only take me a few minutes!"

"Quiet," I snickered to myself. That's why Sara had to come in on her day off. I exhaled the rage building in my system for Victoria's sake.

"What's a loaded brownie?"

"A brownie covered in ice cream and fudge." I raised an eyebrow and laughed at the slow smile stretching her lips. "How about one brownie and we'll split it? It's big and we still have dinner later." I squeezed her shoulder and she nodded without turning around. Wow, when did Phil get here? I was taken aback by the stepfather-like words falling from my lips. I felt . . . responsible for Victoria. I didn't mind it; it was a tad unnerving how natural it was.

"So, did you have fun? Cool place, right?"

"Yeah. I think my dad has to build an extra shelf in my room. I should tell him and Bri later."

The happy kid from a few minutes ago seemed to slip away under my radar.

"I'm sure he won't mind. Something wrong? I thought you had fun."

"I did." She whispered a thank you when Corinne set a glass of water in front of her. "Mommy talks about me a lot?"

"She sure does." I nodded back. "All the time."

"She looks happy. Happier than she used to be in our old apartment. She used to be sad a lot."

My heart sank at the crestfallen expression on her face.

"Well, that's because she was working extra hard, and I bet she was really tired. All she ever talks about is what a great kid you are and how she can't wait to graduate and find a good job, so you can have an even better apartment. She's happy because after she leaves school, you guys are going to have an awesome life. She loves you more than anything in the world, so don't ever think you were the reason she was sad."

"She loves you too, I think. She always smiles when you're around."

"That's because I act like a clown and make her laugh."

I managed to get a giggle from Victoria.

"Do you love her?"

"Yes," I replied without hesitation. "Your mom is . . . beautiful. On the inside and out."

"Do you want to marry her?"

My jaw clammed up as my mouth went dry. I'd been trying to figure out a way to stay together, but I never thought about marrying her—at least not in the official sense. Sure, in the future, some day. Marriage was in the same slot I'd put children, an "of course I want it, but not right now." If I wanted Sara, kids were part of the picture, but it never had the chance to fully sink in until that moment. Did I want a whole gaggle before I turned thirty? Maybe not. But I found myself wanting this one. This shy-at-first little girl who had enough energy to light the sun when you got to know her captivated me as much as her mother did. Did I want to share a bed with Sara every night? *God, yes.* When I fell in love with Sara, no other woman in the world existed. She was all I needed. The thought of leaving her in May twisted me up so much, if I let myself ponder life without her for too long, a blinding panic laced through my system.

"Yes," I whispered with the same certainty as before. "Yes, I do."

"Oh, sorry, Sara. I didn't know you were standing there." My head jerked to Corinne's voice and a shell-shocked Sara gawking at me. *Shit. How much did she hear?*

"Hey, Corinne, would you mind sitting with Victoria for a minute?" I popped off my seat and grabbed Sara's hand, pulling her to the entrance of the empty restaurant.

"Drew," my name fell from her lips as a gravelly whisper as she brought her hand to her chest. "I don't know what to sa—"

I put my finger on her lips. "You don't have to say anything. Look," I cradled her face in my hands. "You have to know how I feel about you by now. I love you. I want it all with you. Just you, and I can't see that changing."

"You're twenty-five. Do you really want all this now? Wife, kid, obligations?"

"You're the love of my life, not an obligation. And maybe not today or tomorrow or next year, but I meant what I said to Victoria. How I feel about you isn't going to fade. It's permanent, no matter what my age is or will be. And I know that's why you're getting upset lately—graduation and figuring shit out—but I'm begging you this time, just trust me, okay?"

She latched onto my wrists, my hands still framing her face. "I love you, too. So much. But I don't want you to get stuck—"

"I'm not stuck, Caldwell. I'm in love." I kissed her lips, lingering for a long minute before I pulled back. "Even at twenty-five, I know the difference."

Thirty

SARA

"I'LL CALL YOU from the train, once I get on, I guess." I wrung my hands in my lap as Drew's car arrived at the train station. "God, I'm so fucking nervous." My hand raked through my hair, pulling at the roots.

He pulled into the parking lot and cocked his head to the side. "Really? I couldn't tell."

I jabbed his arm before unbuckling my seat belt. "This is important. The one restaurant that seemed willing to give me a decent salary and flexible hours. If I don't get it—"

"This . . ." Drew reached over the passenger seat to squeeze my arm and pull me toward him. "This is a formality. You had two interviews when you were in the city the last time. I bet they're bringing you in to make an offer." He pressed a kiss to my temple and cupped my cheek. "They'd be crazy not to hire you."

The corners of my lips lifted despite the crippling nerves. If only the rest of the world saw me through Drew's dazzling dark eyes. The adorable bastard had me almost optimistic at times. It was surreal to have someone so dedicated, so in your corner for every little thing, I wasn't sure how I survived back when I had no one.

"You're the crazy one, Kostas." I cradled his face in my hands and kissed his lips, savoring him for a moment before I pulled back.

"I'll pick you up tonight. And good luck, even though you won't need it." He picked up my wrist and planted a quick kiss to the inside of my wrist. "I love you."

I sucked in a quick breath and opened the car door. "I love you, too, baby."

"Wait." Drew grabbed my wrist before I could step out of the car. "What did you just say?"

"I love you," I scoffed, holding back an eye roll. "I've said it a few times now. This isn't like . . . one of those big moments. We've had those already. Can I go get my train now?" I nodded to the empty track across the lot.

"You called me *baby*." He inched to the edge of the driver's seat and slid his hand to the nape of my neck.

"So? I've called you baby before."

"Eh." A smirk curled his lips before he offered a shrug. "What you say when I'm between your legs doesn't count."

I laughed before I could help it. My head fell into my hands, my cheeks on fire. I'm sure I said a lot I didn't remember pre and mid-orgasm.

I groaned, exasperated but still smiling. "You're impossible."

"Maybe." His lips made a wet trail from my jaw to behind my ear. "Say it again."

"I love you, baby."

Drew growled in my ear, and my neck lolled to the side before I could stop myself. I shrugged Drew away and forced myself out of the car.

"What am I going to do with you?" I asked Drew before shutting the car door.

"I can think of a few things, but you can start by buying me dinner when you get this job. Which you totally will." A slow smile curved his mouth, and as usual, my insides melted. The intensity of what Drew and I had together knocked the wind out of me at times. It wasn't only the connection we had or the combustible attraction. He believed in me and truly cared about me. He was the one I ran to when I had good news and who I would seek out when I was upset.

"Hey," he called out before I stepped into the station.

I turned with a wry half smile.

"I love you." The heat that flashed in his gaze traveled all the way to my toes. All three words were drenched in sincerity and truth. It shocked me every time in the best way.

I shook my head and continued on. Right before I made my way through the door to the station, I craned my head to Drew, the smile still lingering on his beautiful face.

"I love you, too . . . *baby.*"

His head fell back as he mock clutched his chest. I laughed, exhaling a happy gust of air. This man was my everything.

It was wonderful and scary as fuck at the same time.

I RUSHED INTO the restaurant even though I was ten minutes early. Every time I came here, I obsessed over every single detail of my appearance. When I noticed a white stain on my black skirt the last time I was here, I was sure I'd fucked up any chances of making the impression I'd intended. I was acing all my classes at school and learned so much from Loretta at McQuaid's. There was no doubt in my mind I'd be perfect for the assistant chef's position, if only I could get my shit together.

There were other restaurants I'd applied to, but I had my heart set on Blystone. It was the eclectic but traditional restaurant I'd always dreamed of cooking in. Plus, they were still interested after I inquired about flexible hours. Sure, I shared parental responsibility now with Josh and Brianna and wouldn't have to miss a day of work when Victoria wasn't in school or couldn't go to school. Part of the new life I wanted to give her was to be her hands-on mother again, especially after being away from her for so long.

"Sara, so nice to see you!" Aida, the head chef, came out of the kitchen to greet me. "I know it's a trek from upstate."

"No problem at all." I shook her hand and then wiped my sweaty palm on my hip when she led me into the back office, too scared to bring my eyes down and see if I had another white stain. I was so close; it would be heartbreaking to screw it all up now.

I took a seat across from her, exhausted from hiding the shaking in my hands and fighting the urge to let my knee bob up and down. I knew better than to let myself want something—or at least, I used to. I had less than a minute before I screamed, "are you going to hire me or not?" *Put me out of my damn misery already.*

"Sorry, Sara. George wanted to be here, but his daughter was sick. You know how that is; they always get sick at the worst possible time." Aida was a beautiful Hispanic woman, I guessed in her late 40s, with black hair slicked back into a low bun. The crinkles around her eyes when she smiled only enhanced her natural beauty. She had a commanding, yet maternal way about her. Blystone had reservations booked two months out, and while the decor was beautiful, food is what made customers come back to a restaurant. Even if the place is shitty and the workers were nasty, if the food was good it was surprising what customers were willing to tolerate. I'd waitressed in a few of those places. I was anxious to learn from her. Hell, I was anxious period. A drop of sweat dripped down the nape of my neck.

"I do; you can never plan for it." A nervous laugh bubbled out of my chest.

"Luckily, George left all the forms for you to fill out." Aida handed me a thick, manila envelope. "Don't worry about finishing them here. You can take them with you and mail them back. Now, your graduation date is May twentieth, correct?"

"Um, yes, it is."

She nodded, tapping her chin while studying the calendar on the wall. "That leads us to Memorial Day weekend. Would June first be a good start date?"

I gulped, almost swallowing my tongue. "Start date?"

"Yes . . . oh, I'm sorry. I thought you knew that's why George wanted you to come in. We want to make you an offer. The salary information and vacation time is what he said you both discussed. There are insurance and tax forms in there as well. He wanted to give you a tour of the entire restaurant, even though you've seen most of it the three times you've been here. You . . . are still interested, right?"

"Yes," I screeched, wondering what the hell happened to my voice. "I mean, yes, I am very interested and would love to accept the offer. June first would be fine. I have to look for an apartment, but I have a place to stay in Queens in the meantime."

"Great!" She grinned and relaxed her shoulders. "I think you are going to be perfect. I loved your technique." She leaned back in the chair and crossed her legs. "I've had some bad luck with assistant chefs in the past. You have the experience and drive my kitchen needs."

"I've been in the restaurant industry a long time." I forced a smile, ignoring the pinch in my gut that equated 'experience' with 'older.'

"No, that's not it. You have a focus and determination a good chef needs. I think you're going to excel here."

"So do I." I exhaled a long breath and the tension behind it. "Thank you so much."

I did it. I was an assistant chef or would be on June first. The salary was decent, allowing me to afford one of the apartments I'd been looking at in Josh and Brianna's neighborhood. My daughter would be taken care of and would still have both of her parents close by. Elation flooded my veins as Aida showed me around, introducing me to the staff and giving me a sneak peek at their new menu.

I left the restaurant in enough time to get to Penn Station with time to spare for the earlier train. I would have loved to see Victoria, but I needed to be back at school for an early morning exam. Taking the train was much less taxing than four hours of driving back and forth, but when I arrived back upstate I would have spent most of my day in a train car. But, I didn't care. I was relieved and happy and so damn excited. What a difference a year made.

I dialed Drew after I boarded and found a seat by the window. My knee bounced, in excitement—not dread—this time, as I impatiently waited for him to answer.

"How does it feel to be an assistant chef?" I could hear the smile in his voice even with all the distance between us.

"It feels pretty frigging awesome. They gave me the salary and vacation time I'd asked for and I start June first." I shook my head at the long pause, imagining Drew working on the perfect delivery of 'I told you so.'

"And I was . . . right?"

"Yes, show off. Just a formality. Hit me with the 'I told you so' you've been itching to say." I leaned back in the cushioned seat, my eyes heavy from all the anxiety and travel.

"Maybe later." I pictured Drew's arrogant but sexy smile. "I am so fucking proud of you. You're going to be amazing. I have a surprise for you when you get here."

"At midnight?" I yawned, already settling into position for my long nap back.

"Don't get tired on me now, Caldwell. I have plans for you."

"Do the plans involve a mattress and pillow . . . for sleep?"

"You'll see. There may be that gelato you like in the freezer for you when you get here."

"With the salted caramel?" I gasped before another yawn escaped.

"Get some rest. I'll serve it to you naked." I chuckled before a heavy silence fell over us.

"I love you, Gorgeous. I knew you could do it."

"I love you, too. That makes one of us." I laughed as my eyes fluttered. I was already feeling the sleepy effects of the rocking back and forth of the train.

"You need to learn to trust me, Caldwell," he whispered, almost on a plea. "Can you do that?"

I'd been so happy for the past hour, there was no time to think of the other significance of June first. I'd be a New York City resident again, far away from the quaint upstate town and the man I loved. The very reason I'd resisted giving in to any kind of feelings for Drew was coming to fruition: the dreaded complication when school stopped, and real life started. I finally had what I'd been working for, but would that cost me the other most important person in my life? I didn't know what to do or what to say.

The only word I managed to force out, even though I didn't fully believe it, was "Okay."

Thirty-One

SARA

"I AM SO happy for you." Lisa nudged my shoulder as we searched the crowded bar for two empty seats. Even though I came to Night Owls sparingly compared to everyone else, I'd sat on a bar stool more in the past few months than I had in eight years.

"But sad for me. I can't even get a callback." She huffed as she motioned to the bartender.

"It's early. You have a ton of applications out there. Getting an offer this early is a fluke." I handed her the first beer bottle the bartender slid in our direction.

She scoffed before grabbing it out of my hand. "It's most definitely not a fluke. I've seen you in class. I bet you're head chef in less than two years."

"Yeah, sure." I picked at the label on the bottle before lifting it to my lips for a long pull.

"So why so down in the dumps? You'll graduate with your dream job lined up." She snickered. "Ah, your goals aren't so concrete anymore, are they?"

"What? Of course, they are. Get a decent job, find a new apartment for Victoria and me. That's all I care about."

She sighed, tapping an impatient finger on the bar as she awaited me to spill.

"Are you sure that's all you care about. Or who . . ."

Lisa had become a good friend during the time we were roommates. She cared and worried about me and saw how full of shit I was from a mile away.

I shook my head as I stared off into space. "I never should've let it get this far."

"Why are you saying that? Have you talked about what's going to happen after graduation?"

"No," I whispered as I topped off the bottle. My drinks didn't last very long as of late, especially when I was trying to suppress the ache-of-the-bone sadness that consumed me every time I'd think of Drew and me going our separate ways. May was coming a hell of a lot faster than I wanted it to.

She lifted an eyebrow and folded her arms. "You haven't talked about it at all? School is over in less than two months! You're this sick about it but haven't even discussed what your plans are?"

"Nope." My lips made a pop sound at the P before my shoulders jerked with a sad laugh. "Pathetic, isn't it?" Any time we became close to discussing an us after school ended, I either teared up or closed off. This wasn't me. I'd never shied away from anything, but of course, I'd never been this afraid to lose someone. "I can't ask him to move to the city, and I can't relocate here and take Victoria away from her father."

"How do you know Drew wants to live up here? He even has family already in Queens, right?" She leaned forward and squeezed my wrist. "I see the way he looks at you. I bet he'd pretty much follow you anywhere."

I rolled my eyes, trying to summon bitchy Sara and ward away the burning in my nose and thickening in my throat. I needed her. Whiny Sara was getting on my damn nerves.

"You love him, right?"

"I only started letting myself have feelings recently." The side of my mouth lifted in a smirk despite my heavy heart. "Please don't make me talk about them."

"Oh, come on. It's me. The girl who had to text you during class to bring me a tampon the other day. I don't think there are many boundaries between us." We shared a laugh before she leaned closer. "It's okay to love him, Sara."

"Is it?" I laughed. "What happens when school stops and real life kicks in?" I exhaled a gust of frustrated air.

She dropped a hand on my forearm. "I think you guys need to talk and figure that out. Pick up the big girl pants."

I nodded without meeting her gaze. I thought not knowing was the easy way out, but the uncertainty only compounded the dread.

"Hey, ladies." Brian greeted us before ordering a drink. "Congrats on the offer, Sara! Glad some of us know what they're doing after graduation."

"You'll have a master's degree after graduation." Lisa shook her head before taking a sip of beer. "I'm sure you'll figure it out."

"Right," he huffed. "Too bad we can't all be like Drew with a company gunning for us for a year. Asshole doesn't even have to interview."

My blood ran cold as my entire body went rigid on the stool. Drew didn't mention any solid plans or prospects after graduation. I assumed he was applying for different positions and he'd been spending a lot of time on their final project, but he hadn't uttered a peep about any company pursuing him.

"Gunning for him?" I repeated Brian's words, a sting of betrayal piercing my gut. Why didn't he mention this? All he ever said was 'trust me,' and I was so deep in denial about what kind of a future we could have—if any—I never pressed.

"That tech company in Seattle. We talk about owning our own company, but we know that's as likely as hitting the lottery at the same time you get struck by lightning. They're actually the reason why Drew wanted his master's in the first place. He applied there before he even started graduate school. He's had an offer for a year, they're just waiting for him to finish his master's." His face fell as he studied my reaction, most likely realizing I had no clue what he was talking about.

My cheeks were cold, and I was sure I was pale as a ghost. *Seattle?* Upstate was far enough. He had a job offer across the country—an offer he'd had for a year? I sucked in a quick breath through my nostrils in an effort to not lose my shit in front of anyone. Lisa's sympathetic gaze only made it that much worse.

"Listen, I'm sure he's got a good reason for not bringing it up. I mean, maybe he's not taking it. It's a six-figure starting salary but . . . um . . . maybe he changed his mind."

"Stop talking, Brian." My voice was low and dry. The quick breaths I was taking to relax only accelerated the anger washing over me in a red haze.

"Funny seeing you here," a familiar husky whisper fanned against my neck as an arm snaked around my waist. Instead of leaning into him, I stiffened even more. My finger scratched the rest of the beer bottle label off, my insides too tense and pissed off to turn to Drew's voice.

"Hey, what's wrong?"

"What's wrong?" I clipped as my head swiveled around. I

leveled my eyes at Drew's perplexed glare.

"You have an offer for a company in Seattle? A six-figure offer, and you never thought to tell me?" Drew eyes traveled over my shoulder as his jaw ticked at Brian.

"Hey, I didn't know you didn't tell her. I mean, dude, I thought you would have said—"

"Brian, I feel like playing some pool." Lisa shot up from her seat and pulled him by the arm. "Oh, look, I think the table's free. Let's go."

Brian's face crumpled in confusion. "What table? They're all full."

"Ugh," she groaned. "Take a hint and let them talk." She pushed Brian away from the bar and toward the back, giving me a wince of concern before stalking toward the not empty pool tables.

"Sara, I'm sorry." Drew slid into Lisa's vacant seat and grabbed my hand. I let it hang there and wouldn't let him intertwine our fingers. Something inside was about to blow, either in tears or fists pounding into his chest. I was afraid making a sound or a move would set me off, so I stayed stoic and silent.

"Seattle," a humorless laugh escaped me. "All these months you knew and never thought to tell me you were leaving at the end of the year to take a job in Seattle."

"I didn't take it. They've been asking me to come in to finalize the offer, but I never accepted."

"But, it's the whole reason you went to graduate school in the first place. How can you not take it, just like that?" My head dropped into my shaking hands. I pinched the bridge of my nose to ease the hurt, but it didn't work.

"Fucking Brian," he muttered under his breath. "Plans change,

Caldwell. I told you to trust me." His dark eyes pleaded with mine under his long lashes. He was so beautiful. Even while I was furious, he took my damn breath away. My beer bottle label now annihilated, I went after my napkin, pulling it and shredding the shit out of it in a failed effort to calm my nerves.

"It's a little hard to do that after you lied to me for all these months." I regarded Drew with an icy glare, doing my best to be pissed off and not devastated. He reached for my hand again, but I yanked it away.

"Plans change. It happens. When I applied at Ontech, things were different." He inched closer and draped his arm around me. Drew winced when I stiffened and scooted away from him. I couldn't touch him now or have him touching me in any way. I was upset on too many levels: scared, sad, angry, and the worst one, uncertain.

His features hardened as he sat back. "You never exactly factored me into your plans either."

My jaw dropped as my eyes widened. "Drew, I can't uproot my daughter. You know that."

"That's not what I meant." His hand raked through his hair. "I know you can't move from Queens and I'd never ask you to. You won't even talk about what would happen with us after you graduated."

My angry eyes fell to my fidgeting hands. He had me on that one. I couldn't be upset with him not telling me about an offer when I acted as if I never wanted to talk about our future. Truth was, I couldn't handle it. I burst into random tears at the thought of us having to part ways. He caught me a couple of times but never called me on it. I wasn't a crier, but this new stage of my life reduced me to a blubbering mess.

"This is more than just an offer, Drew. It's a six-figure starting salary." My breathing quickened as I tried to digest the bombshell dropped into my lap moments ago. "No one gets that right after graduation." I lifted my head and met his dark chocolate eyes. "It sounds like the opportunity of a lifetime. You can't give that up."

"I got another opportunity of a lifetime." He tucked a lock of hair behind my ear. "I'm not leaving to go to Seattle. I can stay here and do just as well." I squinted in disbelief before he gave me a nod. "Maybe not that well out of the gate, but I'll have my master's and I'm IT; I can work anywhere."

"Before me . . . us . . . you would have said yes without hesitation, right?"

He offered an irritated shrug. "Probably. Maybe. There is a you and an us, so thinking in hypotheticals is a moot point."

"So that's a yes, then?" I exhaled the air that stilled in my lungs since I'd heard the word "Seattle."

"Stop assuming. I don't know what's racing through that brain of yours, but you're more important to me than anything or anyone. I don't know how else to convince you."

What I had with Drew always felt too perfect, too precious to keep. It was as if our love was on loan, and now our time was up. It would be so easy to ask him to stay and give this up for me. I couldn't do that, no matter how much my heart would shatter at letting him go. Our age gap wasn't huge, but it was big enough to have a different perspective. His heart was pure and full of love for me, but it was clouding his judgment. This was only the first concession he'd have to make for a life with me, and even though he wasn't your average twenty-five-year-old, he had the shortsightedness of one. I saw clearly and far into the future, and the vision broke my heart.

"I think . . ." My voice scratched as it tried to form words. "If you don't take this, you'll regret it. And resent me for it." My teeth sank into my bottom lip, the finality of what I was feeling turning my stomach over. A tear snaked down my cheek before I could stop it. There was an odd relief to your worst fear being realized.

"Wait just a fucking minute. Back up. You don't want to be one of my regrets? Do you have any idea how I feel about you? I don't care what I have to sacrifice. Jobs are a dime a dozen as far as I'm concerned. I could settle for something closer." He framed my face and kissed my lips. Although I wanted to with everything I had, I couldn't kiss him back.

"Stop it, Sara. Brian made a big deal out of nothing."

"Sacrifice." I nodded as my hand draped over my eyes. "You have to *sacrifice* for me. *Settle* for me." I grabbed my purse and stood. "Tell Lisa I'll see her at home."

"No!" Drew bellowed and stepped in front of me. His eyes searched my face in panic. "That's not what I meant. I love you. I love Victoria. I'd do anything for the both of you."

I cupped his cheek. "Including spite yourself. You should listen to your aunt. Don't let some woman and her kid drag you down."

Drew's chest now heaved along with mine as he grabbed my wrist. "Are we really back here again? You aren't dragging me down. I won't let you do this. We're so fucking happy. Why would you throw it all away?"

"Because I don't want *you* to throw it all away. All you worked for up to this point. You're not thinking clearly."

"I'm thinking fine, Sara," Drew yelled through gritted teeth. I felt the leering of a thousand eyes on us. "I'm fine with staying in New York, being someone's dad. I'd take on whatever I need to keep us together but you're still fucking running." Drew's jaw ticked as his hold on me tightened.

"Take on?" A heavy sigh fell from my lips as the choice I had to make became achingly apparent. "We aren't your sacrifice or something you have to take on. Take the job, live your life and we'll live ours. Please let me go." My voice croaked as I tore my eyes from his.

"Miss, is there a problem?" A bouncer approached Drew and me, looking between us and the hold he had on my wrist.

"No, no problem. I was just leaving." I gazed into Drew's glassy eyes one more time. Ripping off a Band-Aid was never more excruciating. He was the only man I'd ever loved, and that wouldn't change, no matter what state we both lived in. I couldn't and wouldn't be a burden on him. Maybe he didn't see it now, but in time he would. Hurting him now would prevent him hating me later.

The bouncer was the only reason he wouldn't follow me to my car, and I took advantage of the out.

"Goodbye, Kostas."

Thirty-Two

DREW

Me: Please talk to me. I love you. You have to know that.

I SENT TEXT after text to Sara with no response with calls sent straight to voice mail in between. It'd only been two days, but the more time went on without a reply, the more final it all seemed. I couldn't lose her. Not now. Maybe we were only officially together since Christmas, but I loved her before that. It didn't matter if I was twenty-five or fifty-five, I knew Sara was it for me. The job at Ontech was my goal when I started graduate school, but not anymore. My goals were a beautiful brunette and her adorable daughter, and the amazing life I knew we could have. Not accepting the offer to be with her was not settling or a sacrifice, despite my word vomit at the time. She was what I wanted. I convinced her to take a chance on us, and I would again—if she would just fucking answer me. Every second away from her that ticked by brought me that much closer to madness.

I trudged into the kitchen, tired and hungry and yet restless and sick to my stomach. I needed her back. Nothing felt right or made sense without her.

"Hey, man." Brian cringed at my approach. "You look like shit."

"I feel like shit, too. Thanks." All my free time was spent texting and calling Sara. Shaving and showering dropped low on my list of priorities. Sleeping wasn't happening either as my bedsheets still smelled like Sara. I buried my face in my pillow, breathing in her scent as if I could will her to come to life in my arms. We weren't broken up, we were in a limbo that needed to be fixed. The more I told myself that, the harder it was to believe.

"I'm sorry, man. I had no idea she didn't know."

"It's all right. And it's my fault. I should've told her." I fell into a seat at the counter and poured rice cereal into a bowl. It tasted like sawdust even after I doused it with milk, but I couldn't win Sara back if I fainted from malnutrition.

"So, why didn't you?" Carlos strolled into the kitchen and headed for the blender for one of his protein shakes. "Graduation is in a month and a half, and you still didn't give them a hard no."

"That's because I need the offer in play to negotiate. I found a firm in Manhattan with almost the same position available." I swirled my spoon around in the bowl, forcing myself to swallow with every bite. I knew exactly how she'd react if she knew about Seattle. Before me, no one ever gave her a second thought. She had no friends or family before she came here. She had a hard time believing I wanted to be with her at all, much less relocate myself for her. She still didn't believe the love between us was real, and that burned most of all.

"Where the restaurant Sara will be working at is, right?"

"Yes. Once that offer came through, I would've told Sara right away. She's been so upset lately with graduation so close. I didn't want to tell her unless I was sure." If I didn't get it, I had other feelers out there and a few callbacks. I wouldn't give up, but I didn't want to tell her unless I was certain. I was in this whole stupid mess because I wasn't honest with her, and in my panic over losing her, I said a shit ton of things I didn't mean. Words like burden, sacrifice, taking on. No wonder she wouldn't respond. I picked up my phone, taunted by my blank screen.

Come on, Gorgeous. Text me back.

"So, you really love her, huh?" Brian came over to where I sat and rested his elbows on the counter. "I mean, I've seen you break up with women before—"

"We didn't break up," I grunted as I threw my bowl in the sink. "It's a fucked-up misunderstanding I could correct if she would just speak to me."

"Are you really ready for all of that?" Carlos asked from where he leaned against the counter.

"Ready for what?" I craned my head as I clutched the edge of the sink. The only conversation I was capable of was snapping at anyone who dared to speak to me. I was an angry, heartbroken, ornery-as-hell mess.

"Settling down, being someone's stepdad. I know she stayed here with her kid for a few days, but doing that full-time . . . are you sure you're ready for that?"

Did I plan on falling in love with a woman with a child at this point in my life—no, but it happened. Now, being forced to think of having to live without her turned my stomach.

"Being with Sara isn't settling. She's the . . . she's everything. I can't see myself with anyone else. Maybe having Victoria here for a few days isn't the same as being a full-time stepdad, but I'm up for the job. In fact, I want the fucking job. I want them both. And I'll get them back."

I wanted to believe that, but I wasn't convincing anyone, including myself.

⋎⋎⋎

I PARKED IN the lot by the lab, hoping like hell Sara would be practicing for lab exams tonight. My heart leaped into my throat when my phone finally buzzed in my pocket.

Victoria: Can you help me pick out a birthday present for Mommy? Dad said he would help but you know her better.

Pain seized my chest as if I'd been stabbed. Losing Sara would mean losing her, too. My fingers froze over the keys, unsure how to respond.

Me: Sure. That's an awesome idea. Let me think and I'll get back to you, okay, pretty girl?

Victoria: OK. You're the best Drew.

I strode into the lab on shaky legs, quickly settling at the front desk. Pretending to be engrossed in my laptop screen, my eyes darted back and forth to the door. She usually came to the lab around eight and practiced for an hour before a practical exam. The air stilled in my lungs when I found Lisa but expelled out when I realized she was alone.

"Hey, Drew." Lisa regarded me with sympathetic eyes as she signed in. "It's none of my business," she whispered as she leaned in. "But I hate this for you guys."

I nodded and folded my arms. That made two of us.

"How is she?" I asked, unsure if I wanted to know the answer.

"Miserable. Doesn't say much. Sniffles in her sleep but denies it." Her lips curved in a sad smile. "She's as quiet as she was when I first met her."

It should have made me feel better hearing she was so distraught, but it didn't. Her own happiness was a non-factor to her. She cut me off because she thought it was best for me without any regard for breaking her own heart. I missed her to the point of physical pain, but I was selfish enough to fight for her. She didn't have a selfish cell in her body. She only fought for herself when it meant fighting for her daughter. I hated that she was back to the closed off woman I'd first met all those months ago. She needed me; we needed each other. Why was this even happening? I pulled at the roots of my hair in frustration, wanting to tear them from my scalp.

"She's not coming, is she?"

Lisa shook her head, frowning at the sad sack I was. "I'm sorry."

"Sara's at McQuaid's." Emma signed in behind Lisa. "She said Aaron would let her have the kitchen to herself to practice tonight."

"Aaron?" My blood boiled as I straightened in my chair. Seeing me was too much for her so she went to that slime ball for help? I crushed the pencil I was tapping on the desk so tightly in my hands, it broke in half. "Instead of coming here, she's with that douchebag—after hours—by herself."

Emma grimaced before she headed for an empty station.

"You know nothing is going on, right? She loves you, Drew."

I leaned back in the chair, itching to close the lab and speed to McQuaid's to pull her out of there. But, I couldn't, could I? I wasn't her jealous boyfriend. Not anymore.

"You know that she can handle herself—"

"I'm fine, Lisa. No need to explain." I nodded to the back. "Go practice."

She opened her mouth to say something but closed it before making her way to a station.

Sara and I had a soul-searing, once-in-a-lifetime kind of love . . . but only one of us thought it was worth fighting for.

Thirty-Three

SARA

EVERYTHING I DID, every move I made, seemed to be in slow motion. I was trapped in my own tortured version of *The Matrix*. Drew still texted and called all the time, but although it killed me, I wouldn't answer. Why make the inevitable even worse?

After a long two hours of practice at the restaurant, staying later than I intended to on purpose, my broken heart and I headed back to the dorms. Loretta stayed behind, pretending to only be around if I needed help, but putting a much-needed barrier between Aaron and me. If he hit on me tonight, I was afraid I'd punch his lights out in frustration. I didn't want anyone but Drew, and I had the sinking feeling I never would. After being alone for so many years and never giving the solitude a second thought, now it felt like a death sentence.

I promised Lisa I'd call her the moment I left the restaurant at ten o'clock or else she'd call to check. She didn't trust Aaron alone with me, but as luck would have it, I'd only seen him when I arrived and when I left. Maybe he'd gotten the message or was deterred by Loretta's presence. Either way, I was happy the awkwardness of my internship would soon be coming to a close.

My phone rang at exactly 10:01; Lisa was nothing if not

punctual. She'd been pressing me to open up about Drew, but I couldn't do it. I'd only be able to pull off stoic if I didn't mention his name, no matter how many times his face ran through my tortured brain.

"Hello . . ." I sang after I reached into my bag and grabbed my phone, answering without looking at the screen. "Sorry, I'm fifty seconds late, I'm on my way home n—"

"Did he touch you?" Drew growled in my ear, an unusual menace in his tone.

Shit. My eyes squeezed shut at the sound of his voice. He'd been calling and texting nonstop for days and I'd managed to avoid him, until now. He sounded furious, and as devastated as I was, the love I had for him hadn't changed and probably wouldn't in my lifetime, but I couldn't give in. I loved him enough to do what was best, even if he didn't see it that way.

"What are you talking about?"

"You won't speak to me or even come anywhere near me. You go to McQuaid's, after hours, to be with that fucker who can't take a hint. Emma slipped and told me where you were, and I've been climbing the fucking walls ever since."

"Drew, I've handled a lot worse than Aaron alone. I don't need you to take care of me—"

"But I need you! That's the part you don't get. That you *never* understood. I'm an adult, not a kid that doesn't know what the fuck he wants, no matter how you blow off how I feel about you because of my age. I want *you*, Sara. I want Victoria. This job could pay seven figures for all I care, but if it takes me away from you, I don't want it. What the hell do I have to do to get through to you?"

I winced as his words grew louder and more desperate.

"I don't blame you for what you said. We *are* a lot to take on, and you don't need us to—"

"You don't have the first fucking clue what I need, Caldwell. If you did, you'd be right here with me and not in that asshole's kitchen." My chest pinched as his voice cracked on the last word.

I sank my teeth into my quivering bottom lip, willing the cascading tears down my cheeks back into my eyes. I missed my best friend. I missed his pure heart and fierce love. He deserved the best in life and should feel free to take it without obligation. It was all raw and fresh, but eventually the wound would heal, and he'd move on. I wouldn't, but I was tough. I'd survive knowing he was better off.

"You need to take the offer." A long, heavy silence washed over us. I was about to hang up when his heavy sigh made me freeze.

"Sara, please don't do this." Pissed off Drew I could handle, but heartbroken Drew gutted me right in half. "I love you . . . more than you'll ever know. What I have with you, it's everything to me. *You're* everything to me. I'll come over and we'll talk this out. I miss you so damn much. I can't—"

"No, *I* can't. You need to take that offer and you need to go. Goodbye, Drew."

I hung up and threw the phone on the passenger seat, crying into my hands until I calmed down enough to start the car. I punched out a text to Lisa and headed back to the dorm, white-knuckling the steering wheel as I fought against the overwhelming urge to drive to Drew's apartment and take it all back.

Being the strong one was destroying me.

꙳ ꙳ ꙳

"OH MY GOD!" Lisa yelled as she rushed over to me. I felt like hell, and I supposed I looked like it. I cried the entire drive home. My eyes were irritated and sore, impairing my vision the last couple of miles. If I were honest with myself, I always expected Drew and me to end. It was as if I was working on telling him goodbye before we even said hello. What I didn't expect was the grief and sorrow over losing him to be this excruciating.

"Did that jerk do something?" She grabbed my shoulders and shook. I let out a real laugh for the first time in days.

"I can handle Aaron. He's harmless, especially now that the internship is almost over." I sniffled and moped to my bed. "Drew called me. I picked up without looking, thinking it was you checking up on me. I'm guessing that one of you told him I practiced at the restaurant tonight."

She pulled me to sit and gave me a slow nod. "Emma slipped. He freaked out that you were going to be alone with Aaron and was angry as to why you couldn't be in the same room with him." She swallowed and cringed. "Then, he broke a lead pencil with one hand."

My head fell into my hands with a groan. "This is so awful."

"I know it," Lisa agreed. "He's in bad shape, Sara. And so are you. This is dumb. Why can't you talk this out?"

I shrugged, at a loss as to how to answer. "He basically said he was making a sacrifice to be with me and Victoria and didn't mind settling for something else. If he thinks that now, what about years down the road?"

"Maybe he put his foot in his mouth a little, but isn't love about sacrifice? All you had to do to take care of Victoria. Do you regret any of that?"

My head jerked up. "No, of course not. I wished things were

different sometimes, or easier, but I never regret having her. She's my biggest joy." I smiled despite my misery. She took to Drew so well and so fast, I dreaded breaking this to her. We'd been texting back and forth over the last few days. I was out of excuses why we couldn't FaceTime, but I wasn't ready to face her yet.

"Exactly! You love her, so you did what you had to do. Did you ever stop to think maybe that's what Drew meant?"

"Maybe." I cupped my forehead and rubbed at my temples. "But it's too late now. I can't go back."

"Babe, take it from me. He's miserable without you. You don't break pencils over just anyone. I doubt it's too late."

A laugh escaped me before I pulled my phone out of my purse. I had twelve missed calls and ten voice mails. My heart fell into my stomach when I read my sister's number, not Drew's, on the screen.

I hadn't heard from Denise since Christmas. My mother refusing to speak to me wasn't her fault and I appreciated her trying. She was too young to realize what a lost cause it was. I still wanted to see her, but I was done with any hope I may've had to make amends with my parents.

As I tried to figure out why she was in such an urgent rush to speak to me, the phone buzzed in my hand. A bad feeling washed over me as I hit accept.

"Denise?"

"Sara, thank God. I've been trying to get through for the past half hour." Her voice was shrill, filled with panic. My chest pinched, bracing for whatever bad news she had to tell me.

"I'm here, what's wrong?" My throat tightened as my hands shook. Was she in trouble? How was I supposed to help her from so far away? Even after all these years, she was still my baby sister and I wouldn't leave her like my parents deserted me.

"Mom and Dad . . ." She sobbed into the receiver, the rest of her words were muffled with tears.

"Denise, you need to stop trying. They don't want to speak to me—"

"They were in a car accident, Sara. Mom and Dad are gone."

Thirty-Four

DREW

THE MEMORY OF Sara tortured me everywhere I turned, but in the kitchen lab it hurt most of all. I waited outside for the students to filter out. This was exam week, and I knew Sara would be in there. The thought of her behind that door make my skin prickle with sweat. I loved watching her cook. The peace and joy on her face when she was in a zone enraptured me and made me fall for her all over again every damn time. I rubbed at the ache in my pathetic chest. If she came over to me and said let's forget everything and be together, I would have gathered her in my arms without hesitation. That wouldn't happen, but a guy could dream. I'd give her some space for the moment, but I couldn't stop fighting for her, or loving her. I didn't know how.

I waited until the very last minute to make my way into the room and start my shift, bracing myself for the awkward confrontation when Sara and I were face-to-face. I'd been inside her more times than I could count, yet I didn't even know if I should say hello. How fucked up was that? I searched the room upon entering but there were no more students—and no Sara. That made no sense. She'd never miss a test, no matter what sick or battered condition she was in. Yes, she was avoiding me, but not at the expense of her degree. Something was wrong.

"Drew," Lisa called as she burst into the lab. "Listen, I need to speak to you. It's about Sara."

"What happened?" I rushed over, imagining the worst. The worst took on all different forms in my brain, and it seemed to take forever for Lisa to spit it out.

"She had to leave this morning to go back to the city. I made her take the train because she was in no shape to drive all that way."

"Is it Victoria?" My blood ran cold thinking of that little girl sick or hurt or . . . worse.

"No, no she's fine. Sara's sister called her last night. Her parents were killed in a car accident. Sara is headed back to help with their funeral."

The air drained from my lungs as I fell back on the edge of the desk, stunned and worried as hell. "You're serious? After all they put her through she has to go back and—"

"Yes." Her eyes were pained as she dropped a hand on my arm. "She's only told me bits and pieces, but I know how awful they were. She's going back to help her sister, but this is going to be horrible. This is not my place or my business, but she needs you. She'd never ask you because she's stubborn as shit."

"No kidding," I scoffed, massaging my temples. "She's not thinking of herself or what this will do to her. Do you know her mother hung up on her on Christmas Eve? Wouldn't even say Merry Christmas. Who does that to their own kid?" Sara was so broken that night. At the time I was almost grateful since that was the moment she let down the last wall she built around herself and let me in, but I loathed seeing her that devastated.

"You know," I huffed and lifted my eyes to the ceiling, trying to figure out what the hell to do. "She acts so tough. Never needs any help, can go it alone, but . . ." I trailed off, sick to my stomach at the thought of her on a train by herself, mourning parents who weren't worth a second of her time.

"She can't." Lisa laughed and shook her head. "Not this time. She's used to being the caretaker with no support. The only family she has is her daughter. When I first met her, she was almost surprised I wanted to be her friend. As if she couldn't understand why anyone would waste their time on her." She frowned and let out an audible sigh. "Broke my heart a little for her."

"Mine too," I agreed, staring off into space as I searched for an answer I didn't have. "She thinks of herself as a burden, so me and my stupid choice of words the other day nailed that point across to her," I snickered. "She doesn't want to see me."

"Do you still love her?"

My head snapped in her direction. "Of course, I do. I miss her so much I can't even function."

She reached into her purse and handed me a piece of paper. "Then fight for her. Show her she's worth it. This is the name of the funeral home and information about the services. I asked her to text me when she found out, so I could send something." She offered a sad shrug. "She was too out of it to tell I was lying." She closed my fingers around the paper and squeezed. "She shouldn't go through this alone. I would go but I'm not who she wants. You're the only one that can get her through this. Think about it."

I didn't turn to Lisa's footfalls as she sauntered out of the lab. I plopped into the chair behind the desk, my breaths quick and heavy as if something barreled over me. I unfolded the paper and looked it over. The funeral was the day after tomorrow. It was enough time for me to find someone to cover the lab, dig out the only black suit I owned, and head down to Queens. The fight we had and the time apart didn't matter. She had me whether she liked it or not. I wasn't budging or going anywhere. My only issue was how to not do ninety down the highway to get to her.

I pulled out my phone and shot a text to my boss telling him I had to have someone cover my shift or close the lab.

My place was with Sara. *Always* with Sara. I'd finally make her see she was worth it. She could try to push me away as much as she wanted, but I wasn't going anywhere—ever.

Thirty-Five

SARA

IT'S AMAZING HOW, despite all the years that pass, some things remain exactly the same.

My feet seemed to go on autopilot when I stepped off the train at Penn Station and transferred to the subway. I was thankful Lisa wouldn't let me drive as I didn't remember most of the four-hour ride from school. My mind replayed years of memories, the loss and hurt accompanying them, stinging so badly it crippled me. Why was I mourning parents I hadn't seen in almost a decade—parents who made it clear they never wanted anything to do with me or my daughter? Every year I'd send them Victoria's Christmas picture in the ridiculous hope they'd call and ask to see her—see *us*. That call never came, and now that they were gone, it never would.

Trudging up my old block, I was transported back ten years to the last time I was here—the last time I'd ever see my parents alive. My father remained stoic as my mother lashed out at me as she always had, but with a grim finality in her tone. I left their house all alone in this world other than the tiny pea growing inside my belly. Even with all the anger I'd felt, I never stopped wishing for their forgiveness. I grieved their death and the hope

I never could let go.

When I arrived at my old house, spying the same silver 1776 adorning the top of the door, my heart hammered against my rib cage. I climbed the outside steps with shaky legs and pressed the doorbell with a quivering finger. My demons would always reside here, regardless of what world my parents were in.

The swift clicking of the locks accelerated what must have been an acute panic attack. I grabbed onto the wrought iron rail framing the porch as I tried to slow my quick and shallow breaths. I wished I prayed. Who I was praying to or what I was praying for escaped me, the only thought echoing through my troubled brain was "please help me."

When my eyes popped open, I was tackled with a hug. I fell back onto the railing I clutched for support and dropped my bag. A tall and slim mess of black curly hair cried and whimpered into my shoulder, and all I could do was lean my head against hers and weep along with her.

"Hey, DeDe," I whispered in her ear, making her sob harder. "I'm here."

I grabbed her shoulders and pushed her back, studying the little girl I was forced to leave ten years ago. Did we always look this much alike? She could be my twin other than all the dark waves surrounding her face, as my hair was always pin straight. Even as a child, she was the emotional and sensitive one. She needed my comfort after countless sad books or movies or even commercials. My mother would regard her with an annoyed grunt or mutter a "suck it up," but I always loved that about my sister. This house and everything that went on here turned me into an emotional iceberg at a young age. Denise still had passion and fire and wasn't afraid to show it.

Fire and ice.

I missed Drew so much, I ached. But I couldn't call him when I was upset anymore, could I? Even though he was the only one in this world who could make it better. I blinked away the second wave of grief and focused on Denise.

"You got tall, baby sister." I cupped her cheek. "And so pretty." The bashful glint in her eyes reminded me of Victoria. Everyone who came in contact with my daughter found her easy to love, and she inherited that from her aunt. I sucked in my bottom lip and straightened, ignoring the impulse to fall at her feet and beg her forgiveness for not finding a way to see her all these years. We had a ton to catch up on, and I had loads to make up for.

"I missed you so much," she sniffled. "I'm so sorry." Her voice cracked as she squeezed my hands. "I'm so sorry you couldn't come back before this."

"I'm sorry I didn't find a way to see you. I should have answered your call on Christmas Day. I've been a terrible big sister, but I intend to make up for it starting now."

Her gaze dropped to the floor. "You had a baby by yourself. And Mom and Dad were so awful about it. I just wish—"

"I wish, too." I cut her off. "I wish for a lot of things, but that won't help us right now. Right now, we need to get through the next couple of days. We can hash all that out later." My tears slowed as the caretaker in me came to the surface. It was always easier to focus on taking care of others and ignoring my own needs. I guessed it was a coping mechanism, but I embraced it for the moment. I'd worry about the lasting effects of burying parents who disowned me later.

"Come in," she whispered as the same brown eyes as mine pleaded with me. I didn't realize I froze for a beat, tension seizing my body before I crossed the threshold.

"Right behind you," I croaked as she yanked me inside by the hand. The sour scent of lemon furniture polish assaulted my senses as soon as I stepped through the door, the familiarity thickening my throat.

I studied the living room with an odd anxiety bubbling in my gut. My mother was dead, yet I was expecting her to run out of the kitchen and scream at me for being here. There was nothing like the sinking feeling of being a trespasser in the home you grew up in.

"You'll stay here, right?" Denise's voice was small. "Your bedroom is still empty. Please, Sara? I can't be here alone for another night."

I'd booked a hotel for tonight, unsure if I could sleep in this house, much less my old bed.

"Yeah, DeDe." I pulled her into an embrace, her weary head falling onto my shoulder in relief. "Of course, I'll stay."

⸙ ⸙ ⸙

I TRUDGED UP the stairs, bracing myself for the memories that would flood me at the top. The ugly brown rug still covered each step and the entire second floor. Bracing myself, I tiptoed to the door, still somehow afraid my mother would come out of the woodwork and throw me out. My old room was the same. Same sheets I remembered, same curtains, my personal effects gone long before my parents cut me off. I plopped on the bed and let out an audible sigh. This wasn't my room for many years, but I remembered every second I spent in here, itching to be old enough to go out on my own. But I was never really on my own.

I remained tentative and careful—other than the night I took a stranger home and conceived my daughter. Did I ever really feel free of this place?

The answer came to me in a quiet yes. When I found someone to love me for who I was, but I pushed him away.

"Hey," Denise called from the doorway. "You don't have to sleep in here. My bed is big enough for both of us. You must be tired. What do you say we order Chinese and head to bed?" She wrapped her arms around her torso, her nose scrunched up exactly as when she was a little girl—the little girl I loved and never meant to desert like I had.

"Sounds good." I rose from the edge of the bed and dropped a hand on her shoulder. "I'm not leaving, DeDe."

"No," she sighed. "But you will. And that's okay. I'm glad you're here now."

I squeezed her hand and swung it back and forth like when she was little, and we'd walk together. "I'm glad too."

¥ ¥ ¥

"I FOUND OUT something today," Denise said as she fixed her eyes on the ceiling. She still had the glow-in-the-dark stars along the rims of her ceiling fan blades. I remembered standing on her bed and almost falling off numerous times, trying to get it just right. They still worked and illuminated the entire room.

"What's that?" I mumbled as I fought against my heavy eyelids.

"Mom and Dad got married a year later than they said they did. I noticed when I was searching through their papers for an insurance policy."

My head jerked to hers. "A year later? When was their real

wedding date?"

Her chest shook with a laugh before she turned to me. "Two months before you were born."

My mouth fell open in the darkness. That was one hell of a missing puzzle piece.

"She was only twenty. That's probably the reason Dad was always so checked out and Mom was always so bitter. They had to get married." Mom saw me as her missed opportunity, her burden. That stuck with me for my entire life.

"Well, no one *has to*, Sara. Everyone has a choice. Although, I think her parents were super strict and made her feel like she had to. That's probably why we only knew Dad's parents. I miss them."

"Me too." Our grandparents' home was our sanctuary until they passed away, and the only memory of love I had as a child. Maybe my mother's parents did the same thing to her when they found out she was pregnant. My very existence was a large thorn in my mother's side, and I was beginning to understand why.

"But again, who really knows? It's not like they were ever straight with us. I guess I was a big oops after the fact."

"Stop," I scolded as I nudged her with my elbow. The bed was big enough for both of us but didn't have a whole lot of extra room. "And whatever you were to them, you were *my* gift." Her head fell on my shoulder.

When they brought her home from the hospital, swaddled in pink and already with a tuft of black hair piled on her head, she brought joy to an otherwise sullen house. Mom didn't smother either of us with love, but she spared Denise of the malice she always directed toward me. I guessed my sister wasn't a breathing reminder of the detour her life had to take. I had the same reminder, but she was my blessing—not my downfall. I pitied my mother in that moment for never enjoying her daughters like I enjoyed mine.

"Tell me more about school." Denise yawned as she cuddled closer to my side, assuming the same position she always had during a thunderstorm. "Any boyfriends?"

"Nope. Not anymore. It's . . . all still new. I don't want to talk about it right now, DeDe. Let's focus on one tragedy at a time." I patted her arm.

"Me neither. My friends think I should go into therapy. I always pick the assholes I know will break my heart. It's like my own insurance from getting too invested."

"You're twenty. Dating assholes is a rite of passage. I dated my fair share."

"Like Victoria's dad?" She turned on her side and propped her elbow on the pillow.

"No, he actually turned out to be a nice guy. I didn't know him long enough the first time we met for him to be an asshole."

We shared a laugh. "Toniann even made an appointment with her therapist for me next week."

"Toniann is still around?" She was always a cute kid, even if she was Queens' answer to *Full House's* Kimmie Gibbler.

"Yeah, she's still herself," she snickered. "But she was always someone I could talk to. When you left . . ." She trailed off. "I was pretty lonely. I think I'm going to go. Just the once, at least."

"Good. Now go to sleep, sis. It's going to be a long day tomorrow."

She fell back on the pillow and nodded. "Okay. Goodnight, Sara."

"Goodnight, kiddo."

"I love you," she breathed. My eyes drifted to my sister, out cold already.

I smiled into the glowing stars on the ceiling, an odd peace drifting in with my turbulent thoughts for tomorrow.

"I love you, too, baby sister."

Thirty-Six

"AT LEAST THE funeral home is in walking distance, right?"
Denise offered a nervous laugh as we turned the corner.

The funeral plans were clear for every step, odd for a couple
in their fifties. In her search for some sort of insurance policy,
Denise stumbled upon a large envelope with all the paperwork
we'd need for the funeral and reading of assets afterward, complete with all necessary contact information. Everything was paid
for and planned; she only needed to call the numbers listed. By
the time I arrived, everything was already set.

The painstaking detail in their final wishes brought a whole
new level of sadness to the day. They must've known their daughters—or anyone for that matter—wouldn't know them well
enough to have any idea what their wishes would be. There
would be no church service, only a priest saying a few prayers
at the funeral home before a car drove us to the cemetery. We
locked eyes and sucked in a long breath before strolling inside.

Two closed caskets lay at the front of the long room with
two floral arrangements on either side. I ambled over to read the
cards. One was from my mother's sister who only lived in New
Jersey and didn't come in person to pay her respects, and a couple

were from my father's job. I contemplated sending flowers, but why? Why would you send a gift to someone in death who would probably throw it back in your face if they were alive?

My eyes drifted around the room, avoiding my parents on purpose. When they landed on the wooden boxes, my gaze clouded. Part of me wanted to pound my fists on the wood, demanding an answer for shunning me for so many years. The other part wanted to collapse in tears and beg them for forgiveness for not being the daughter they wanted. I cupped my throat, rubbing away the growing lump that was almost asphyxiating me.

Other than a half a row of mourners in the middle of the room, it was empty. A morbid thought of my own funeral entered my mind. Would it be as empty as this? Victoria would have a ton of people there for her I was sure, her father and Brianna and all the friends I knew she'd cultivate over the years. No matter what I did in this world, I was leaving behind something precious in her. A tear snaked down my cheek for my parents and the life and love they squandered.

"Sara, remember Toniann?" The little blonde pixie's eyes filled with tears as she embraced me in a hug. I was relieved someone other than me was here to give her support, especially today.

"Where's the priest?" I asked my sister as I impatiently searched the back of the room. It was a long day already and I wished he'd arrive soon to get the show on the road.

I found him as he closed the door behind one last mourner. When the man in the dark suit lifted his head, all the air expelled from my lungs in a whoosh.

"Drew?" I croaked as my eyes slow blinked at the sight before me. He buttoned his suit jacket before making a quick stroll over to me. He had to be an illusion, some kind of mirage my troubled mind conjured to get me through this awful day. How did he know, and how did he get here?

"Lisa." The corner of his mouth lifted in a half smile as he came closer. "She found me at the lab and told me. I left campus yesterday afternoon."

My quivering jaw dropped. "You drove all the way here? Why?"

He gave me a slow nod and shrugged. "Why wouldn't I? I love you. I won't let you go through this alone." He lifted an eyebrow as he closed the distance between us. We were almost chest to heaving chest.

"But . . ." My mouth parched as I forgot what I was about to say. I took in a sharp breath through my nostrils and did the best I could to stand straight.

He inched a fraction of a centimeter closer, still not touching me, but holding my watery gaze with a dark, burning glare. Time stopped along with my heartbeat. Drew shook his head, as if he was reading my thoughts, and opened his arms. I once again collapsed onto his chest in choking sobs.

"I love you. I'll keep saying it until it sinks in," he rasped into my hair. "The rest, we'll talk about later."

I burrowed my head deep in his chest, breathing him in and praying this wasn't a dream. He always seemed too good to be true.

"I'm Denise." My sister rushed to Drew with an extended hand, giving me a quick side-glance. I nodded, answering her silent question that this was the ex-boyfriend I didn't want to talk about.

"Drew." He took her hand and gave it a shake with his other arm still wrapped around my waist. We still had a lot to talk about, but having him here and so close to me felt too good to question for the moment. Maybe I didn't have to question it at all. The past couple of days were a painful reminder of how my family gave me shelter, but not a home. My home was Drew.

A hint of a smile danced across his mouth before he took my hand and laced our fingers together. Tears flooded my eyes as I squeezed back. I rested my head on his shoulder, letting my eyes shut as an odd peace wafted over me through the sadness. Even after everything, Drew was my someone. My person. He gave me something I never had before—unconditional love through the worst of circumstances.

I let my hand drift down the lapel of Drew's jacket. "You clean up really well, Kostas." He caught my hand and brought it to his lips.

"Always so gorgeous," he whispered. His hand slid to the nape of my neck as his eyes searched mine.

A sad chuckle fell from my lips. My eyes were heavy, and I was sure circled with dark puffy bags.

"You're delirious, Drew."

He drew me into his side and rested his chin on the top of my head.

"Maybe. But I'm not going anywhere." He pressed a kiss to my temple. "Whether you like it or not."

Thirty-Seven

SARA

THE PRAYERS WERE short and sweet as the priest didn't know my parents personally. I wished them the peace in death they couldn't find in life. They disowned me years ago, so my grief wasn't about missing them. I mourned for what *should* have been. As I waited for my sister in the living room this morning, my eyes searched the room as I imagined all the moments we *should* have had: Victoria crawling over the carpet as a baby; her grandparents reveling in each milestone; congratulating me with pride in their eyes when I found a way to go back to school; the moment with my mother when I told her about falling in love for the first time with Drew. When we left my parents at the cemetery, the finality of what I never had sunk in, and I was sadder for them and their wasted years than I was for me.

The car dropped us back off at the funeral home and Drew drove us to the lawyer's office—the air in the car thick with uncomfortable silence. I wished the lawyer hadn't insisted on reading the will an hour after the funeral, but it was probably best to get it all over with. I worried about my sister. Yes, she was an adult, but a young one. The thought of her living in that house all alone didn't sit right with me at all.

"Sara, Denise, come in." A stocky man in a tight suit motioned to us to come into his office when we arrived. For a reason I couldn't explain, my stomach twisted. The cemetery was our final goodbye, but this would be the permanent confirmation of how they felt about me—or how *little* they felt about me. I expected absolutely nothing and only came along to support my sister. My chest tightened again at all these big decisions about to fall into her lap before she was ready.

"I'll wait out here," Drew whispered.

"No, you're coming in with me." I rose from the chair and pulled him up by the hand. I didn't want to experience the final "eff you" from my parents alone. We ambled into the office and sat down on the leather couch across from his desk.

"I'm sorry for your loss." He looked between Denise and me as he unfolded the papers in his hand. "Your parents were very specific in their wishes, so this shouldn't take very long."

"I bet they were," I huffed to Drew. He draped his arm around my shoulders and rubbed my back.

"The house and any savings are in a trust for Denise Marie Caldwell until her twenty-first birthday. She can sell the house at that time but not before. A trust of $50,000 was left to a Victoria Elizabeth Caldwell."

"Wait." I grabbed the edge of the desk, positive I heard that completely wrong. "They left a trust in my daughter's name? Why?" I stammered as my body went rigid with shock.

He pushed the rim of his glasses up as he nodded. "Yes, and there is also an annuity in her name as well. Your parents knew how to invest, and your father had a great pension. Looks like you have a little help with college tuition." He leaned over to hand me an envelope. "All the information is there."

All these years, they never bothered with either of us or even opened up a Christmas card to see her picture. Is it possible they regretted cutting us out of their lives? I couldn't describe how I was feeling. It was a cross between getting punched in the stomach and holding a winning lottery ticket.

"When did they set this up?" I whispered as I grabbed the envelope with a shaking hand. "This has to be a mistake."

"They added this in January. I assure you these were their final wishes."

This was a dream, right? A month after my mother hung up on me—on Christmas Eve—my parents set up a trust for my daughter. As much as my head ached from trying, I couldn't connect the dots.

I draped my hand over my mouth in an attempt to control the myriad of emotions rushing through me. Help in paying for Victoria's college tuition and whatever else she would need as she grew was a dream come true, but my bigger dream was having them be a part of her life. I'd never understood what was in my parents' heads or hearts and never would.

I guessed some mysteries were never meant to be solved.

"LONGEST DAY EVER, right?" A nervous laugh shook my sister's shoulders as we shared a pizza at my parents' kitchen table. Most of the afternoon was spent in stilted and awkward conversation after we arrived back from the lawyer's office. Denise's eyes darted between Drew and me, a thousand questions dangling between us—questions I had no clue how to answer. I loved him for what he did, for rushing all this way to be with me when I needed him the most, but nothing had changed. He was still a young man with the world at his fingertips, and I refused to be the woman who got in the way.

"Are you staying, Drew? I can get you some pillows and blankets for the couch. It's actually pretty comfortable."

"That would be great. I thought I could stay with my aunt, but I forgot they're all away. I could use some sleep before the drive back up. Thanks, Denise," he answered as his eyes caught mine.

"I'm looking at an apartment tomorrow," I said to my sister while ignoring the heat of Drew's stare. Not the best thing to bring up in front of him, but in my desperation to divert attention from the discomfiture in the room, it was all I had. "And I'm seeing Victoria tomorrow. Would you like to come?"

She gasped and fell back into the seat. "I . . . you'll let me meet her?" She nodded with a quivering chin.

"I always wanted you to meet her." I dropped my eyes to the table. "All of you," I whispered to myself.

"Do you think she'll, you know, be weirded out by an aunt she doesn't know?" My sister's pleading eyes begged me to say no.

"She wasn't weirded out by a father she didn't know," I chuckled. "You'll be fine." I dropped a hand to her forearm and squeezed.

"She's pretty lovable," Drew added. "In fact, she's impossible *not* to love. Knows her comics, too." He regarded us with a sad smile before rising from the table and tossing his paper plate into the trash. "Bathroom is upstairs?"

My throat was too thick to utter a reply. I motioned toward the stairs with my chin.

"What's going on with you guys?" Denise's whisper tore me out of my thoughts.

"It's complicated, DeDe." I stood to clean off the table.

"Doesn't look so complicated. I've known him less than a day, and it's obvious he adores you. Hasn't today taught you anything about waste?" She clucked her tongue before storming out of the kitchen.

That talk needed to happen tonight, but I didn't know how I could let him go a second time.

Thirty-Eight

SARA

I TIPTOED INTO the living room after I lingered upstairs, taking much longer than usual to get ready for bed and face Drew. I rested against the banister and watched him fuss with the pillows and sheets my sister gave him, and as I did when we first met, ogled him from afar. His tie was undone under the collar of his shirt. My eyes drifted over his torso and the crisp, white fabric stretching across the lean muscles of his back I'd memorized with my hands and my lips. I rubbed at the ache in my chest as I shook my head. I'd always be his, but he couldn't be mine anymore. It wasn't fair.

"Are you going to come talk to me or keep staring at my ass?" His head swiveled to where I was frozen in place. "You have many talents, but being stealthy isn't one of them."

I fought the twitch at the corners of my mouth before I ambled into the living room and sat on the far end of the couch.

"Thank you for . . . everything. I don't know what I would have done if you weren't here today."

"Why didn't you call me when it happened?" He sat on the edge of the couch and rested his elbows on his knees.

"I wanted to, believe me. But I couldn't . . . it wouldn't be fair."

He took in a long breath and exhaled on a groan.

"You have a screwed-up vision of what's fair and what's right. You wanted me there, I wanted to be here for you, but you went alone because you thought that was the fair and right thing to do. You make no sense lately, Caldwell."

"It doesn't matter how I feel; you can't throw a huge opportunity away because of me—"

"What does this say?" Drew whispered as he pressed his fingers into my chest, right over my heart. It sped up at his touch and hammered against my rib cage. I lifted my head and our eyes locked, the heat and love in his eyes pinning me to the couch cushion. "Your heart, what does it say right now?'

"I love you." I sank my teeth into my bottom lip to hold in the tears.

The side of his mouth quirked up. "I know that, Gorgeous. What else does it say?"

"I can't be the reason you don't take that—"

"Stop. That's your head running interference." He tapped my temple and shook his head. "Not interested in that. This . . ." The pads of his fingertips delved deeper into my skin. I prickled with goose bumps at their proximity to my breast. Combined with how much I missed him and all he'd done for me today, the sight of him was enough to make heat pool in my belly and drip lower. He had to stop touching me before I lost myself and gave in.

"Well," he rasped as he lifted an eyebrow. "Tell me what you want. Not what you think is right or what's best for me. What. You. Want."

"I don't want you to go," I blurted in one hysterical breath. "Not to Seattle or upstate. I want you here. With me. I want you to move in with us. I know it was only for a few days but when I was with you and Victoria, I was . . . happy. Purely fucking happy." I sniffled while Drew's expression didn't change. "And it's all too soon and you're young and having a kid around all the time isn't something you planned for right now. I want you to not end up hating me for tying you down so early. But if you want to know what I want or what my heart wants, it's you. But I can't have—"

"How do you know you can't or that's not what I want? Or that I wasn't just as happy when you and Victoria stayed with me? You remember what you overheard me say when Victoria asked me if I'd marry you? I said 'yes,' and I meant it. You're it for me, Sara. Maybe I'm twenty-five and you always dismiss whatever I'm feeling for you as temporary, but I can assure you it's not." He grabbed my hand and held it with both of his.

"You're not a sacrifice or a burden. I'm sorry it came out so wrong that night." He lifted our joined hands and pressed a kiss on the inside of my palm. "I'd never see you or Victoria like that. You're the love of my whole damn life and I'd be miserable away from you—like I've been the past few days. Maybe now, I could get that through your thick skull."

"Drew—" He pressed his thumb over my lips and shook his head.

"You didn't get the love you deserved in this house. But from me, you have it. Always. You have it without asking because it's yours. I want what you want. All of it. So this time we wasted being apart is all pretty ridiculous, isn't it?"

A sob bubbled out followed by another and before I knew it I was bawling. Drew inched closer and slid me onto his lap.

"Believe it or not, I'm not a crier. Like, at all." I laughed as the tears cascaded down my cheeks. I'd always been well-versed in channeling tears into anger or general abrasiveness. I wiped my cheeks with the back of my hand. "Before you, I never felt loved before. And every time you would say something or do something that made me feel . . . everything about you is a beautiful gift, and the thought of the day I'd have to give it all back turns me into a blubbering idiot."

He swiped away my tears with his thumbs as he shook his head. "You never have to give me back, same as I'm sure as hell never giving you back."

"This is crazy," I croaked as I snaked my arms around his neck, resting my forehead against his. "You really want to move in with me? With us?"

"Ask me," he whispered, my tears slowing from the heat flooding my chest, and other places. I cupped his cheek, feathering my hand down the cropped bristles along his jaw.

"You shaved." My thumb glided across his chin, skating around the outline of those plump lips that tasted every bit as delicious as they looked. *Jesus, Sara. Focus.*

"I needed to look presentable. Plus, lately I haven't given a shit what I looked like, so the beard became scraggly anyway." He shifted underneath me, the steel of his erection pressing into my hip. "Want me to grow it back?"

"Yes," I hissed, embarrassing need dripping off the word.

Drew laughed and pulled me closer. "Maybe. Now ask me, Gorgeous." A shiver rippled down my spine as he cupped my neck.

"Do you want to move in with us?"

He tapped his chin as if he was mulling it over. "I probably need a job. It's a good thing I have an offer in the city already."

"You what?" The sexy moment was over as my jaw dropped. "Where? How?"

"A company about two blocks away from Blystone. Pretty

much the same salary as Ontech, too." His arm looped around my waist to pull me back. "I told you to trust me, didn't I? I had a plan, and it always included a life with you. The only regret I'd ever have would be losing you." He backed away and lifted my chin with the tap of his knuckle. "And that is not happening, Caldwell. Ever."

I grabbed his face, peppering kisses across his cheek before he covered my mouth with his. I exhaled against his lips—relief and happiness filtering through me.

"So, yes. I would love to move in with the both of you. It's not sudden. It's right. That's what we are, Sara. Nothing we do could be wrong if we're together. Numbers don't matter, not in time or age. What we have is timeless."

I crushed my lips to his, fisting the edges of his tie before I yanked it off and threw it behind me. My fingers dove for the buttons of his shirt as our kiss became hungry and sloppy. All the sadness and all the longing came rushing to the surface as we grabbed at each other's clothes.

"Upstairs," I murmured against his lips. I'd never even had a boy over for dinner, but I was about to have sex in my old bedroom. There was something disrespectful about that, but it wasn't enough to make me hesitate. My last memory here would be a happy one, without one bit of guilt.

I rushed up the stairs, pulling Drew behind me. The door wasn't all the way closed before his lips were back on mine.

"I missed you so fucking much." Drew grabbed the hem of my T-shirt and peeled it over my head, muttering a "fuck" when he found me braless underneath.

"You're trying to kill me," he growled against my mouth. Heat flared in his hooded eyes as he hooked his thumbs into the waistband of my pajama pants and inched them down my legs.

"My Sara," he breathed in between long, open-mouthed kisses along the inside of my thigh. My balance wavered as he ascended higher. My fingers dug into his shoulder as I tried not to fall over.

"I told you," he rasped as he lifted his head, offering a sexy curl of his lips as he hooked my leg over his shoulder. "I've got you."

A guttural whimper escaped me when he sucked my clit into his mouth. I was drenched, swollen, and two seconds from coming apart on his tongue. Drew always liked to tease me when his head was between my legs, but this time he dove right in, kissing me long and deep while digging his fingers into my ass. He wouldn't let me move as he devoured every inch of me.

I leaned into him, my legs shaking from the tremors pulsing down my spine and through my core. I'd never been afraid of an orgasm before, but I feared this one would tear me in half. It was the need radiating from Drew, the muffled grunts and groans he made—that alone made my head spin. I squeezed my eyes shut and braced myself as I tipped over the edge.

"So good," he whispered as he painted kisses across my stomach and ran his tongue along my hip. He rose from where he knelt on the floor and weaved his fingers into my hair, fisting a large chunk before he crushed my lips with his. He took my mouth with the same hunger as he ravaged my core: deep, determined, and knee-buckling. Drew was an intense lover by nature, but I'd never seen him this crazy with want.

My hands shook as I fiddled with the buttons on his shirt, everything below my waist still aching with a dull throb. My head fell into his chest, planting a wet kiss on every newly exposed inch of lean muscle.

"Take it off," I demanded as I dragged my lips over his

collarbone. His chest rumbled with a laugh as he peeled his shirt off his shoulders.

I leaned over and nipped down his torso. Drew groaned before he grabbed my head and yanked me up to stand.

"I'm ready to burst. I need inside you before I lose my damn mind."

He lifted me by the waist and brought me closer to the bed, his lips back on mine as he backed me against the mattress. Once the back of my knees hit the edge, I fell back and flipped us over, so I was on top. His fingers tangled in my hair, both of us battling to get as close as possible. I unbuckled his belt and pants and pushed them down his thighs until his rock-hard erection bobbed free. I wasted no time straddling his waist and scooting myself down until I settled over what we both wanted.

Drew let out a hiss as I sank down on him, willing myself to go slow and take in every glorious inch. We had all night to feast on each other, but right now I needed this, *we* needed this.

"I love you." Drew's gravelly voice stilted as he lifted his hips to get deeper inside. "Don't forget that again."

"I love you, too," I breathed, my own voice hoarse and straining. Drew sat up, grabbing my hips and sucking my nipple into his mouth. The new position rubbed against my still sensitive clit and the wet warmth of his mouth as his teeth bit down on the rigid peak tripped an even stronger orgasm than the first. My thighs quivered as I buried my head into his neck. A tortured whimper escaped me as I tried like hell not to scream. Drew stiffened as he came hard inside me. The thrusting and panting slowed as we fell into each other, my hair sticking to my sweaty forehead as the rest of my body went limp.

"I mean it," Drew whispered as he brushed the sticky strands away from my face. "I love you, and you're all I want. The rest is only details." He gave me a soft kiss and lay back on the bed, cuddling me into his side.

"You're the only boy I ever brought here, you know?" My hands drifted up and down his chest.

"Is that so?" He rested his chin on the top of my head.

I nodded without lifting my head. "This is the only time I've ever been in this room and not felt lonely. Or worthless."

"You shouldn't. You aren't alone anymore. And you were never worthless." He tapped my chin with his knuckle for me to look up. "You're worth *everything* to me."

I smiled before dropping my head back on his chest. I felt grateful, loved, and was ready to leave without looking back.

That was another first in this room.

Thirty-Nine

DREW

MY FINGERS GLIDED through Sara's hair as she slept on my chest. Without glancing at my watch, I guessed it was close to two in the morning. I was a blissful type of exhausted, the two rounds of epic make-up sex knocking the both of us out, but I still couldn't sleep. My eyes stayed open and glued to Sara. The lights from the outside streetlamp filtered through the blinds, illuminating a peace on her face I'd never seen before.

The relationship I had with my father was sketchy at best, but I never wondered if my parents loved me. I hated how alone Sara was for most of her life, but she had me now—and we were permanent. After months of dreading it, finishing my master's couldn't come fast enough. I was itching to take a look at that apartment and couldn't wait to see the look on Victoria's face when I told her I was moving with them, too. Sara would probably need some convincing from time to time that being with them wasn't a hardship, but I'd prove it to her every single day if I had to. It may have been unexpected, but it was all I wanted. *They* were all I wanted.

"Why are you still up?" Sara's groggy voice startled me.

I kissed the top of her head and shrugged. "I'm a little hungry."

"I'm sure." She turned her head and planted a kiss on my chest. "You were a busy boy."

To my surprise, my cock thickened under the sheets. I figured it was as tired as I was, but I wanted this woman all the damn time. Getting my fill of her wasn't possible.

"Well, that." I tightened my embrace around her. "And I haven't really eaten much over the past few days." I picked up her hand and laced our fingers together.

"Me neither," she said on a yawn. "There's still pizza downstairs, I think. And I couldn't sleep last night so I made brownies."

"From scratch?" My head perked up. Falling in love with a chef sure as hell didn't suck.

"No, I found a mix, but I gave it my own spin." She rested her chin on my shoulder and gave me a wink. "If you get one, grab one for me." She pecked my lips and settled back on the pillow. "They should be wrapped in foil on the kitchen counter."

"I'm so damn in love with you." I kissed her lips and jumped out of bed.

"Hey, Drew." I swiveled my head after I grabbed my shirt off the floor and slipped it on.

Her dark hair spilled over the pillow as she leaned into the crook of her arm, hiding a smirk. When her weary eyes met mine, her swollen lips—swollen from my kisses—pulled into a smile. She'd never stop taking my breath away.

"I love you, baby." Sara rolled over and stretched her arms over her head, a contented smile lifting her cheeks.

I laughed, my own smile wide as I made my way back to the bed, leaning over to paint kisses across her cheek and down the sensitive slope of her neck.

"I love it when you call me baby," I whispered before nipping at her shoulder. This was the Sara I fell in love with, the one I always knew was there but never had a chance to come out. All she needed was love.

The house was pitch black as I headed down the carpeted staircase, with only a couple of nightlights in the living room and by the kitchen. I found the light switch on the wall and spotted the tray of brownies.

"Hey, Drew," Denise greeted me from the kitchen table, causing me to jump out of my skin and almost drop the tray.

"Holy shit, you scared the hell out of me." I laughed until I noted the crestfallen expression on her face. She was a younger, sadder version of Sara. Whereas Sara put up a hardened wall to the people she met, Denise showed a softer, vulnerable side.

She dropped her gaze to the table and with a wistful smile, said, "I don't usually hang out in the dark. This house is . . . It's a little weird being here, I guess. Funny since I technically own it now, right?" She picked up a ceramic mug off the table and huffed around the rim before taking a sip.

I slid into a chair across from her, recognizing the vacant stare I'd seen so many times from Sara. I was raised to not speak ill of the dead, but after witnessing the number they'd done on their daughters, I had a hard time giving their parents even the least bit of respect.

"Maybe you can rent it until you're ready to sell. I have a cousin who's a real estate agent who could help you. You can get your own apartment with whatever rent you get."

She nodded, still fixed on whatever was inside the cup. "I could. I'm not brave like Sara. Or smart. I remember all the jobs she worked when she was in high school. She saved every cent she made so she could move out and be on her own." She shrugged as she set the mug in front of her. "My mother always called me a baby but never showed me how to be an adult. I guess I'll figure it out, right?"

"Your sister isn't Superwoman, even though she tries not to show it. Your parents had the same effect on her, too. I'd bet she was just as scared when she went out on her own. Everyone is."

"I'll manage," she sighed before she gave me a half smile. "So, I guess you guys are okay now? I mean, I'm assuming since you slept upstairs and there was some . . . noise coming from her old room."

My nose crinkled as my face twisted into a grimace. "Sorry about that."

"Don't be sorry." She waved me off. "I'm so glad she has you. You have no idea. I'll never forget the day my parents threw her out. Or my mother did, and my father just watched. I've thought about her and her baby so many times. They forbade me to speak to her, but I should've called her. I wish I'd seen Victoria when she was a baby." Her voice cracked as her face crumpled into tears. "How doesn't she hate me?"

I shook my head. "She absolutely doesn't hate you. You were a kid. She's worried about you here all alone. We're looking at apartments tomorrow. Maybe we can find one with an extra bedroom for you. I think you guys have a lot of time to make up for."

Her eyes widened. "An apartment together. Wow, that's great. Don't make arrangements for me. Sara should live her own life now." She leaned back in the chair, giving me a once-over under her crinkled brow. "You love her a lot, don't you?"

I gave her a slow nod. "More than I ever knew it was possible to love anyone. I love Victoria, too. She's going to be crazy about you."

"I'm already crazy about her." She zoned out over my shoulder. "Every year I'd rush to the mailbox to look for her picture, praying Sara would keep sending them. She always did, and I shoved Victoria's picture in my parents' faces. Last year was the first time they looked for more than a minute. I'm glad they did right by her with that trust." Her finger traced the rim of her mug before she lifted her head. "Take care of them, okay?" Denise pleaded with glassy eyes. "My sister deserves the whole happily ever after."

"You have my word. That is one thing you never have to worry about."

"Thanks, Drew. It helps more than you know." She stood from the table and trudged out of the kitchen.

"Denise," I called before she made her way up the stairs. "You're welcome to come live with us. Think about it."

She swiveled her head, a smirk playing on her lips. "You're a good guy, Drew." She continued up the stairs without looking back.

Forty

SARA

"THAT WAS A nice place; you guys think you'll get it?" Denise's voice had a nervous shrill as she wrung her hands in her lap. She was equal parts excited and terrified to meet her niece, and as soon as Drew found a parking space by Josh and Brianna's apartment, her chest began to heave, and her words fell out of her mouth at a rapid rate.

"I think so. One of the apartments anyway." I craned my head and gave my sister the most reassuring smile I could pull off. It always worked when she was little, and I prayed I hadn't lost my touch. "Hey, she's going to love you; no need to be nervous at all." I reached back to give her knee a squeeze. "She'd love it if you'd live with us, too."

Both Drew and I kept extending the invitation to live with us, but for the moment she wouldn't budge.

Her eyes rolled as she shook her head. "I'm fine, Sara. I'll come visit but I don't need a room in your new apartment." Drew shot me a side-glance before we stepped out of the car. The apartments we viewed today had plenty of room for more than the three of us and part of me yearned for the chance to make up for lost time with my sister. I'd have to settle for visits, but I was overjoyed to have her back in my life in any capacity.

Our parents had just died, but after the initial shock faded, all I'd felt was relief. Always sadness for what we should have had and what could have been, but mostly closure.

"I told Victoria I had a surprise for her so she's probably chomping at the bit until we get inside." I nodded in the direction of their front door, attempting to urge my sister to move from Drew's back seat. I ignored my own tension to ease hers.

When we left the landlord's office, I should have been elated. This was my goal, what I worked so hard for over the past year. We'd have a great apartment and a lifestyle much more comfortable than the one I was barely holding onto. But, after being with her father for so long . . . maybe she didn't want to leave. Josh did a stellar job stepping into the role of full-time parent, and the old Sara would have resented the shit out of him for it. This one only wanted happiness for everyone involved. If Victoria wanted to stay with her father, I'd be devastated but would deal.

"What's wrong?" Drew whispered in my ear as we ambled up the block.

"What? Nothing."

He pulled back and squinted at me. "If you bite your lip any harder, you're going to draw blood." He snaked his arm around my waist and pulled me close as Denise trudged in front of us. "It's not the good kind of biting your lip, either. So, spill." He pinched my side and made me jump.

"Victoria may not want to leave." His shoulders dropped in irritation when he caught my gaze.

"Are you serious right now? The same little girl Josh had to pile into his car in almost tears when she left my apartment and left you? You're her mother. She's always going to want to be with you."

"Maybe, but they made a nice home for her here. Is it selfish of me to pull her out of it?" My eyes drifted to their apartment windows and the Wonder Woman window clings decorating the panes in Victoria's room. "I took her away from her father before, and all it did was hurt her."

"You didn't know him before; you thought that was the only choice to make. He's a reasonable guy, you're more or less reasonable now." I punched his arm when he let out a snicker. "You both can make it work so that she's not *pulled* from either of you."

"Right." I reached for my sister's hand before I rang the doorbell. "Neither of us get to chicken out." The corners of my lips lifted into a smile at the scampering of feet followed by the locks clicking.

"Mommy!" Victoria leaped into my arms and clutched my waist. She was so tall now that her head grazed my chest.

"Surprise," I whispered in her ear.

"Drew's here, too!" She gasped when she caught sight of him next to me.

"Hey, pretty girl." He kissed her forehead and stepped aside, revealing where Denise hid behind him.

"Who are you?" My daughter's brow furrowed as she brought her eyes back to mine.

"This is your Aunt Denise. My sister."

"You have a sister?" Her nose crinkled at me. "Since when?"

I laughed. "It's a story for another day, but she's dying to meet you."

Denise's eyes welled as she leaned over to be eye to eye with her niece. "Hi, Victoria. You're even prettier than your pictures."

"You're like, my *real* aunt?"

She laughed and gave her a slow nod. "Yes, I am. And you have no idea how happy I am to finally meet you."

"Cool! Want to see my room?" Drew and I shot Denise our best "I told you so" glare before Victoria dragged her away by the hand.

"Hi, Sara." Josh ushered all of us in before he shut the door behind us. "This had to be an awful couple of days for you. I'm so sorry."

I shrugged, still unsure of how to respond when someone offered their condolences. I thanked him for the gesture, but my parents were gone to me a long time ago. I mourned, but I wasn't bereaved.

"Josh." Drew extended his hand and Josh took it like they were old friends, a huge comparison to how he looked him up and down on Christmas.

"Hi, Sara, Drew." Brianna came behind him and offered me a warm smile.

"I actually have things to discuss with you. Can we go into the living room?"

Josh nodded and followed us inside. He took a seat on the couch with Brianna as Drew and I settled on the loveseat across the room.

"Well, I have some news. I got that assistant chef job in Midtown."

"That's awesome! Congratulations!" Brianna beamed with pure and sincere happiness. "When do you start?"

"June first, and I may have an apartment. It's actually pretty close by—walking distance, in fact."

"That new complex by the train station?" Josh asked with his elbows resting on his knees.

"Yes, we looked at two of the vacant apartments. One has a terrace and one doesn't, but Victoria will have her own room, plus a spare—"

"'We'?" Josh's eyes darted between Drew and me. "So, you both are making this . . . permanent, then?"

"Yes." My abrupt answer came out just as tense as my sister's on the way here. Drew rested his hand on my thigh and gave it a squeeze. Why was I so nervous? Josh always had Brianna, so why did it seem as if I had to ask permission to move in with someone? A pang of guilt twisted my gut remembering how I'd purposely made Josh and his then girlfriend squirm whenever they wanted to take my daughter anywhere.

His mouth stretched in a smile as he caught Brianna's gaze. She returned the same wide grin.

"Good for you." He nodded at us. "Vic will be happy. She talks about Drew nonstop."

Drew nudged my leg with his and threw me a wink.

"I'll be working nights and I'm sure a lot of weekends. I'll be living close enough that she can go back and forth without too much trouble. I . . ." I lifted my eyes to their expectant but so damn good-natured expressions. "I don't know how I'll ever thank you. She's happy and healthy and . . . you're great parents to her. The last thing I'd want to do is take her away. I kept her away from you for a long time, and it's a little hard to forgive myself for it."

"Sara, we'll work it out as we go. Not that I don't think she likes it here, but we aren't you. She'll have you back and that's all we want. She's got a lot of love, more than I had as a kid." Josh huffed out a laugh. "There are worse things for a little girl, right?"

"Oh, yeah." I nodded with a sad chuckle.

"I don't think we've met formally. I was dragged past you on my way in. I'm Denise." My sister came into the living room and shook Josh and Brianna's hands.

"Sorry for your loss," Brianna offered. Denise nodded, unlike me, still getting used to not having her parents around.

"Victoria wants a sleepover, so I guess I'll be staying at your apartment at least once." She laughed as she pulled Victoria into her side. My soul sighed, their similarities as they stood side by side overwhelming me. My sister passed her boisterous spirit along to her niece, and I knew if they could only meet, they'd be instant best friends.

"Of course, she does." I scoffed. "She probably won't let you leave."

Drew leaned back on the couch and extended his arm on the cushions behind me. "Lovable as hell, right?"

She smiled and crossed her arms over her torso. "Absolutely. I have a lot of spoiling to catch up on."

"Mommy!" Victoria barreled over to the couch where Drew and I sat. "Aunt Denise said you got a new apartment!" Her eyes widened.

I pulled her to sit between us. "Almost. I'll probably move in at the end of May, and Drew is moving in with me. With us."

She popped off the couch and gaped at the both of us. "You *are?*"

"I am." Drew nodded before she flung her arms around his neck, and the elation on both their faces almost had me in tears.

She ran back over to where I sat, eyes wide and hopeful. "That means I can go home? Let me get my stuff."

I caught her arm before she made a mad dash to her room. "Not yet, and it's not the same home. It's a nicer one, though. Much bigger and nicer."

"You won't go away anymore?" Her voice was small and caught me right in the chest.

"Well, I'll be working some nights, and you'll still stay here sometimes, too, but yes. I won't be away anymore."

"Yes!" She tackled me with a hug so strong my head fell back. I enveloped her in my arms and buried my head in her neck.

My chest flooded with warmth and relief. All this time I worked my fingers to the bone to give Victoria a better home. But she didn't care where home was—as long as it was with me.

Forty-One

SARA

"THIS IS SILLY, Drew," I sighed as I shrugged on the chef's jacket and hat. Instead of the traditional cap and gown, the culinary school students graduated in chef's jackets and hats in their own separate ceremony from the rest of the college commencement activities. It was the same uniform I'd worn at the restaurant and during class, but it seemed ridiculous to pull it on for the sake of sitting in an auditorium.

"You worked hard for this." He wrapped his arms around me from behind and dropped a wet, open-mouthed kiss to the back of my neck, causing all the tiny hairs to stand up along my spine "And after the ceremony, maybe you could keep the hat on and lose everything else."

"You want to fuck me in a chef's hat?" I turned to Drew's sexy smirk and shrug.

"I want to fuck you in anything," he growled as he pulled me flush to his body. "But the chef's hat . . ." Drew hissed out a breath before crushing his lips to mine.

"We could stay here . . . and I could get naked now," I mumbled against his mouth as my back hit the edge of Drew's kitchen counter. I attempted to hoist myself up and wrap my legs around his waist, but he wouldn't budge. I scoffed and frowned at the shake of his head.

"Nice try. Let's go."

I leveled my eyes at him with a petulant huff. "Fine," I clipped before grabbing my purse.

"Listen to me." Drew grabbed my hands and enclosed them in his. "Today is something to celebrate. Why don't you want to go?"

My eyes left his and fixated on the floor. "Everyone will be there with their families, and the two people in my family are four hours away. It feels more depressing than celebratory." I never asked Josh if he would drive Victoria up here because I didn't see the point. I saw graduation as an insignificant formality, but in spite of how I blew it off, I wished my daughter and sister were here today.

"I'm not enough?" His bottom lip jutted out in an exaggerated pout.

My chest shook with a laugh before I planted a kiss on his lips. "Yes, you are. Always. This is just a day when . . . not having parents beaming with pride stings a little."

"What about having the man who loves you more than anything in the world beaming with pride?" He kissed where our fingers were still joined. "Because I am proud *as hell* of you."

He rested his forehead against mine, his chocolate puppy dog eyes pleading under his long lashes.

"Why are you so fucking wonderful?"

He chuckled as he kissed the top of my head. "It's a curse, Gorgeous."

❧ ❧ ❧

THE CEREMONY WAS thankfully short and sweet. The culinary graduating class wasn't very large, and we weren't called up one by one. I searched the audience for Drew, but seats were mostly taken, and he was hard to find in the crowd in the sea of congratulations balloons. I smiled to myself at the thought of having someone in the crowd—here only for me. In a year's time, so much had changed. I was in love, I had a sister, and finally a career—not just a job. The lonely lifestyle I thought was my life sentence had been lifted and the future filled me with excitement instead of dread. Birthdays and holidays were something to look forward to, not a reason to panic over how I'd be able to afford it or how I'd get through it alone. Drew was right; today was a day to celebrate.

The class filtered out of the auditorium, making it even more impossible to spot my boyfriend. I was about to dig out my phone to text Drew when a hand wrapped around my waist.

"Congratulations, chef." Drew pressed a light kiss to my lips when I craned my head around, giving my bottom one a little suck before he pulled back.

"*Assistant* chef," I corrected him before I snaked my arm around his neck and gave him a peck. The crowd shimmied us back and forth as more spilled out of the ceremony. I kept the annoyed New Yorker in me in check as I focused on the joy of the moment.

I turned around and drifted my hands down Drew's black button-down shirt. "Where were you sitting? I couldn't find you." My fingers traced along the edge of his collar. This man made me so damn happy. Drew loved me enough to make me believe I was worth it, that I deserved someone as amazing as him in my life and in my corner. Maybe moving in together so soon was a touch impetuous, but I'd had my life on hold for so long it was as if it never had a chance to ever begin. Now, I was starting a brand-new life and sharing it with both the man I loved and my daughter.

It was surreal when the dreams you never let yourself have come true.

"I was toward the back, I had people to meet up with."

"People? Who?"

Two arms wrapped around my torso from behind and almost made me fall.

"Surprise, Mommy!" My daughter whispered into my back.

I gaped at Drew, his mouth tipping up into a smirk.

"How did you . . . ?"

"We took the train in last night and stayed at the hotel down the road." My sister came out of nowhere and flung her arms round my neck. She'd been visiting with Victoria quite often since our parents' funeral, and the two of them had become close. In a year's time, my family multiplied. That, along with my degree, was my biggest joy.

I glared at Drew through her unruly waves, elated that they were here yet clueless as to how he made it happen.

"Hotels are cool!" Victoria's eyes widened as she tightened her grip around me. "These are for you, Mommy!" She hoisted a huge bouquet of flowers at me before releasing me from her bear hug. She must've been clutching onto them for dear life throughout the ceremony since the petals on the squished outer flowers were falling off.

"And we got a room in the same hotel for tonight." Drew's lips found my temple. "We also have a special dinner planned, so . . ." He peeled one of my hands off the crinkled paper surrounding my bouquet and laced our fingers together. "Ready?" He nodded at my sister and Victoria walking up ahead.

I allowed myself to get lost in his smile for a minute. Accepting love was still a bit out of my wheelhouse, but with Drew, I had no choice. He surrounded me with it, melting away the last shards of ice to bring the fire out, the one burning in my belly for all there was to come.

"Yes, I am."

Forty-Two

DREW

Six months later

"YOU'RE COOKING?" VICTORIA crinkled her nose as she came into the kitchen. Quinn, the Yorkie we begged Sara to allow into our home a month after we moved in, stirred in her arms, regarding me with the same "what the hell" glower as Victoria.

"I can cook," I huffed as I slipped the London Broil into the bag of marinade and laid it on a plate before stuffing it into the fridge. She had me. I most definitely didn't cook. I called my mother in a panic for something easy and non-screwupable and she suggested broiling steak, provided I didn't ruin it by cooking it too well done, was fairly simple. Ordering something would be a hell of a lot easier, but I wanted tonight to be special. We both deserved better than takeout on a night like this.

"Why haven't you cooked before?"

"Because your mom is a whole lot better than me. And stop with the twenty questions." I tickled her side and ruffled the soft fur on Quinn's head before I checked the fridge one more time. Steak, veggies I could steam in a bag, her favorite dessert from the bakery since I sure as shit wasn't attempting to bake—all check. It appeared I had it handled for the moment. I only hoped I didn't fuck it all up in the execution.

Victoria turned on a giggle to head back into the living room. All of us acclimated to our new routine without much trouble. My hours at the new job were reasonable, but Sara's shifts were long. Victoria still stayed with Josh and Brianna most days during the week but came here whenever Sara had a night off or if Josh and Brianna had something to do. We lived close enough that the back and forth wasn't too taxing. We both wished Victoria could be with us more but as the newest employee, Sara didn't have a lot of say in her schedule yet. Despite the hours, she loved her job and came home every night all lit up because of a recipe they let her test or a new pairing she thought of. That weary strain in her eyes she had when we first met dissipated into happiness. She was doing what she always wanted to do, and no one deserved to finally enjoy her life more than Sara.

Victoria was curled up on the edge of the couch, engrossed in her tablet, when I sat next to her.

"I wanted to ask you something."

She lifted her head and leaned back into the cushion.

"Okay." She rested the tablet on the arm of the couch and the dog jumped in her lap.

"It's about the dinner I'm making for your mom tonight. I'm . . . I'm asking her a question, and I want her to say yes, but I think I should ask you before I ask her."

Her face scrunched as she regarded me with a confused gaze. "Why do you have to ask me first?"

"Well." I sat up and wiped my sweaty palms on my jeans. If asking Victoria was this stressful, I'd give myself a heart attack when I asked Sara. "I want to marry your mom. And this dinner I'm going to try to cook . . ." I winced and drew a laugh out of her. "It's so I could ask her tonight. But I should ask you if it's okay first."

"What would be different? You'd still live here, right? Just Mommy would have your last name?"

"Mostly things would stay the same, I suppose. But when you marry someone, it takes everything to another level."

"What level?"

I stretched my arm behind her on the couch. "Well, she'd have my last name, but when you marry someone, it's because you want them in your life forever and want to make sure everyone knows it. That's why people have weddings and give each other rings. I love your mom and want to spend the rest of my life with her and marrying her would seal the deal." A grin split my mouth. Making Sara mine was all I ever wanted. And she was, but it was time to make it official.

She nodded, mulling it over as she bit the corner of her bottom lip. "Like when Dad married Bri. They lived together first, but they got married later. Dad told me they got married because he wanted to spend the rest of his life with her and tell everyone."

"Exactly." I slapped her knee. "So, it's okay? That means you're stuck with me. Are you sure you're all right with that?" I smirked as I nudged her knee with mine.

"I'm not stuck with you. I love you. And I love Bri, too. My friend Emerson only has two parents. You and Bri make everything more fun. I feel bad she doesn't have a Drew or a Bri." Her lips fell in a frown. A laugh escaped me at Victoria's sullen expression. "You can ask her." She met my eyes, her nod resolute.

"Get over here." She scooted toward me on the couch and I wrapped my arms around her. The dog yelped, reminding me she was between us. "I love you, too, kiddo."

"I hope she says yes!" She folded her hands under her chin. *Shit, so did I.*

❥ ❥ ❥

SARA TEXTED SHE was running a few minutes late. I ran around the kitchen, searching for the candles I swore we packed when we moved in and uncorking her favorite Malbec. She always called me a hopeless romantic, but tonight she was half right. In an effort to make everything as romantic as possible, all I felt was hopeless. Dinner seemed edible and the wine was poured. I only needed my girl to come home.

At the jingle of the keys and click of the lock, I sucked in a nervous breath. She was the one, and I knew that deep in the marrow of my bones. We shared our lives, so why not share a last name? It was the logical but scary next step. Not scary because I was unsure; in fact, I'd never been surer of anything. What the hell would I do if she said no? I squeezed my eyes shut and shook off the horrible, intrusive thought. Failure wasn't an option, and I wouldn't allow my tortured subconscious to entertain the possibility.

"Who's a good girl?" She cooed at Quinn bouncing at her feet. I couldn't help but laugh. Victoria and I worked on her for a week to finally convince her to bring in a pet, but somewhere along the way she became Sara's dog before ours. My secret softie.

"I'm sorry I'm late." She breezed over to where I stood against the sink in the kitchen. "Fridays are insane but at least I have tomorrow off . . ." She trailed off, pausing right before she kissed my lips, her eyes darting from the candlelit table to me.

"Did you cook?" Her nose crinkled. "Steak?"

"London Broil, string beans, I nuked a couple of potatoes. Don't look so shocked." My lips found her forehead.

"Didn't you eat with Victoria?"

"Victoria's at Josh's tonight." I slid my hands along the curve of her hip and pulled her closer. "Tonight, it's just you and me. I haven't seen much of you this week."

Her confused gaze faded into a contrite wince. "I know, I'm sorry, baby. George and Aida have been really great, but I can't refuse if I have to stay."

"Don't apologize, Gorgeous." I pressed a light kiss to her lips. "I wanted to do something for you since you've been working so hard. Sit."

The corners of her mouth curved before she framed my face and planted a lingering kiss on my lips, then another, then one tiny peck before her tongue glided along my bottom lip.

"Oh, no," I groaned. "I worked too hard on this dinner. Plenty of time for that later." I peeled her hands off my cheeks and nodded to the table.

"Fine." She sighed as she plopped into one of our dining room chairs. She cut into the steak and brought a tiny piece to her mouth. "Wow, this is good, Drew. You sure you made this?" Her mouth tipped up in a smirk around the rim of her wine glass.

"Yes, I'm sure." I glared at her from across the table. "Wasn't all that hard." I shrugged before digging my knife in my own steak.

"Did you call your mom for help?"

I sneered back without answering.

We ate in silence the next few minutes. Sara happily devoured her dinner, but I only picked at my not-so-bad attempt at an edible meal. My eyes glossed over the chocolate brown eyes that changed to almost black when she was pissed off or turned on, the long chestnut hair kissing the tops of her breasts, and the way her tongue darted out to lick her bottom lip between bites. There was no one else for me and there never would be. She owned me, and if she said yes tonight, I was tempted to head to city hall as soon as it opened on Monday morning. I exhaled a tense gust of air as I leaned back in my chair.

"You're weirding me out, Kostas." She lifted an eyebrow as she took another sip of wine. "What's with the staring?"

"You're gorgeous," I rasped as I set my fork down. "*So* fucking gorgeous."

A blush tinted her cheeks as she rose from her chair. She climbed into my lap and looped her arms around my neck. "So are you." Her hand feathered down my cheek. "I was only teasing you. Dinner was perfect—"

"Marry me," I pleaded in an almost guttural whisper.

"Drew . . . I . . ." Sara stammered, causing my heart to race in a panic. Talk about fucking it all up in the execution. Shock was not the emotion I wanted reflected back at me. I had an entire speech planned, but having her in my arms, so content and full of love, I blurted it out without thinking.

"I love you more than you could begin to imagine. I want to spend the rest of my life with you and make you mine in every possible way. Make us forever and tell the whole world." Her bottom lip quivered as I tucked a stray lock of hair behind her ear.

"Caveman," she teased as her eyes welled up.

"When it comes to you, you better believe it. Wait, stand up. I need to do this right." Patting her thigh before I lifted her off my lap, I knelt down on one knee as tear after tear snaked down her face.

After digging the two-carat platinum ring I'd been paying off since my first paycheck out of my pocket, I took in a deep breath to calm my compounding nerves.

"I had a whole speech planned but screwed it up." I gave her a crooked grin. "All I have left is: Sara, will you marry me?"

She gulped as she brought her eyes to the ceiling. Her chin quivered, her face was soaked, and I had zero clue how to read any of it.

"Sara," I pressed, now scared to death she was thinking of a way to turn me down.

"Yes. Of course, yes. You really thought I would say no?" She shook her head at me. "You . . . you're my everything." She threaded her fingers through my hair. "My reason and my purpose along with Victoria. You made the impossible possible. You changed my life and gave me a better one than I ever could have imagined. So yes, I'll marry you." She wiped a tear away with her knuckle.

I slipped the ring on her finger before I stood and took her mouth in a hungry, brutal, and relieved-as-fuck kiss.

"Can we do this soon?" I murmured as she backed me out of the kitchen and toward the hallway leading into our bedroom. "I can't wait that long."

She pulled back, a wide smile lighting up her entire face; the smile that captured me and never let me go.

"Monday too soon?"

Epilogue

SARA

Five years later

"THIS PLACE IS packed!" Aida gushed as we stole a glance out of the tiny glass window on the kitchen door.

"It sure is," I marveled, equal parts excited and exhausted. It wasn't unusual to be this packed on a Saturday night, but now that I owned a share of the restaurant rather than just worked here, it was a wonder to behold. Paying customers demanding more, a long line of patrons waiting to get in. Dollar signs and hearts clouded my ecstatic gaze.

Although I fought her tooth and nail, Denise split the money with me when she sold the house and moved to Florida. I hated the thought of her leaving—especially after I'd just gotten her back—but the distance didn't hinder our bond. We spoke all the time and visited each other a couple of times per year. She needed to get away from the ghosts that held her back, and as I dealt with the same specters at times, I couldn't say I blamed her.

Parking the money into a savings account, I refused to touch it for a few years. I was well paid at Blystone, moving up to chef after only a couple of years and didn't need what I considered a consolation prize from my parents. I didn't want their help then and I wouldn't accept it now.

George was the sweetest restaurant owner I'd ever known, and in my previous life I'd met a slew. He was smart and kind and simply a good man, why all of his employees rallied to take on more when his health deteriorated. He'd let Aida manage most things for the past year, but when he called us both into his office a couple of months ago, I was sure it was to inform us he was closing. Instead, he offered to sell a piece of the restaurant to both Aida and me. He still wished to be a partner but was ready for retirement and over the day to day. I refused at first, as I believed Aida deserved a greater share, but he insisted, saying that no one cared more about the success of his baby than I did. I couldn't disagree, and as of yesterday, I was a signed and sealed co-owner of a successful Manhattan restaurant.

To celebrate the first night of ownership, I was observing, not cooking for a change. Even though I took great joy in directing the kitchen, it was nice to sit back and watch patrons enjoy what I created. Josh and Brianna came to celebrate with us. Somehow—and against all odds—we became a happy, extended family. My daughter was growing up with an abundance of love and wouldn't have the same issues her mother and her aunt still fought against. Even more than the restaurant, I considered that my greatest success—even if it entailed accepting help. Despite how my husband teased me, I was almost easy going these days. *Almost.*

"I'll take a look outside. Be back in a minute." I squeezed Aida's arm and headed to the dining area.

Drew and Victoria were seated with Josh and Brianna in the large corner booth. Their son, Chris, had just turned two and fidgeted on Brianna's lap as I approached.

"Hey, Mom, still need me to give out the menus?" My daughter offered as she slid out of the booth. She was itching for a job at the restaurant ever since I'd told her I was an owner, and for a couple of hours I let her hand out menus when guests were seated tonight. She was about to turn fifteen and was almost my height. Victoria looked much older than she was, and each time a male glanced for more than two seconds in her direction, Drew and Josh were ready to pounce. Brianna and I shared a ton of eye rolls as this poor girl had an uphill battle if she ever dared to bring a boy to either of her homes.

"I think the rush is over, but I'll let you know. Thank you." I brushed her thick caramel hair over her shoulder and kissed her forehead.

"Maybe I could do something else . . . you seem tired."

I cocked my head as I soaked in my daughter's concern.

"I'm fine. Everything is great and all under control."

"Sure." My husband scoffed as he came behind me and drifted his hand over my swollen belly. "Because you aren't eight months pregnant or anything. Take a break, Kostas," he scolded with a clenched jaw.

"I don't need a break." I held in a groan at my husband's frequent hovering and forced a smile. "As I just said, I'm fine."

"When was the last time you sat down? You're the boss now, so why don't you goof off for a little bit." He nodded to his now vacant seat and nudged me onto the cushion.

I exhaled in defeat, hiding my wince from Drew. My feet were swollen and killing me. I didn't remember tiny things taking so much effort when I was pregnant with Victoria. But I was much younger back then, and never took it easy because . . . I couldn't. Drew opened his own company with Carlos and Brian a year ago and his hours were flexible. Lately, most of his hours involved loitering at one of our tables with his laptop, watching me like a hawk. I loved him from the deepest depths of my soul, but I would throat punch him soon if he didn't stop treating me like a china doll about to fall and break.

"Excuse me." One of my long-time customers came over to our table with his teenage son. Lucas was a business lunch regular but never came in with his children before. This young man shared the same piercing blue eyes and sandy brown hair. It was too much of an identical resemblance to not be Lucas's kid. "I'm sorry to bother you, Sara. We haven't gotten a menu yet, and this one is always hungry." He laughed and motioned behind him where the handsome boy of, I guessed, sixteen or seventeen offered a sheepish smile—until he spotted Victoria over my shoulder.

"I'm sorry, Lucas." I rolled to a standing position and nodded to the front. "It's a little busy but I apologize for the wait. I'll pick them up for you."

"I'll get them!" my daughter offered before bolting out of the booth.

"Thank you," the boy replied for his father before ambling toward Victoria with a wide grin. "I'm Joey. You are?"

"Fourteen!" Josh and Drew answered in unison with the same menacing glare.

"You don't need my daughter's name. Have a nice dinner," Josh clipped as all the blood drained out of this poor kid's face.

"Sorry," I mouthed to Lucas who, thankfully, gave me a knowing smirk before heading back to his table.

Victoria huffed at her father before heading to the front to pick up the menus.

"I need to be scarier," Drew lamented as he stuffed his hands in his pockets. "Josh has the whole ink thing going for him." He nodded toward Josh, now trying to get Chris to sit still on his lap.

"The little guy has some, too," Brianna laughed as she turned Chris's arm over, showing multi-colored scribbles on his pudgy arms. "He wants to be just like Daddy. Washable markers, my ass." Chris splayed his chubby hand on his mother's cheek and shot her a heart-melting-toddler grin, reducing Brianna to nothing but a puddle on the seat.

Laughing at the frown on my husband's face, I rubbed his shoulder. "Remember Aaron? When you picked me up on my last day at my internship, he almost pissed himself. You'll be fine." I kissed his cheek.

"Yeah, but . . ." He rubbed my belly with a frustrated sigh. "I need to be better. It's hard having daughters knowing how boys like *that*," he tilted his head to Lucas's son, stiff in his chair and most likely terrified to turn around, "think because you were the same kind of asshole."

"Tell me about it," Josh grumbled as he bounced his son on his knee.

"It's a girl! I didn't know you were finding out!" Brianna squealed with her hands folded.

"Yep," Drew wrapped his other arm around my middle. "I'm completely outnumbered. Even the dog is a girl."

"And you love every single second." I elbowed his stomach but fell back when a strong kick followed by a blinding cramp shot across my abdomen.

"What's wrong?" Drew stepped back, clutching my shoulders in a panic. "You don't look so good."

"I'm fine." I waved him off. "This one is a kicker. I don't

remember if Victoria was one—ow!" I clutched the edge of the booth in mind-numbing pain. Two more kicks were followed by a horrid cramping of the entire lower half of my body that set off my own panic. It was too soon; she wasn't due for another three weeks. We didn't even have a name yet.

"We're leaving." Drew grabbed his jacket. "Victoria can go home with Josh and Brianna."

"Wait, maybe it's just Braxton Hicks or whatever. It's too soon for—fuck!" Another contraction hit me so hard, I tumbled over, unable to straighten without Drew's help.

"They'll tell Aida you left. I'm not playing, Sara. Let's go." I kept my mouth closed and waddled beside him as he led me outside, as this was the one time my husband's overprotective alpha ways were a comfort not a nuisance.

"I'm scared," I whispered when he piled me into the front seat of the car, lifting my legs because pain hindered every move I made below the waist.

"What do I always say? I've got you. *Both* of you." He leaned over and kissed my lips. "Everything is going to be fine. Relax, Gorgeous." Drew massaged the back of my neck and gave me a wide smile.

"Okay," I panted out, wishing I didn't blow off those breathing classes as bullshit. "I trust you."

※ ※ ※

DREW

I WAS FUCKING terrified.

I thought we had at least three more weeks. Sara's age made this a high-risk pregnancy, so we played everything as cautious as could be. I knew she wanted to punch me in the junk at times for hovering, but that never stopped me. She was too important. *They* were too important. I wasn't leaving a thing to chance, although chance was laughing its ass off at us right now.

"My wife is having contractions. She needs a doctor," I blurted to the emergency room clerk as Sara folded into my side. The contractions were coming fast and furious.

"What's her name? I need your insurance card."

Cursing under my breath, I dug into my wallet and fished out the card. "Sara Kostas. Dr. Rodriguez is her doctor and we already called to let her know we were coming. Can someone please take her in?" I was past the point of pretending to be calm.

"Have a seat, sir." The clerk's gum snapped as she nodded to the waiting area with her chin.

"Have a seat? Are you fucking kidding me?" I took a leap forward, ready to pounce through the plexiglass separating us.

"Stop it," Sara whispered as she pulled me away. "I'd like to not have my husband hauled off by security. Let's sit without the ruckus, okay?" Her words were strained from pain, only adding to the terror pulsating in my chest. They had five minutes to call us in before I lost it.

"This is my fault," Sara sniffled as she eased into a seat.

"What is, the baby? I was there too, Gorgeous. Not all your fault." I smiled, willing myself to calm down and not add to her distress.

"I worked until almost the hour I had Victoria. I had contractions almost my whole shift and only left a half hour before it ended. When I made it to the ER, I was still in my waitress's uniform. Now, at the age I am, I should've taken more precautions and I didn't. I felt tiny cramps earlier but ignored it. I didn't think and now what if she's—"

"She's fine, you're fine," I said as evenly as I could while offering that statement up as a prayer. "You're a little woman with a lot of baby." I glided my hand across the swell of her stomach, almost hoping my daughter would sense me and calm down. "I'm sure you've had little cramps and pains here and there for weeks; you can't beat yourself up for that." I cupped her cheek and kissed her lips.

"You're all right, Kostas." A laugh bubbled out through her watery smile.

"Right back at you, Kostas. And they have four more minutes before I make a ruckus look like a kid's cartoon."

"I love how you take care of me. Of us. This baby is a lucky little girl."

"Mmm, I don't know." The side of my mouth tipped up into a smirk. "Not sure if you loved it so much the past couple of weeks."

"Maybe," she panted as she leaned forward. "But you were right, I should've been taking it easy. Aggravating, but right."

"Unfortunately, that's not something I can stop. You're stubborn as hell and maybe sometimes I overdo it, but I love you too much. If anything ever happened to you, I . . ." I stopped, as I was already on the borderline of going apeshit on the ER clerk for not moving fast enough. "There's no me without you. So, I'll always be the pain in the ass, overprotective husband and father. Sorry." I patted her stomach and dipped my head to whisper. "Sorry, baby girl. Daddy is a little nuts."

Her head fell against my shoulder. "What would I do without you?"

I kissed the top of her forehead and rubbed her back. "Good thing you never have to find out."

⸎ ⸎ ⸎

SARA

WHAT WE WERE assured was routine labor turned into an emergency C-section. I was wheeled into the OR after the baby's heart rate fluctuated as the contractions intensified. When they finally got her out, the little troublemaker had the cord wrapped around her neck—twice. When they laid her on my chest, her big eyes shining at me with innocence, I had the feeling this one would keep us on our toes for a lifetime.

"She needs a name," Drew whispered as his fingers sifted through her silky swath of black hair after we were rolled into a room. The birth of our baby was the first time I'd witnessed my husband left without words. He stared at her in awe from the second she came out.

"She looks like you. The big eyes and the dark hair." I threaded my fingers through the thick locks on the back of his neck. She even had the same sweet but sneaky curl in her lip.

"You're never dating anyone—ever. Isn't that right, Princess?" Drew's thumb drifted back and forth over her chubby cheek as the perfect name popped into my head.

"Diana."

His weary head perked up. "Diana? For her name?"

"You know my royal family obsession." I laughed as I cuddled her into my chest. "And wasn't that Wonder Woman's real name?"

He lifted a tired eyebrow at me. "I'm impressed you know that."

"Funny. Want to take her for a minute?"

A grin split his mouth before he scooped her out of my arms. When Victoria was born, no one else held her in the hospital besides the nurses. Tears flooded my eyes at all the love this baby already had.

Drew walked her over to the window, kissing the top of her head and whispering in her ear. I had happy memories with Victoria as a baby, but even the best ones were sad because I was alone. Joy is always better when you can share it and sharing everything with Drew made life wonderful.

I'd teach both of my daughters they didn't need a prince to swoop in and save them, but when a real one came into their lives, appreciate it for the wonderful blessing it is—and make damn sure not to let him go.

THE END

Acknowledgments

I'M GOING TO do my best to keep this short and sweet, but as I'm long winded and sappy—and am blessed with a lot of friends—it's a challenge.

To my husband and son, my superheroes, my reason, and my purpose. Thank you for supporting me through this crazy writing journey, even when it takes me away from you at times. I love you more than you could ever imagine.

To my mom, I watched you work your fingers to the bone and take care of me all by yourself and never truly realized how hard you really had it. I admire and love you very much, and I hope you know how grateful I truly am. All that I am is because of you.

To my betas: Bianca, Joanna, Christine, Franci, Saffron, Shannon, Lara, Ella, Jessica, Angie, Christine, and Lisa. Thank you for helping me perfect the slow burn and for helping me make Sara someone you could love, even if you started out thinking she was the villain.

Jodi and Julia, for completely derailing my writing schedule and lobbying for this book in the first place and then reading chapter by chapter at all hours. I'm so glad you made such a great case. Your support and encouragement are what made me write the fastest 80,000 words of my life. I love you guys.

Laura, you always help get my brain on the right track. Thank you for helping me with the blurb, title, and always making sure

I know when *The Godfather* is on. You're a class act, sister—and I appreciate you more than you know.

To Jenn, my official blurb editor forever. Thank you so much for stepping in and making it perfect.

Jaimee, my wonderful friend who always finds the little things in my drafts that make the biggest difference. I love your big heart and eagle eye and hope my lack of geography knowledge gave you a good chuckle.

Beth, you came in to read when I was ready to set the whole thing on fire, and knowing someone like you loved it saved it, and saved me. I'll never forget that, and now you're stuck with me.

Mila, my brilliant friend who always makes time for me and my books to be my last pass. I'm elated you loved my slow burn romance and I treasure our friendship.

Kaitie, thank you so much for being my last review, and as always, your attention to detail is impeccable and invaluable. Thank you so much for being so thoughtful and considerate, so glad my books brought us together.

Barb, the wonderful soul who became my best friend and always has my back. Thank you for being both my cheerleader and my center and pushing me to make this book the best it could be. I couldn't function without you, and I can't wait until we unleash Cole and Tierney out into the world. I love you and thank you will never be enough.

To Jenn, the world's best PA. You're insanely organized, huge-hearted, and funny as hell. You get me and know how to handle me. I don't know what I'd do without you and never want to find out.

Najla, my cover designer with loads of both talent and patience. Each cover is my new favorite, and you captured Drew and Sara perfectly, as always (and never laugh at my weird ideas that usually don't work out).

Mary Ruth, thank you for making a beautiful announcement teaser! I'm always in awe of your talent and wonderful heart.

Daniela, thank you for your gorgeous edits! I can't wait to show them off!

Mitzi and Marisa, thank you for making sure my baby was clean and tight, and making me laugh along the way. You guys are true professionals and I learn something new from you each book.

To Christine, you run Type A Formatting with a flawless professionalism and tolerate nut job clients like me. You are truly the best and are stuck with me for life.

To the readers and bloggers who took a chance on me and this book. I always remember how when I first published, I said if ten people who weren't related to me bought my book, I'd consider it a success. This, all the support I've received across 6 books and three novellas, continues to blow my mind. It's a blessing I'll never stop being grateful for.

Thank you Give Me Books and Enticing Journey for organizing a wonderful cover reveal and release event. Thank you for helping get my baby out there.

To the Rose Garden, my happy place on social media. Thank you for all the support and encouragement and tolerating my daily free association. I love you all and thank you from the bottom of my heart for staying with me.

To the father who acknowledged me in death more than he ever did in life, I'm sorry for all you missed and pray you found peace.

About the Author

STEPHANIE ROSE GREW up loving words and making up stories. Being able to share them with readers is her dream come true. This lifelong Bronx girl loves Starbucks, wine and 80s rock. Her voice often gets mistaken for a *Mob Wives* trailer.

She married her prom date and has a LEGO obsessed son. She believes there is nothing sexier than a good guy who loves with all his heart and has made it her mission to bring as many as she can to the page.

Follow her everywhere, she loves hearing from readers!

Find Stephanie Rose online at:
www.authorstephanierose.com

Facebook, Twitter, Instagram and Goodreads

Books by Stephanie Rose

THE SECOND CHANCES SERIES

Always You

Only You

Always Us

Finding Me

After You

STANDALONES

Rewrite

Intimate Strangers,

St. Helena Vineyard Kindle World Novella

Made in the USA
Middletown, DE
07 June 2021